I0595807

HEARTS ECLIPSED

L.C. SON

Hearts ECLIPSED

a
Beautiful Nightmare Novel
by

L.C. SON

Hearts Eclipsed © 2019 by L.C. Son

All rights reserved. No part of this book may be used or reproduced in any written, electronic, recorded, or photocopied format without the express permission from the author or publisher as allowed under the terms and conditions with which it was purchased or as strictly permitted by applicable copyright law. Any unauthorized distribution, circulation or use of this text may be a direct infringement of the author's rights, and those responsible may be liable in law accordingly. Thank you for respecting the work of this author.

Hearts Eclipsed is a work of fiction. All names, characters, events and places found therein are either from the author's imagination or used fictitiously. Any similarity to persons alive or dead, actual events, locations, or organizations is entirely coincidental and not intended by the author.

COVER ART & INTERIOR: RMGRAPHX
EDITED BY: DARK RAVEN EDITS
ISBN: 978-1-7336503-3-5

Dedication

To my loving husband and kids, thanks for living through this fantasy world with me. Your support brings worlds alive and characters to life. Thank you.

Dear Reader,

Thank you for purchasing Hearts Eclipsed! I hope you enjoy moving past the nightmare of Damina's dreamscape and hear directly from the men in her world, Jackson and Dalcour. To ensure a pleasurable reading experience, be sure to read Beautiful Nightmare (Book One) FIRST. Hearts Eclipsed is a companion novel chronicling the events of Beautiful Nightmare from Jackson and Dalcour's perspective. It is not a retelling of the first book in the series, but assumes the reader understands nomenclature from the first book.

If you haven't read Beautiful Nightmare (Book One), visit my website at WWW.LCSONBOOKS.COM to purchase the book in both digital and paperback.

Again, thanks for your purchase and happy reading!

Dream Well,
Author L. C. Son

Hearts
ECLIPSED

Chapter 1

Jackson

Walking out of her door is the hardest thing I've ever done. The look of want in her eyes. Desire radiating from her skin. If it weren't for her parent's portrait crashing to the ground, I have no doubt the honeymoon would have preceded our nuptials.

Why not?

I love her.

With the exception of those two sacred words, "I do," and our long-awaited consummation, I think of her as my wife in every way. In fact, I can say with all assurance that I have loved her since the very first day we met.

She had a look of helplessness without surrender. The two contending bidders were doing everything they could to best one another in obtaining the Charloque de Posse oil painting all while causing quite a stir in the auditorium. While she was noticeably frustrated with both gentlemen, she held her own. I liked that. Immediately, I knew she wasn't a pushover, but I also knew she needed my help.

Raising my paddle, her eyes met mine with the sincerest look of gratitude. Followed by a small smile in the corners of her perfect peach-colored lips, she bowed her head slightly and whispered the sweetest "thank you" my ears ever heard. I knew nothing about her. Not even her name. She was the subbing auctioneer and somehow, I guessed she wasn't the Martin Trask listed in the program. But I knew one thing. I loved this woman with no name.

I was only at the auction to reclaim two relic effigy bowls that were once my great-grandfather's. My plans were to gift them to my aunt as an offering to her for caring for me after my father's death. Sophie always said my grandmother, or as I called her Pokni Natika, sold many of our family's belongings to traders to ensure the status of our pack.

I got the bowls. Only five hundred a piece. Seems like a steal compared to the insane twenty-eight thousand dollars I belted out to end the bidding war. The last bid was only ten thousand, so I am not sure what possessed me to offer such an amount. Well, actually I do. I simply wanted those idiots to shut their pie holes. Mostly, because I could tell they both were only trying to flaunt their wealth and impress her.

Not that I blame them. Damina is the most beautiful woman I've ever seen in my life. Ever.

I'd gladly do it again. There's no amount of money in any currency that would be sufficient to spend even a moment in her presence.

I knew that then and I know it now.

But it was the moment she agreed to go with me to dinner after the auction that I knew I'd never let her out of my sight. Even though I've often teased she was the most expensive first date ever, I'd gladly do it all over again.

I've gotten no farther than just outside her door and everything inside me is screaming for me to return to her. Leaning against the cool marble tile walls adjacent to her entrance, I try to allow its coolness to relieve the sweltering sweat masking my skin. My heart is racing and I'm working hard to catch my breath. I haven't felt like this since I ran the 10K.

My, what that woman does to me.

I know one thing. If I don't leave now, I have no doubt I will claim her as my wife. In every way. And by the way, her gaze deepened into mine, I'll be equally claimed. Right now, I am all too eager to comply. But our promises of chastity rein in my inhibitions. At least a little.

Leave now, idiot.

Or we could just call Pastor Holmes to pronounce us man and wife right now. He owes me a few favors. I had to utilize a lot of my contacts to get the Ward to agree to the expansion of his church parking lot.

Besides, after running into him at the Indian bistro in Chantilly with a woman who looked nothing like his wife Patricia, I doubt he's in a position to chide my reasons for wanting to speed up the nuptials.

Everything about the moment was so right. The way she smelled. Like vanilla and Eucalyptus. Calming and sweet. I recount the way she kissed me, locking her tongue with mine. The way her fingers grazed my chest as her luscious mouth gaped open full of wanting made my heart throb straight to the seat of my pants. Her peasant top did little to hide the glistening sheen along her breastbone and the rise and fall of her breathing as her body folded into mine was almost my undoing.

Sure, I could blame it on the nearing of the full moon. I've spent five years planning business trips and other excursions around the lunar cycle just to douse my desire for her. While we wolves are never shy a mating season, the full moon makes our desires almost too hard to resist. One summer's eve in the pool with Damina was enough to know not to tempt fate. Especially since I'm not sure I can guise my wolf when I'm in full bloom.

I've yet to tell her who I am.

The wolf is everything. All rage. All desire. Ferocious and fearless.

Yet, the moment we share our vows we invoke the copula ritual. She will finally be able to see me. All of me. I hate holding this part of myself back from her. But I will do what I promised to keep her safe, even if that means keeping my true self hidden from her until that time.

It's been five years. Five years of want, desire, and ice-cold showers.

None of it has been easy but I know making love to Mrs. Damina Nash will be well worth the wait. Besides, I want to do it right. I have every intention of doing so. She deserves the best I can give her. Not a romp on the couch for her first time. Our first time.

I've planned everything for our honeymoon. A rose petal covered honey-milk bath by candlelight is how I plan to start. I want to wash away all her cares as I caress every perfected inch of her. Though she exudes strength all her own, I need her to know that she can depend on me to wipe away every stain or vexing of her heart. After, I'll carry her to our bed and make love to her over and over again under a moonlit sky.

With moonlight our only light, I'll share my wolf with her, marking my scent over her body. Imprinting myself over her completely. As I drape her with my essence, I'll bind her Altrinion nature with mine, keeping her safe from all who would seek to hurt her kind.

All I have to do is wait the night out.

"Tomorrow," I whisper to her door with my hand pressed against its seam. I inwardly chuckle at the light imprint my sweaty palm leaves behind. The next imprint I make will be on her body and I look forward to that moment with the grandest delight.

Dalcour

"DALCOUR!" I hear Jerrica screaming my name before I even make it up the staircase. I'll never know how she hears me coming like she does. I love her dearly, but she drives me insane.

"Yes, I'm here," I mutter with dread. The last time Jerrica was this chipper we nearly started a war with the wolves. Sure Abraham could have used the money but purchasing their land for her strip mall endeavor would have cost him his already fading alpha status. I trust Jerrica so emphatically I began signing the deal between her and Abraham without reading the fine print. Not a normal practice, but she's one of the few people who can catch me off guard. Though just a ragged pack of Dunes wolves, had the others heard of such an allowance I have no doubt the war my brother Decaux always hoped for would ensue.

Her bright smile is ear to ear as the squeaky door opens. Jumping up and down with her phone in hand she is beaming with joy. If I didn't know better, I would think she just won the lottery; not that she needs it. I could just read her mind to understand what's the cause for such ruckus, but with both Charlotte and Brian musing about, her thoughts will be chaotic at best and I have no desire to work that hard to discern the inner-most parts of her mind.

"I guess it would help if I knew what we were excited about," I continue dryly.

"Oh look who just came up from the pit! Ladies and

gentlemen, Mr. Darkside," Braelyn scoffs perched atop the high landing.

"Happy to see you too, Braelyn," I reply forcing a smile to match Jerrica's enthusiasm.

"Well, I'm always glad to see you too, D, but you know I have no desire to hang out with you know who." Braelyn's arms are folded, and she pouts out the corners of her mouth while slurping her evening gorge through her straw.

"Aw, are you and Titan still at odds? You know he's just a bit gruff about the edges. I think he was really coming around to the whole monogamy thing."

"I seriously doubt it. Not to mention he's way too controlling for my speed. I spent half a century ogling the man from afar. It only took a week to see the real beast. Better single than miserable."

"Yeah, you say that but then you can't take your eyes off Abraham's boy."

"Whatever!" Braelyn snaps, taking another swig from her straw.

"Are you really going to continue with the whole sippy cup thing?" Jerrica quips over her shoulder, pausing enough to stare at Braelyn with her lips curled in disgust.

"Look, I'm trying to go incognito. A large glass of blood is a bit telling don't you think. Besides, with smoothies all the rave these days, I just seem like one of those juicing nut jobs. No one is the wiser." Brae replies leaping down from the landing onto the chandelier.

"Hey! Can you get off that? This isn't a gymnasium! Well, you know what stay up there! That's what I wanted to talk to you about, Dalcour."

"What? You called me up here to talk about the chandelier? I was in the middle of something you know."

"I saw those grizzly pawed heifers Titan had lined up for you two, you're not missing anything!" Braelyn laughs as she jumps from the chandelier onto the dusty floor. "Just hear her out, D, you might just like this."

"It had better be good, Jerrica." I find my patience waning. Titan managed to swing by the cheerleader tryouts. He has a few disappointed damsels that I'm sure we can find a way to cheer up. I'll hear Jerrica out but I'm looking forward to drowning myself in the most pleasurably depraved way possible.

"Okay, just hear me out okay," Jerrica begins grabbing my wrists tight. Her smile is bright enough to jockey for the sun's position.

"I'm all ears," I answer after a deep exhale.

"Well, you may recall Sue Burgin has given us the green light to revitalize the mansion as a submission to the Garden City project."

"Yes, and I offered my estate for that purpose. Braelyn has all the covenants. Once we make the necessary updates you can go forward. Is that it?"

"That's only part of it. I think I found a way to finally make your dreams come to pass!"

"My dreams?"

"Yes, your grand plan of civility. Remember?"

Braelyn adds rolling her eyes still slurping through her straw.

"If you disregard her sarcasm you may find truth in her words," Jerrica says in a softer tone aimed at calming my irritation with Braelyn. I nod and motion for her to continue.

"As I was saying, Dalcour, your dream—your plan for civility the answer for it all is contained in the notification I just received from the postal service."

"The postal service?" Both Braelyn and I squeak our words out in unison. Although I thought Braelyn was in on Jerrica's enthusiasm, she seems just as baffled as me.

"Well, yes, Brae, I didn't get a chance to fill you in before he came upstairs. You know how you've worked to bring about civility through your work at the CC? You've worked for years bonding, bridging, and building the rift between those in the supernatural world. Wolves, vampires, bulwarks, changelings, and even Altrinions all owe the peace we've recently enjoyed due to your efforts."

"Thank you, Jerrica, but I'm not sure I follow."

"Yep, you're losing me too JJ!" Braelyn adds.

"I found her!" Jerrica shouts ripping through both Braelyn and me.

"Who?"

"Your one true love. Listen, she's an Altrinion, but she hasn't a vampiric strain, so she's pure. Her mentor, and my friend, Harry Emmerson, attests to her talents and beauty."

"Okay, this is about an Altrinion? I thought you said something about the postal service?" Braelyn says coolly.

"Jerrica, listen, if this is just another attempt at setting me up with someone—no thanks. I've had my fill of the parade you've brought before me over the last few years. Besides, if there were still an Altrinion bearing the fated mark of the Great Oak, I think I would know—"

"Not if she's been hidden. Just look at my phone. I sent her a package to come join us for the revitalization project. Here's her electronic signature. That means she got it. If Harry was right about her, there's no way she'd pass on something of this magnitude. Think of what that will mean for the cause of civility. For your heart."

"Jerrica, if this venture makes you happy, then, by all means, you know you have my support. Braelyn will help you however you have need. As for anything concerning business you know I trust you. But my heart, well that my friend is locked away in the depths of my tortured soul. There isn't a defibrillator among men or the supernatural strong enough to revive it."

I shift my movements from the stairs and whisk myself away before Jerrica has a chance to reach out and touch my face. I know my dear friend means well. She always does. Both Jerrica and Braelyn only fear my brother's retribution should I not stake the supernatural world in civility and find true love soon. We've now reached the final year of Decaux's threats and while I've done much to bridge the world in a more civil manner, I've yet to aid the plight of Dunes wolves or fall in love.

While I'm close to aiding Abraham's family, the largest Dunes pack in this parish, thus signaling a truce with the wolves, I've found none to be my equal. The funny thing is, I've looked. Sure, I've never strayed from a pretty face or curvaceous figure, but someone to love who will love me for who I am, tortured soul and all—that I have never found.

Finding someone to revitalize this old mansion requires someone of impeccable talent and skill. But finding someone to revive my dormant heart requires a talent capable of straddling the gates of both heaven and hell.

If indeed she exists, I'd love to meet her.

Chapter 2

Jackson

Well, if I ever needed something to jar my thoughts away from going back to Damina's place, seeing Allyson propped against my car with her typical condemning glare is enough to keep me focused.

I really don't like her.

"Took you long enough to come out of there," Allyson quips through her gum-chewing, examining her nails.

It takes everything in me not to rip into her. These are the rare times where I wish I had a sister who could do to Allyson what I cannot.

"I didn't know I was on a clock, Allyson," I respond with a dull forced smile.

"Save your faux pleasantries for someone else.

I'm one of the few folks still not fooled by your charms Nashoba."

"How many times do I have to tell you that isn't my name!"

"As many times as you've looked your fiancé in the eye and deliberately lied to her!"

"I've told you before, I'm not lying about anything. And in our own time, not yours, will she learn everything! Anyway, why are you here?"

"I'm here because I wanted you to know when your house of lies comes crashing down, I will be there to help Damina put together the fragments of her life."

"You have no idea how to help Damina. You couldn't even fathom what it means to be what we are. You're just another self-righteous human wishing to live vicariously through the life of one you couldn't possibly understand. You humans see everything in black and white, but we don't. There are colors you've yet to see, feelings you've never felt, and a life you'll never live. So how could you possibly promise to be something for her when you can barely comprehend who and what she is."

"And you do? You think you understand her? You think you love her? Sure, I may not know what it means to be what you are, but I know what love is and what it isn't. Secrets and lies are not the makings of true love—and you know this. But you're so far gone you've become too chicken to tell her the truth. But that's okay. The truth will prevail and when it does, I'll be there for her. I promise you. That's the promise I'm making to you today Nashoba and my promises never fail."

Allyson brushes past me hard bumping my shoulder as she walks away. She wants me to know that she has no plans of just letting me and Damina be happy. While I agree that Damina should know the truth, Allyson has no idea how all of this will dramatically change Damina's life.

Forever.

Seeing Allyson only reminds me I need to speak with the only other person more vested in ensuring Damina's truth will not be disclosed prematurely—Delia.

Patting my pockets, I realize I don't have my phone. Crap! As tempting as it would be to retrieve it from Damina's place, I still know that's not the best thing. There's no way I can resist her a second time!

It's nearing the eve of the next lunar cycle and I'm already running hot. Thankfully, I know exactly where to find Damina's aunt, and it's only a few blocks from here.

I reach the church where I know Delia will be prepping the sanctuary with all the frills and flowers she chose for our wedding. I'm kinda glad I have an excuse to be here. If I cough or sneeze just once I know that idiot florist found a way to sneak in the aconite flower.

The florist, I think her name was Kelly or Kim, was a bit too presumptuous. Insisting since Damina's favorite color was purple we should mix in a few.

Hopefully, Delia reined back that snippy and overly expensive little florist. I'd hate for a church full of sick wolves to be Damina's first introduction to our world. Sure, only poisonous if ingested by a human, but for my kind, just its buttery scent alone is enough to sicken us to the point of death. I guess that's why we called it wolfsbane.

I feel my eyes well with tears the moment I open the double doors to the sanctuary, but it is not from aconite. An overwhelming feeling like butterflies tingles all over me as my mouth drops at the sight of the wedding chapel. Everything looks impeccably amazing. Everything. Delia went above the call of duty to ensure this day was special for Damina. While I know Damina is not as frilly as her aunt and cousin, she certainly appreciates beautiful things.

That's what I love about her.

From the large floor votives that accent the church aisle, to the silk lavender poms wrapped in lace hanging along the pews, every detail is flawless. I can't help but imagine how lovely my bride will look as she gracefully strides down the aisle. Once more my eyes fill with tears at the mere thought of my wife-to-be, and I am now certain that tomorrow can't come quick enough.

"Jackson," Delia's tone is soft yet husky enough to break me from my musing.

Quickly, I blink rapidly, tossing my head back to vanquish my tears as I clear my throat forcing her name from my lips in a more commanding tone than I intended as I turn on my heel to meet her gentle smile.

"I didn't expect to see you here until tomorrow," Delia continues in the same quiet manner, examining my face.

Crap she can probably see my glassy eyes.

"Yeah, I was just leaving Damina's and I thought I'd stop by." I fake a sniffle and pull my handkerchief from my vest pocket.

"Well, what do you think? Do you think she'll like it?" Delia replies after a slight knowing pause. I'm happy she's refraining from her normal motherly pandering. I hate anyone making a fuss over me.

"Everything looks lovely, Delia. I'm sure Damina will be very pleased."

"And the groom?"

"Yes, I'll admit I had to catch my breath once I opened the doors. But to be fair, I expected nothing less from you, Delia."

"Oh, don't make this old lady blush, Jackson—but do go on!" Delia exclaims with a bright smile that softens the mood as she rests her hand on my shoulder.

"I never doubted your skills for a moment, Delia. But I did come to chat with you—just not about the arrangements."

Delia's smile weakens and her eyes fall almost knowing my reason for coming.

"Did you—"

"No, Delia. I didn't tell her, but I came pretty close."

"What do you mean you *came close*?"

"Delia, it's killing me keeping this from her. So I

tried to use the orb and show her, but I couldn't. My emotions and everything were running amuck!"

"So, you didn't tell her? I mean after you called me this morning I thought for sure, you'd tell her—what made you change your mind?"

"Let's get this straight. I didn't change my mind. I still think she should know. And she needs to hear it from me. But I made a vow to her father that I would keep her safe."

"I'm glad, Jackson. Like I told you the orb works best after consummation or at least when her heart is open to accept this truth. And we both know the only way for that to happen is if she's accepted who she is and who you are. Only then can she receive the orb from her father. More importantly, once you consummate, she can see your wolf. She *needs* to be able to see your wolf. If you use the orb to show her too soon it could—"

"Kill me. Yes, I know."

"Exactly. It would kill you because you'd need a great deal of strength, enough to summon the Prime Wolf within you, to show her—and since you have yet to accept your Prime status, I doubt that would work. Please know that no matter how much we may disagree on the best way to tell her I would never want anything to happen to you."

"Look, Delia, I appreciate your sentiment, but I know how the order of the Primes work. I only wanted you to know that I didn't tell her. Still, it's not me you have to worry about. It's that pesky Allyson DeSantis. She's relentless. I'm afraid she'd tell her tonight if she could."

"I wouldn't worry too much about that. Dacari has just dropped Doodle off at home and is going to pick up Damina's gown. She'll be at Damina's place in no time. I have no doubt Dacari can keep Allyson at bay."

"Still, I don't trust her. I have a feeling—she's up to something."

Dalcour

LOCKED AWAY in the quietness of my room I can still hear Jerrica calling my name from the foyer. Braelyn's voice is more muffled, but I gather she's complaining about me and all men in general. While I know Braelyn refuses to be labeled by outdated binary rules, it's the male species that always gets her worked up. Sometimes I wish she would just stick with the ladies; she seems way more at ease with them.

Jerrica, on the other hand, is way too invested in my love life.

I wish she wasn't.

As my phone buzzes in my pocket I'm momentarily relieved, hopeful that Titan has finalized our plans with the cast-aside cheerleaders. I could surely use the distraction from Jerrica's incessant demand of my attention. But my hope is short-lived when I see my brother, Decaux's name on my screen.

What the hell does he want?

An exasperated sigh is all I have to give upon answering.

"Well, it's good to hear from you too, brother," Decaux remarks in a grainier tone than his normal slithering sound.

"What do you want, Decaux?" I hope the gruff and stiff sound of my voice meets his ear like nails on a chalkboard. I don't have time for this.

"Ah, so you prefer to get right to the point I see. Fine, I'll be brief: your clock is winding down."

"That's why you called? To remind me of your little games. You could've saved yourself the trouble."

"Oh, is that right? Is that because you've completed the scores of balance little brother? Are your precious Civility Centers sating the appetites of vampires and Altrinion-vamps alike? Do the wolves finally have sacred yards to reduce their hunt? Have the Dunes pack reclaimed rights among their ranks? And alas, my favorite, have you, my brother, found a love to wander you out of the shadows of night?"

Decaux shoots off his series of questions as he intends, like an assault rifle of threats. While just his presence on the other end infuriates me, I know well to take exception to his questioning. And I also know he's just getting started.

"What if I said no?" I know better than to bait my brother, but I need to either see through his guise or at least gesture a parley—he's extended his deadline at least twice before.

"Ha! What? Do you think I'd give you the floor for a parley? Surely you jest! And what, pray tell do you have to offer in exchange for such a negotiation?"

He's right. In the past I've been able to offer him something of worth or value to him. At my first request I gave him Chartreuse Grenoble; the younger sister of his slain and one true love, Calida. Though his affection for her was only as one would dote on a small child, she gave him pause. That is, of course, until he turned her into one of the most lethal, sadistic, and villainous vampires I've ever known. The second time was over twenty or so years ago when I offered a post of Guardians back to him, but he surprisingly refused. He was distracted with a woman. And for the first time in a while I thought I had my brother back. Yet, I never knew whether this new woman warmed his black soul like that of Calida, it was short-lived.

He's never mentioned her name, but I wish I knew who could steer his course so far from his beloved bloody shore.

I gaze around my room, looking for anything to barter. Holstered over my bed are two Diablo Blades. There's no way I'll ever part with them. Besides, he has no idea I have them. These are the only swords with the ability to sever the power of the Great Oak. The roots of the oak in the earth are said to hold the power that binds Altrinions to the curse of the sun and Wolves to the moon. Decaux would want nothing more than to sever our ties to the tree. Which is why he will never get it.

I also see the rice paper scrolls Trieu gave me with the Latin *Canticum Incantationum*, song of enchantment, embroidered in ancient Vietnamese script. Though

Decaux is too lazy to comprehend its meaning himself, he would torture some unlucky victim until he got what he wanted. The last thing the world needs is Decaux with the power to speak the ancient language of our creation. He would surely misuse it only to bring about some decrepit, vile, and sinister being worse than either Chartreuse or Scourge.

"Well, brother what is it? What do you have for me?" Decaux snaps through the phone. His patience with me is fading.

"I have nothing more than my word to give you, Decaux. I told you I would bring about a balance and I'll do exactly what I said. When have I ever gone back on a promise?"

"Never my brother, never. So I suppose it is a luck to the world that the words of your mouth hold so much honor. I look forward to seeing your promises fulfilled."

"*Sh—*"

"Wow did you talk to your mother with that mouth, sir?" Braelyn chides before I can complete my curse as I toss my phone across my room. Standing at my doorway with her arms folded shaking her head in amusement, I'm both irritated and slightly thankful for her interruption.

"Why do you insist on coming to my room unannounced and unrequested?" I snap. I'm still bothered by my brother's call. Besides, I refuse to let on that I appreciate her bullying her way through my funk.

"Ah! So you're in a mood too?" Braelyn counters as she walks around the fissure of light from the setting sun. Quickly I glide to the corner of the terrace and pull the drape cord. No need for either of us to get burned. Or worse.

"Look Braelyn, I'm sorry. There's just a lot going on."

"It's okay, I get it." Braelyn replies in a softer tone before making a loud slurping sound through her straw. "So was that big brother on the phone?"

"Yup. The one and only." I answer as I drop onto my wingback chair near the terrace still holding onto the drape cord.

"Well, that's why you need to hear Jerrica out—all the way this time!"

"Oh no! Look, I really don't want to hear anything about finding me a true love or any crap like that. Like I said, I'll pull my weight and help with the mansion. Heck, I'll even choose Mark and make it official for the Dunes Pack. Titan's got a good hold on the Guardians for now and Dranoel and Jerrica's little mutt Brian will make sure Abraham's boy can pass his Alpha valuation. So you see, nothing to worry about."

"But there is something to worry about—or rather someone. You." Braelyn's big doe-eyed stare cuts straight through me as she speaks.

"Braelyn," I gently reply as my speed carries me to her side at the doorway. "There's no need for you to worry. I've held my own against Decaux many times before. I'll be just fine," I add with a strong hold at her shoulders and a quaint smile.

"Hey, I'm not doubting your skills Big D. But what's the sense of going through all the trouble of making life worthwhile for our kind if you're not around to see it—or worse Decaux destroys it. All I'm saying is, if you give this girl a chance to win your heart maybe it will be all worth it."

Gazing into Braelyn's tear-filled eyes I see both sincerity and fear. No matter how much of a jerk I can be, she only wants the best for me. Sure, I may have been instrumental in aiding her transition from a Scourge, but her little sister-like antics bring an air of joy to my dark soul.

"Okay, Braelyn, I promise I will talk with Jerrica. Even though I've yet to experience a love to capture the beat of my heart, perhaps this mystery woman is worth the five-century wait," I answer while nudging Braelyn's chin.

Braelyn looks up at me and smiles wide, happy with my response. Without warning, she wraps her small arms around my waist and squeezes me tight, burying her head in my abdomen. Before I can return her embrace, she quickly pushes me aside, shaking herself as she does when she's shown too much emotion and walks to the door.

She grabs the door frame and looks back before exiting and says, "Who knows, maybe just maybe, she's been waiting for you too."

Chapter 3

Jackson

"Jackson, dear are you alright? You look more troubled than a man about to wed should be."

"I'm sorry Sophie, just a tad contemplative I suppose," I answer as my icily stoic reflection stares back at me from the mirror over my sofa. As I stand to greet my aunt, the ache in my tailbone reminds me I've been seated on the wooden pub chair in my basement for over an hour.

I'm still having a hard time shaking off Allyson's presence.

"It's only understandable, my dear," Sophie begins as she lightly strums through my hair, trying her best not to fuss over me. "You're about to marry tomorrow. And while you should be thinking of your bride, your brother was up to his usual machinations. I mean bringing Kyra to your luncheon was just— reprehensible!"

"Oh yeah. That." Kyra showing up at our luncheon pales in comparison to Allyson's meddling.

"That? Well, I wouldn't just brush *that* off if I were you, Jackie! Your brother is up to something. I just know it." Sophie counters with her hands rested at her hip. My brother is the only one I know who can ruffle my aunt's nearly perfect feathers.

"Promise you won't call me Jackie during your speech at our reception, please," I jokily respond as I pull her in for a light hug and kiss her forehead and walk to the bar to grab a bottle of water from the mini fridge.

"Jackson, I'm being serious!" Sophie yelps and snatches the bottle from my hand and begins drinking it for herself.

I grunt and smile as I grab another bottle, shaking off my aunt's typical bouts of entitlement. "Of course, I know you are but so am I. What did you always tell me, what you practice is what you perform?"

"Yes, and Kieron has practiced nothing but deceit and treachery since the day you refused his challenge for rank."

"No worries Aunt Sophie. I'm not worried about Kieron in the least. He just wanted to get a rise out of me is all."

"Well, I think it's time you start worrying about him. And it wasn't you he hoped to get a rise from—it

SON

was Damina. From the looks of it, I think he may have succeeded."

"Sure, he may have annoyed her a bit, but I assure you it was the last thing on her mind when I left her today."

"Please don't tell me you told her—did you show her—oh Jackie, please say you didn't!"

"No, Sophie I didn't. You're beginning to sound like Delia," I reply awaiting my aunt to snap at me for comparing her to Delia. She doesn't. Instead, her eyes become glassy pools of water and frown lines form at her brow.

"Well, we both know just how harmful it would be to you if you tried and failed. The outcome could be deadly. Besides, Damina deserves better than an ill-fitted orb. She deserves to see her groom for who he is because she loves him, not out of fear—that way it makes the process easier to take."

"Ah! So I see you've warmed up to the bride? I'm glad since tomorrow is the big day."

"And I see my tough demeanor fooled you as much as it did the blushing bride. I only did it to ensure she had what it took to stand side by side with an Alpha. Besides, you are no mere Alpha wolf. You are a Prime Alpha marked with lordship. There's no room for a wimpy mate."

"So I take it she passed?"

"Well, she was raised by a Peyroux, so I hardly doubted her dexterity. There were never any weaklings in Elias' bloodline. Despite your brother's coaxing, I

L.C. SON

28

was impressed to see a glimpse of her Altrinion nature arise at the sight of Kyra. You've told me of her innate ability to master nature, but today I saw in her the capacity to do much more."

"Now I'm curious. What did you see?"

"Not only did the sky darken at her dismay, but I saw fire rising from her skin and burrowing flames encased in her eyes. She was quite a sight."

"Now I'm worried. Did anyone else see it?"

"No, I kept my eyes on the crowd, they were too busy eating and taking selfies. Even Delia was in awe of her niece's transformation. I doubt she's ever seen Damina so—"

"Herself." Suddenly, it hits me. I knew seeing Kyra upset Damina, but she must have felt threatened by her. "Delia has spent years cloaking that part of her. The only time Damina has come close to such a transformation was on her birthday."

"Ah yes, when you purchased the red car."

"Yes and that was the day my suspicions were confirmed. But now that you tell me, I'm troubled as to why Kyra's presence set Damina off so bad. With both Delia and I cloaking Damina her nature should have been dormant. I mean since her birthday she's barely done more than clip the weather from time to time. How could she go from zero to a hundred so effortlessly?"

"Ha! Ha!"

"How is this funny, Sophie?"

"My dear Jackie, one day you will assume your place

as the Prime Alpha of the highest court in all the world, but today you are still as daft as any man."

"Excuse me? I suppose since you're laughing there's a point to your humor."

"I'm sorry my dear nephew. I don't mean to poke fun. But I thought it was obvious."

"What?"

"Damina loves you."

"Huh? Well, of course, I know that."

"Jackson, it's no mere infatuation for your bride. She loves you with her entire being. And today, Kyra was a threat to that love. I suspect she would go to the ends of the earth—to whatever end if anything or anyone were to come against that love. My dear nephew, there is no woman worth her salt that wouldn't protect what was most precious to her. So it is clear to me why not even the cloaking of an alpha or Alpha Prime could keep her defenses at bay. She loves you."

While it's no shock that Damina loves me, for the first time the enormity of her love for me is overwhelming. I love her with every ounce of my being, so I know what it means to love someone so deeply. The difference: I know who and what she is. It pains me to know she cannot say the same.

Our wedding night can't come fast enough.

"Are you okay, Jackson?" Sophie asks as she squeezes my shoulder trying to regain my attention.

"I'm sorry Sophie. It's just hard knowing how much she loves me without truly knowing me, is all."

"I know, dear. Soon she will know everything, and

she will know you for who you truly are. And with the love you two share, you will be able to conquer anything."

"That's just it. Will we? Can we truly conquer anything? How do I know she will forgive me for keeping the truth of not only her lineage but my own a secret for all these years? She may never look at me the same! You saw it today, Sophie. Her nature buckling at the bit, trying to force its way out. Damina has always told me that no matter how hard she tries to be refined and settled; she still feels chaotic. And I'm the author of it all!"

"Stop it, Jackson!" Sophie commands interrupting my rant. "Get yourself together, my dear. You are not weak. And neither is she. True love will always cover a multitude of transgressions. And what you have is love in its truest form. Not only that, you will have the orb from her father. Once the orb manifests itself in her Altrinion nature, her frenzy will settle, and she will understand her true purpose. Besides, there is no one, whether supernatural or mortal who can do what you can."

"What Sophie? What can I do?"

"You, Jackson, are the only person in this world with the power to bring order to her chaos."

Dalcour

BRAELYN'S WORDS still ring through me as I lay on

my bed staring up at the ceiling bouncing my leather hacky sack back and forth. She's right I need to talk to Jerrica and at least hear her out. Jerrica has never stirred me wrong in the span of our more than one-hundred-year friendship. Even though she came into my life on what was likely my most violent period to date, she's been a reliable and honorable friend and ally.

Thankfully and with the friendships of she and Braelyn, I'll never be that man again. Ever.

Beyond my brother's continual need to control me with this wrenching challenge, it's the thought that I could become *that man* again. Violent. Bloodthirsty. Above all—I would be alone again. Gone would be the comfort of the Civility Center, rallies for donations with the nobles, or even these little pet projects like the mansion revitalization that Jerrica is known for. No, it would all be gone. I know if I fail to meet my deadline, Decaux would unleash his secret herd of Scourge, more importantly, a bloody reckoning would arise—one so strong even I wouldn't be impervious to its lure.

I jump up from the bed at the thought of Decaux releasing the Scourge upon this world. Chills race up my spine because I know neither me nor even the most disciplined vampire could resist the blood flowing freely through the streets. Bloodlust would surely steer us in its path and the outcome for humans would be catastrophic.

"D, come quick!" Braelyn shouts as she blows

through my door in an instant, yanking my arm all while forcing me to shove my wandering thoughts aside.

"Braelyn, slow down! What's wrong?"

"Scourge attack. Come now!" Braelyn tugs my arm with all her might, enough to pull me to the doorpost. I look back at my terrace door and see only a slither of sunlight remains, piercing beneath the curtains. This is strange. The sun hasn't even set and there's a Scourge attack? Things are getting bad already.

We race through the hall and are down in the foyer in an instant.

"Dalcour, stop him!" I hear Jerrica bellow, with a tear-stained face as she points to Brian. I'm more concerned to see Lux and Cedric guarding the door, pushing Brian back blocking his exit.

"Let me out now!" Brian growls forcing himself between them.

"What's going on!" I demand, pitching my voice an octave lower so that it reverberates through the room, muffling the sound of both their snarls and growls.

"The Scourge, Dalcour, they attacked at the borders of the Tremé," Jerrica responds through her sobs as Braelyn maintains a hold at her waist.

"Let me out!" Brian barks once more, this time with enough force to push Cedric aside but Lux remains steady.

"Fine, I'll have Titan send the Guard to the Tremé right away. I'm sure he's already on it."

"You don't understand, D, Titan was the one

who told Lux and Cedric," Braelyn answers, gently approaching me. My attention is squarely on Brian's rage. I know the full moon is in a few days and wolves are bound to get testy, but his aggression is atypical for his normal stoic posture.

"Then why is Brian trying to tear my house down?" I snap, my gaze still set on Brian as he leans hard into Lux with all his brute force.

Turning quickly on his heels, Brian aims his attention for me, eyes glowing bright with a deep growl that burrows through his chest. I do not back away. He and I have never been much for pleasantries, but something is different. As I stare into the bright hue arising from his eyes, I notice what I didn't expect to find. Tears.

Grabbing his shoulders, I hold him tight at arms-length. Cedric and Lux come to my aid and hold his arms behind him as he locks his body stiff, muffling his growls through his canines.

"Dalcour, it's his home. His people. Salvadorè Abahana," Jerrica speaks slowly in between Brian's grisly sounds.

Then it hits me. Salvadorè. The man who raised him. Orphaned by the death of his parents when he was only a pup, Brian never knew his true family. He had no family. That is until Salvadorè found him the morning after a full moon. Salvadorè, one of the oldest pure Altrinions I know, was a close friend of Jerrica's father. He cared for Brian as if he were his own. But that's what Salvadorè did best, caring for people.

"Brian, I am so sorry," I begin, softening my tone. "What would you have me do?"

"Let. Me. Go." Brian seethes through his teeth.

"Cedric. Lux. Let him go. Let him be," I say as I watch small drips of water leak from his narrowed eyes. Immediately, both men let go of their hold as Brian shakes them loose. He snarls one last time, bows at me, thankful for his release and races out of the mansion.

"Hey, D! You're not going to let him go alone are you? He could get himself killed out there!" Braelyn quips.

"No, but there was no need to restrain him. Cedric, get my car now."

"Dalcour, please hurry. Brian is in no condition to go after the Scourge alone. If Titan had to call for the Guard it must be a great number," Jerrica says in a grim tone with a bleak expression to match.

"I know that's what worries me too. Don't worry dear friend, I'll bring back your furball," I answer in a gentle tone, wiping Jerrica's tears before nudging her jaw. Seeing her in pain is both unsettling and out of the norm for her.

Cedric beeps the horn of my Audi and Lux and I dash out the door, jumping into the car in a blink. I look back and see Jerrica and Braelyn standing at the door with Ms. Zamora, Jerrica's servant now at her side.

No one knows the back roads of New Orleans like Cedric and thankfully his skills get us to Salvadorè's home in no time. As we jump out of the car, the smell of freshly spilled blood fills my nostrils before I even see it, making me work hard to resist my bloodlust.

This attack was bigger than I thought.

Bodies, mostly human and Altrinion from what I can tell, lay in the courtyard. Most are torn apart and drained of blood. It's probably the most sickening sight I've ever seen. As if seeing children among the dead wasn't disgusting enough, the sight of a woman with her abdomen ripped open sends burning bile to my throat. I've done a lot of villainous things before, but this is sadistic. Evil at its core.

"Look what the vermin have done!" Lux says pointing to a small sac of fluid next to the woman's outstretched hands.

"Is there nothing sacred?" Cedric exclaims covering his nose and turning away with disgust.

"Wait a minute," I begin.

"What is it, Lord Marchand?"

"Shh—did you hear that?"

"A baby," Cedric says in a questioning tone as our eyes search the cobblestone yard for the child.

The cries of the infant grow louder, and we race inside the doorway where the sounds are loudest. Cedric slips on a pool of blood at the entrance, crashing into a vase and a small Scourge turns toward us and lets out a hideous hiss. Strange, however, it doesn't approach us, and I notice its legs are torn from its body. Still, it continues its screeching cry.

Once more, the baby cries but it's nowhere in sight. Lux, Cedric, and I search the area where we stand, looking for the baby, yet watchful of an attack.

While we've only seen one Scourge, we must remain vigilant. They never hunt alone. The baby makes one last cry and suddenly its sound fades. Thoughts of a Scourge with its clammy claws on the child send my thoughts into a frenzy.

"Search everywhere. Kill any vile thing that approaches. Whatever you do, find that child!" I order and Lux and Cedric spring into action.

The disheveled Scourge before us shrieks again and stretches toward Lux, wrapping its hand around his ankle.

"Kill it!" I shout.

Cedric pulls his katana blade from its holster as Lux turns away, readying himself to sever the creature's head from his body. Just as he whips the blade in the air, Brian's large foot slams into the creature's skull, smashing it dead to the ground.

A proud smile crosses my face at Brian's feat, and he smiles in return. But before I can congratulate him, a small gurgling coo comes from behind Brian's blazer. We all sigh relief when he opens his jacket, revealing the small infant wiggling alive and well in his arms.

If vitality remained in my doomed and damned heart, I'm most certain it would leap for joy.

Chapter 4

Jackson

"**G**ood grief Jack-o! How much did you have to drink?" Gregory laughs as he slaps my back hard. "Looks like you and Tye got the party started without us."

As much as I'd like to rebuke Gregory for irritating me, I can't form a response. I'm not sure if it's the mugginess of the evening or this hooch Tye gave me, I'm wrung. I know better than to drink without food. Yet, with Sophie ordering Tye to give me a proper last night out and demanding I stop my sulking, I took my first gulp just to satisfy her. While Tye claimed the tonic in the jar was from his grandfather's stash, the way it burned like acid in my throat makes me think otherwise—probably something he found from the street vendor by the boardwalk near his home.

My throat feels raw too, making every word I speak almost intolerable. Still, this is my last night as a "free man." I should be able to cut loose at least a little.

"Give the man a break, Gregory!" Shawn answers in my defense.

"Aww, he knows I'm just giving him a hard way to go, right Jack-o?" Gregory responds with another backslap. "Besides, seems like they're wrapping up with practice anyway. We should get going and head to the pub. Gotta get some wings, potato skins, and nachos in this man stat! There'll be nothing but veggies and wholesome homecooked meals after tomorrow." Gregory adds as the others join in the laughter.

"I'm sorry, he's right Jackson. Damina's family are very healthy eaters from what I remember. So you better get used to eating a lot of leafy greens and all other sorts of rabbit food!" Brandon teases and grabs my bottle from me. "So I'll take this from you, for now."

"Nope, I'm afraid I can't let you have that!" Tye barks, snatching the bottle from Brandon.

"C'mon man! This is supposed to be a party! Share a little with a brother!" Brandon replies, sounding as if he's already had one too many.

"This is special and for the Groom-to-be only. But no worries, I got you guys covered!" Tye answers, pulling out several small bottles of Smirnoff and Jim Beam from his jacket pocket. The guys all cheer, patting Tye on the shoulder, appreciative for supplying more booze.

"You know what—" I begin, my voice still scratchy but just loud enough to preempt their celebration. I grab onto the fencing and look up to the lights and try to get my bearings. As I gaze back at the guys, there now seems to be two of each of them. My balance shifts and I tilt over the fence to vomit.

"Eww gross!" Shawn shouts.

"Alright guys, we gotta get something in this guy before he does it again," Gregory says, coming to my aid.

"No worries, I got him," Tye says quickly pulling me from Gregory's arm.

"Hey! Listen up! I got myself! I am not weak. I am a grown man and the Prime Alpha—your alpha! Am I not?" My words are a bit sluggish, but I shout them out, shaking loose from Tye's grasp. Though their images are blurry, I see each of them stare at me, their faces filled with awe. "Good, I thought so," I finish and turn to walk away.

Before I know it the smell of freshly cut grass tickles my nose as I find my face planted in the ground just an inch from the curb.

"Geez Jack-o, now Damina's gonna kill me if you show up to your wedding tomorrow all tattered and bruised. You barely missed the pavement. Now come on and get up," Gregory says as he and Shawn lift me to my feet. "Tye, dude, what did you put in that hooch?"

"Nothing. Just a little extra fermented is all. It's been on grand's shelf for a minute," Tye quickly responds, his hands twitching as he holds the bottle close to his hip.

"Yeah, whatever just help us get him in the truck," Shawn snaps.

"No, it's okay. I got him. He can ride with me," Tye answers, pulling me from Shawn and Gregory's hold.

"Dude, there's more room in the truck!" Gregory protests.

"Please, stop fussing over me like I'm a frigging child!" I slobber and shout as I shake loose from their tight grip. "I'll ride with Tye. Gregory, you and the guys get our tables ready and order me some wings or something. I need to go home for a bit and change anyway," I add as I wipe my grass-stained knees.

"Alright, looks like we have our orders fellas," Gregory says in a more cheerful tone than his scowl suggests as he eyes me with concern. He quickly looks over his shoulder and gives a haughty grin to the guys, assuring them all is well before giving Tye a stern nod. Tye nods in reply, moving immediately to my side to seat me in his car. "Jack-o, I'll text you two the details and see you soon!" Gregory adds as he walks toward his truck.

"Sounds good. We'll see you in a bit," I reply leaning my head out the window for air as Tye speeds off.

While I'm thankful Tye is driving with a sense of urgency, I wish he'd slow down. My head is still spinning from gorging in more alcohol than normal. I'm not sure how long his grand's hooch has been fermenting, but it's quite potent. As much as I'd like to scold him for his head-whipping driving skills, I don't have the energy. I'm wasted.

This can't be good.

I lean my head against the seatbelt post, allowing the cool air of the evening to bring relief to the light-headed bout of nausea slowly forming. The streetlights all seem to combine into one long white stream of light while the twinkling stars shimmer blinding light into my irises. My senses are also all over the place. With the next full moon so close I'm used to a bit of lycanthropic overload—but this feels different.

Strange.

Thankfully, I don't have long to try to shake off the lingering effects of the alcohol as Tye's racecar-like driving has us at my place in no time. Still, my legs feel like gelatin when I rush myself to stand to get out of the car. Once more, Tye is a welcome companion and at my side in an instant. I pull my key out of my pocket and hand it to Tye, and we proceed down the walkway.

While I'm rather sure there are no more than five steps to climb to the landing of my townhome porch, tonight it looks like the stairway to heaven. I try one step, but my legs flail with just the bend of my knee.

"Perhaps we should just go around back," Tye suggests. My head nods in agreement before I have an opportunity to speak and Tye laughs slightly as he leads us to the backyard. I'm sure he's quite amused. No one has ever seen me intoxicated before. Not even me.

I hate doing things in excess just for the heck of it. Even more, being the Type-A admitted guy that I am, always used to being in control, this is not my norm.

But hey, I guess if there were ever a night to take a break from the norm, tonight is the night.

We're in my basement in an instant and Tye helps me to Damina's favorite chaise lounge chair. Tye offers to get me some water and rushes upstairs before I can remind him there's water at the bar. Again, my lips are too slow to respond.

Laying on the chair, Damina's fragrant scent of vanilla and Eucalyptus is woven into every fabric rising to meet my nostrils. Closing my eyes, I inhale deeply, thankful for just the aroma of her presence. In a flash, a replay of our passion earlier today sparks through my mind and my heart races with both excitement and desire. Tomorrow can't come fast enough.

As I reminisce, I hear a lilting chuckle that sounds familiar but is hard to place. I call out for Tye, wondering if someone else is here, but he doesn't answer.

I open my eyes and see Tye's shadowy form in front of me. It still feels like someone else is in the room with us, but I don't see anyone through the now murky coating of my eyes.

Crap! What was in that hooch?

"Here's your water," Tye says in a low and slightly gruff tone.

"Thanks, man," I answer, gulping the water down to cool the heat rising within me. "Is there someone else here?" I question, trying to ignore the salty taste of the water which does little to sate my thirst.

"You—um—do have a visitor I suppose."

"Who?"

"Well, I hope I'm more than just a visitor," a soft feminine voice calls to me from behind. As an hourglass silhouette rounds the chaise, Damina's scent glides past my nose in the wind carried from her movement and the chair.

"Damina?" I question trying to discern through the muffling sound of my own breathing. Tye places another tray on the lounge in front of us and quickly leaves my view. I squint and wipe my eyes, trying to see through the veiling of my own intoxication, but I cannot. It doesn't matter, I'd know her sweet tone anywhere. Though her footsteps sound heavier than usual, all I can think of is having her in my arms again.

Desire sweeps over me as it did this afternoon the moment she places her hand in mine. But this time is different. I don't think I have the strength to let her go. Perhaps it's the alcohol having its way with me, but I don't care. I don't even know what brought her here. I'm just glad she came.

Pulling her into my embrace she straddles my lap, pressing me down into the chaise and our passion rekindles just where we left off this afternoon. Strength rises in the seat of my pants once more and I now have no doubt that waiting another day to make her my wife is no longer an option.

She is mine tonight.

Dalcour

CHASING THE remaining Scourge from the premises isn't my idea of a night on the town. We barely had a moment to relish in the fact that Brian saved the baby before four other vipers made their presence known. However, they were easily beaten when Cedric's wife Abigail and her companions surprised us with their aid.

In the last five decades, we've added more women to the Guardian's detail; much to Titan's displeasure. His old-world charms are archaic and certainly out of touch with the times. He still believes women are for nothing more than his pleasure. While I've undoubtedly indulged myself with a parade of women at his side as of late, it's not because I think of them as objects only for my enjoyment as he does. I just haven't found my equal.

Frankly, I've given up hope that such an equal exists despite Jerrica's claims.

Still, watching how Cedric and Abigail fight side by side, stealing kisses from one another all while fending off attacks in such harmony, I can't help envying their pairing. They are happy and completely in love.

Cedric and his brother, Lux were born both half-Altrinion and half-Wolf. Born with the luxury of deciding their own fate, Lux always knew he wanted to embrace his wolf while Cedric remained undecided. That is until he met Abigail. She and Braelyn were in the same cell block of rogue Scourges that Titan found on his patrol. Braelyn was easier to tame than Abigail—probably because she never wanted to be a vampire in the first place. Abigail, on the other hand, was a different creature altogether. She embraced her nature, fearing neither death nor pain.

Titan was convinced that we would have to put her down, but Cedric persuaded Titan that he could tame her. I'm still not sure just what happened in the taming wells of the Civility Center between Cedric and Abigail. What I do know is that when they came out on the other end, they came out together.

"My lord," Lux begins as he pulls me back when I near the edging of the Bayou Bienvenue. I've let my mind wander too far. Jerrica and Braelyn's pleas for me to find love are beginning to get the best of me.

Shake it off.

"I'm good," I snap, freeing myself from Lux's grasp. I don't need another person trying to save me. He stares at me as if he wants to say more but restrains himself.

"No worries Lord Marchand, the mighty duo won't let those vile beasts get any further than the bluff," Lux continues with a haughty laugh while proudly pointing to his brother and sister-in-law as they tear the creature's limb from limb, tossing them into the water.

"Very well then," I reply, squeezing Lux's shoulder in agreement.

"We found something!" Cedric shouts, waving for us to come to him.

"What is it?" I question.

"I'm afraid it's for you, my lord," Abigail adds as she pulls a bloodied shirt from the lifeless creature's hand.

Horror fills my soul as I read the words, *"The Countdown Has Begun"* smeared across the chest of the fallen creature.

This is no mere warning. Decaux is declaring the start of his war.

"What is the meaning of this Lord Marchand?" Lux asks as though he doesn't understand the reason for the dread expressions now marred across Abigail and Cedric. But as the three of us stare at the bloodied lettered words we immediately understand its intent.

"It's my brother, Decaux. He's warning me that my time limit is nearing its end," I reply, snatching the shirt from Abigail and stuffing it into my pocket.

"I don't understand, the Civility Centers are thriving and your treaty with the local Dunes Pack is running smoothly. Why is he trying to cause panic now?"

"Because there is still more to fear," I say, hardly above a whisper. Abigail clinches Cedric's fist, squeezing it as they both exchange worried glances.

"Lux, all that matters now is that we keep these borders safe. Take some of Abigail's company with you and let Titan know the remaining Scourge have been disposed of. Cedric, you and Abigail tend to this area for a duration and ensure no more Scourge remain near this post. I need to return and see that Brian is well. Jerrica will have my head if I don't."

"But my lord, perhaps one of us should go with you just in case," Cedric says, grabbing my arm preventing my exit. I snatch my arm back without hesitation. The thought of Decaux threatening me is more than irritating. I need to be alone.

"I'll be fine, my friend," I respond, attempting to rein in my rage as Cedric's fear-wrought eyes gaze back at me. Squeezing Cedric's shoulder reassuringly, I smile, and he nods in kind. As I look up, I catch Abigail watching our exchange. I can tell she is more worried for Cedric than she is for me. And she should. My temperament hasn't been steady as of late, but I wish to keep it without incident. Widening my smile, hopeful that it meets my eyes, I nod to Abigail and once more at both Cedric and Lux before racing back to Salvadorè's home.

Every curse and expletive in every known tongue erupts from my mouth like a volcano. My feet can't move fast enough against the wind to catch flight. I need to soar above the city just enough to shed myself of the weight of it all. My mind is a crammed cluster of rage and fury tinged with a grain of hopelessness.

As much as I want to put an end to my brother's schemes once and for all, I am becoming doubtful such a feat is possible. Every time I think I've gained ground; I realize I'm far from the goal.

Too far indeed.

I scan the city from as far as the Quarter to the Tremé in a blink all while I do my best to quench the torrent brewing within me. The last thing I need is to draw too much attention to myself and bring more Scourge out from hiding. Hovering over the city I inhale deeply and try to detect the putrid smell of either Scourge or Skull and am relieved to find neither. But my relief is short-lived when the aroma of drying blood fills my nostrils causing a twinge of nausea to ripple through me.

The smell leads me straight to Salvadorè's courtyard. While I'm thankful the onslaught is contained to just this location, seeing Brian's grim expression sends a barreling pain straight to my gut. With the baby still wrapped in his blazer in one arm and the tattered body of Mr. Abahana in the other, terror strikes the core of me seeing Brian is such a grisly state.

Approaching slowly, I walk through the puddles of drying blood and human remains, trying to discern Brian's disposition. The most troubling part is since he is a wolf, I can't read his mind or hear his thoughts. I don't know what he's thinking right now. And I dare not ask.

As I get closer, I see the baby wiggle a little in his arm and Brian responds with a firm yet gentle sway, calming the child back to sleep. The baby is small—too small to survive without medical treatment for long. I would guess the newborn is no more than four pounds at most.

"We should get the baby to a hospital, Brian. I can compel the doctors to treat him immediately."

"There's no need," Brian responds in a grim tone.

"Brian, just let me help you," I answer, kneeling to meet his eyes.

"Can't you smell it?" Brian's eyes are dark as he glares back at me.

"Smell what? What are you talking about, Brian?"

"Death. It's all around us."

I watch as Brian's whispered words echo like the wind through the courtyard and his golden eyes blaze with both fury and sadness. Looking around the courtyard all I see are corpses. Mostly human, a few wolves and vampire but mostly human. From the looks of the cracked pinata and festive décor I now see the violence interrupted a party.

"Brian, we must get the child out of here and to the hospital," I plead once more, hopeful for Brian to regain his focus as his hand caresses Abahana's entrails and his open body.

"There's no need. He's already gone," Brian responds, now squeezing the hand of his mentor.

As I part my lips to protest, Brian swings his other arm around and places the baby in my hands. My mouth remains open as I watch in horror as the baby squirms, taking one last breath and his now bluish body goes still.

One lone tear falls from Brian's eye but his gaze pierces straight through me. And while I can't read his mind, one thing is clear: He blames me for it all.

Chapter 5

Jackson

If the sound of glass crashing into a thousand pieces against the wooden floors of my basement was my only problem tonight, it wouldn't be a problem at all. Instead, it's the shattered pieces of Damina's broken and bleeding-heart laying before me now that plummets my soul to its reckoning. Seeing the pain, hurt, and fury in her eyes lets me know that I am no longer the broker of her heart's joy.

I am the death dealer of her heart's soul.

I am her enemy.

Her heart, the one thing I claimed was most precious to me—the one thing I vowed to protect with my very life is the one thing I have destroyed.

I care not for the perpetrator now laying at my feet.

The moment Damina crossed the threshold I watched in disgust as the changeling before me was released and Kyra's duplicitous form was revealed. Throwing her from my lap to the cold floor was the nicest thing I could think to do. With my bride-to-be before me, I dare not show further cruelty by enacting on Kyra something more fitting of her treachery.

Even still, I sincerely doubt I could look any worse in the eyes of my beloved.

How could I be so stupid? How could I be fooled by the oldest trick in the lycanthropic lore? There isn't enough wine and spirits in this world or in the world of men that would make me succumb to Kyra's tempting. I never wanted to bed her before, and the thought alone sickens me now.

And she knows it—that's why she used a changeling.

Yet as much as I want to understand the how and why of it all it doesn't matter. I only want her out of my sight—*before I kill her.*

There's little I can do to quench the alpha within me from rising as a vicious, *"GET OUT"* roars through me. Kyra trembles at my feet—as she should. But she dares not cross Damina's fiery-eyed path. I don't blame her. Fear strikes a chord within me as well, but I know I must endure whatever pain necessary before this night meets its end.

As Kyra retreats, I catch a glimpse of myself in the mirror and notice my wolf-form piercing its way through as my muscles protrude and my stride lengthens. Clinching my jaw tight, I do my best to calm myself. I don't want to phase in front of Damina like this for the first time. That would be too much to bear.

"Damina, please let me explain. Please," I plead, softening my stance to meet her pain-staked face. She instantly steps back, wary of my touch. As she stares at me through flame-filled eyes, I know with all certainty that my touch is the last thing she wants.

She quickly turns away from me and runs to the patio. Her body immediately convulsing as she steps into the grassy area and vomits. Watching tremors rage her body with the aftershocks of nausea caused by my betrayal crushes my pride and I rush to her aid, giving no thought for the broken glass piercing my feet as I race to her side.

Even with the pain of glass fragments piercing my flesh, I wrap my arms around her, hoping to steady her as she sways back and forth. The only thing that matters to me is her. Damina's body feels hot like a furnace. A flame-like glow emanates through her reddened pores and I'm almost afraid to touch her, but I press my body forward, cradling her into my chest.

There's no injury too brutal that I wouldn't endure just to have her in my arms right now.

But alas, I've spoken too soon.

With a thunderous bolt of power, Damina sends a hurling energy through my body, shoving me hard with her hand clear across the yard, knocking me into the nearby pergola. Thankfully the hammock at my back takes the brunt of my impact.

53

"Jackson!" I hear Gregory shout from the fence with Dacari at his side. I'm not sure just how long they've been here or how much they've seen, but with the daggered-eyed gaze Dacari is giving me I know she's seen enough to hate me too. This won't end well.

Gregory speeds across the yard and is at my side in an instant. Dacari keeps her sights on me as she walks cautiously toward Damina, obviously wary of her cousin's newfound and luminous form.

"Where is Tye?" Gregory asks, propping me up against a lounge chair. Hunching my shoulders, I nod with uncertainty. It's a good question, but not the most pressing. I need to find a way to calm Damina before she explodes. Sophie mentioned that Damina sparked a little fire earlier at Sonfries when she first saw Kyra. This pales in comparison.

"What did you do to my cousin, you jerk?" Dacari shouts with a bright golden hue flickering quickly in her eyes. Her eyes too reveal a deep wound as tears freefall down her cheeks, but I don't have time to concentrate on it. Gregory squeezes my shoulder, and we both stare at one another fearful that both women might induce their supernatural form for the first time tonight.

Delia will be pissed if that happens, but she is the least of my concern.

Gregory signals to Dacari to calm her temper as he points to the neighbors beginning to take watch from their windows. Crap! Now we'll have to smooth this over if they see too much. I gaze at Damina and am hopeful to see the flaming light around her fading.

"If you laid one hand on my cousin that will be the last thing you'll ever touch, you moron! I'll kill you if you've touched her. Even just once!" Dacari's venomous words shoot clear across the yard as if she stabbed me in the chest. The thought that I would ever willingly hurt Damina is unconscionable.

But I did hurt her.

"I didn't touch her, Dacari!" I contend. Though I know I should keep my voice down, any suggestion to the contrary pains me to my marrow.

"Hey, everyone needs to settle down. Let's go in the house and stop giving these people a show," Gregory says in a tone softer than I've ever thought my hardline ally capable.

Rising to my feet, I make my way as close as Damina's watchful glare will allow. The hurt and anguish written on her face plummet a sense of dread in the pit of my core. Still, I can't allow her to leave. Not like this.

"Damina, please let's talk. Don't go," I beg, with one hand on the gate lock bar, preventing her exit. It's all I can muster.

Damina gazes at me searching my face for hope but it's obvious she only sees her betrayer. For the first time in the existence of us, Damina eyes me as though I were an abhorrent stranger. A grim mar of disgust slowly frames her face as she watches me once more through flame-filled eyes. Just then a faint tint of her former glow rises from her body as anger pulls her in at the sight of me.

I need to find a way to comfort her but I'm still not sure what to do. Mostly, I just don't want her to leave me. Lightly placing my fingers around her wrist, I grimace as her heat stings my fingertips. But I don't care. I need her to stay. My hands are only on her for a millisecond before she shoves me with a brute force I thought her petite frame incapable of producing.

Once more my wolf rises to the occasion as I dig my feet in the ground, dragging both cobblestone and dirt in the hollowed path beneath me. I feel my muscles retract and pulsate with the alpha within desiring its release, but I stifle my rage. Gregory echoes in kind, his lycanthropy aching to take over, but he follows suit only allowing a low snarl to ripple through his chest.

Still, Damina is not moved. She cares not for my foreboding friend nor my callous attempts of regaining the grace of her presence. Not even Dacari can assuage Damina's rage as she almost rips into Dacari for merely touching her. I watch in awe as she stiffens her stance, squaring her shoulders daring Gregory to react. One low rumble from me and Gregory steps back as I nod for him to step aside.

Although I don't want her to go, it's obvious she has no desire to stay.

Why would she?

Just as I begin to accept my fate and let her go, *for tonight*, a shuddering cry erupts from her that breaks through the quietness of night like a bolt of lightning. I watch in horror as my bride-to-be topples to the ground of the front yard. She clinches her hands into the grassy carpet sobbing and screaming in grief. Shawn races to her side, after giving Gregory a nodded warning and asks Dacari's permission to get Damina to the car.

Cries score through me as well as the weight of the pain I've caused her knots the core of my soul into my gut. I care not who sees me cry. What care I that my pack now have their first reveal of my vulnerability.

Tonight, I'm not an alpha. I hardly feel like a man. A man loves and covers his woman. A man protects what he loves because he loves to protect. At least that's what my father taught me as his father taught him. Tonight I am not that man. I am the fool who had a blind eye to the troubles brewing beneath the surface. I am the idiot who didn't follow his own inclination, but rather took the advisement of others and kept the truth from my beloved.

How could I be so foolish? If I could do it all over again, I would do it different. I should have done it different. But I didn't. I've failed her. *I've failed us.*

Now, whatever happens next, I must accept my fate.

Even if it means rewriting my destiny.

Dalcour

THERE ARE very few times when disobedience is acceptable. Tonight is one of those times. Although I clearly instructed Cedric to guard the post with

Abigail, I was happy when he and his wife showed up at the Abahana estate. Had they delayed their arrival I have no doubt I would have killed Brian. It doesn't take a genius or Altrinion telepathy to know he had every intent on unleashing his fury on me. Nor does it take a genius to know had he acted on his impulse only one of us would remain standing.

The odds are not in his favor.

Not long after their arrival, the remainder of Abigail's company returns prepared to provide the Guardian's Defusal Services. Over the last few centuries, the Guard has become adept in cleaning up behind supernatural messes such as these. We even have Tolu and Baron who oversee our faux PR team in New Orleans. Whether the task requires compelling humans to forget what they have seen or making a scene such as this look like a random gas explosion, Tolu and Baron are as crafty as they come.

While I'm always impressed to see the Guard come to our aid, tonight I especially marvel at the caring manner at which they handle the victims. At the very least, I hope it would bring some comfort to Brian that those he considers his family will be given the dignity of both proper treatments and burial. Though, I can tell there is little hope in reining in his anger.

"Lord Marchand," Cedric begins, tapping my shoulder lightly. "We should get you back to the mansion. No need for you to be here when the press arrives."

"What of the child?" I ask curiously of the preemie's whereabouts.

"Abigail will take him to the *Infantia Sacras Cripta* at the edge of the Hall of Isis maze. She's spoken with Brian, and he is well with the arrangements, my lord," Cedric replies.

"Was the child of lineage?"

"Brian believes so according to Abigail, but he isn't entirely sure. The mother was young, and the father not identified."

"It's no matter. Well done," I answer in a grim tone. The thought of a child getting caught in the crossfire of Decaux's nonsense sickens me. In any case, the Sacred Child Crypt is a fitting place for the baby. Although normally used for supernatural children who die prematurely, this certainly fits the situation. Since supernaturals caused his death, we should at least take responsibility for it.

"Abigail, inform the others I'm escorting Lord Marchand back to the mansion. Have Lux accompany you on your way back and keep your eyes peeled," Cedric says. Abigail acknowledges with a brief nod and opens her mouth to respond when Brian jumps in front of her.

"What? Not willing to get your hands a little dirty after all the trouble your family has caused? Or is it more fitting for others to do your work for you? Ha! And they call you lord—"

"Watch your tongue!" Cedric jumps to my defense. Abigail hands the swaddled infant to one of the Guards in her company and stands guardedly at her husband's side.

"Why should I? What has he ever done to be esteemed among any of you? And you Cedric—you are an embarrassment to any drop of canine essence to ever run through your veins! Now you're just another viper!" Seething snarls and hissing sounds erupt within the courtyard and the dutiful deeds of the Guards come to a screeching halt as each of them eye Brian with contempt. Though we've added several wolves to the Guard as of late, tonight only Altrinion-Vampires and former Scourge Vampires stand among the company.

Brian is literally barking up the wrong tree.

"Stop it, Brian! Your issue is with me. Leave it there!" I contend.

"As you wish!" Brian barks back.

"Look, I know these people are your family and I can understand how this hurts you but—"

"But what? The fact remains that every one of these dead bodies can be laid at your feet. You claim to be a leader yet and still you fail to do what is necessary to ensure massacres such as this cease."

"What would you have me do? We are all doing what we can to maintain balance in the supernatural world!"

"Kill Decaux!" With Brian's declaration, my instincts straddle between both ending him swiftly and giving him a Mercy Blade myself to use against my wretched brother. I stand frozen and gaze at the watchful faces of those in the courtyard. Most likely agree with his sentiment but are too fearful to speak. Only a handful like Cedric understand that the situation is far more complex than merely taking my brother's life.

"Lord Marchand—as you call yourself," Brian resumes, "you know as well as anyone here that Decaux is the root and cause for such turmoil. Sure rogue Skull and Scourge exist, but he is putting together an army whose sole purpose is annihilation!"

"Don't you think I know that?" I lash back, lunging at Brian with only Cedric's arm at my chest to hold me back. "Listen to me and hear me well, you stand here among my Guard in the city I call my home and dare hurl insults at me? Don't you dare forget that if it were not for me Abahana wouldn't have had the very land where your feet now rest to call his home. I and I alone have stood countless times against my brother not just for my own grievances but for the good of you all."

"For our good? Please tell me how we benefit from your good! Guardians globe-wide have increased their numbers due to the steady influx of Scourge and Skull. And the reality is you're not the one out here sacrificing life and limb—no you're held up in your mansion. The truth is you are no better than Decaux. You're just a necessary evil!"

"Brian! Mind your words!" Dranoel says now appearing at the entryway of the courtyard. I have no idea how long he's been here, but he clearly disapproves of Brian's charges against me.

"It's quite all right Dranoel. Let him think whatever

he will. Brian, I don't need you to understand the sacrifices I've made; which have ultimately given you the freedom to even stand here with your self-righteous indignation before me now. But you were right with one thing. I am *the* necessary evil and it would serve you well to never forget it!"

Brian charges me, baring his canines with his eyes a bright golden hue and sweat beading across his brow. He swings his right arm, but my movements are too swift, and I duck under his arm and tug his leg, sending him to the ground. Standing over him, I dig my feet into his chest and use my other to hold the heel of my boot at his neck. He grimaces, squirming beneath me but is unable to free himself.

Dranoel comes forward, his arms up pleading with me not to end Brian.

But my rage is kindled.

"Is there anyone else here who shares the sentiment of this mongrel at my feet?" I shout while scanning the room for any who'd seek to defy me. Most look away, hopeful not to catch my eye while others bow their heads in full submission. "Is there no one else? Let me be clear to all under the sound of my voice—I have killed others for far less than the actions of this mutt. I will not hesitate to do so now. So this is your chance. Now is your one opportunity to speak up."

"My lord, please he's just grieving," Dranoel says approaching me slowly, his eyes filled with terror as he casts watchful glances down at Brian, cautioning him to surrender. I know if I press my heel any deeper into Brian's throat, I will kill him. It's no more than he deserves. "Please, my lord," Dranoel begs once more.

Cedric holds his position stiff at my side, keeping his watch of any others with similar intentions. I gaze down at Brian, and he grimaces beneath my boot and am slightly impressed he hasn't given in so easily. As I look at him, thoughts of Jerrica fill my mind and it becomes clear I have let this go on long enough.

"Well then, if there are no takers let us be done with the matter!" I shout. I push my foot into Brian's sternum before kicking him over on his side as I saunter into the middle of the courtyard. Dranoel and his daughter Sonja are at Brian's side in an instant while Cedric remains guarded at my back. "Lest my claims of nobility and civility cloud your view of me, let tonight be a lesson to you all. You do have cause to fear me—*your necessary evil.* So I urge you, choose now the vice for which you stand. Whether it be Decaux, Scourge, Skull, human or me—the evils for which you contend and guard against are always present among you. Still, I promise you this. I will fight for the balance and harmony that we once shared in this earth long ago. And if you stand with me there is nothing we can't do to rebuild this world for the better. But, if you stand against me, not even the light of the sun will protect you from my retribution—that is a promise."

Chapter 6

Jackson

"Does this look like love to you?"* Those six words invade my very being, piercing my soul and heart in one blow. Sure, Damina had more to say about my disloyalty and betrayal which also rage my thoughts, but it's that phrase—that question to which I must give an account.

How I wanted to pick her up from the ground and hold her in my arms! I wanted to console and comfort her, but I knew to her, my touch was the most unwanted thing in the world. To see her so filled with sorrow and anguish is hard to bear. But knowing it was my own doing is where my struggle remains.

I almost wished Gregory hadn't stopped the cellphone Damina hurled at me from hitting my face.

At least I would have felt some connection to her. Just having the last thing she touched—touch me would have comforted my disconsolate heart. Now, I have nothing.

Nothing about tonight looked like love. Instead, it most resembled torment, heartache, and pain. I have given her every reason to revile and hate me. In all my worrying about Allyson and Sophie's concern of my brother, it stands to reason I am my own reckoning. I have authored my own heart's destruction.

I could blame Damina's family for making me vow to keep her lineage a secret; thus binding my own. I could even fault my family and pack for how we've led a life of secrecy in the world of supernaturals. Still, I know it all pales in comparison to the truth. Of my own volition, I kept hidden the things that should've been shared. I made a conscious choice to deceive her.

How else did I expect this to end?

"Just a few more to go, Jackie," Sophie says softly as she tweezes hunks of glass from my feet. Though I feel her heaving the fragments out and puncturing my flesh with each tear, none of it hurts more than recounting the grief-worn look on Damina's beautiful face. Knowing I am the cause is more painful than the sting of the glass etched under my skin.

"I've tried calling Delia, but she hasn't answered," Sophie adds. She stops for a moment and holds my left foot steady on her knee and stares back at me likely awaiting a response. But I am mute. I haven't said a word since Dacari sped Damina away in her Jeep. I can't help recounting the events of tonight in my mind, over and over.

"I can only imagine the vile things Dacari must be telling Delia—filling her mind with all manner of untruth," Sophie continues as she tosses a large bloody shard from my foot into a glass bowl.

"Truth, Sophie. It's all truth," I reply just above a whisper.

"How can you say that, Jackie? Nothing about tonight is the truth!"

"How can I say that? Let's be serious here, Sophie," I shout jumping up from my seat. I've grown tired of sitting here as Sophie plays nursemaid. "I've had five years to tell her the truth—five years, Sophie! Yet in one night those years have been shredded to nothingness! All because I didn't tell her the truth. What else do we expect Dacari to tell her mother? Delia will not be happy that we've let it come to such a pass."

"Well, Delia has her own part to answer in all of this Jackson! We did not set Damina's course alone!"

"There is no we, Sophie. There is only me and Damina. But I allowed the we to play the bigger part and that is all on me. The only one who chartered Damina's course to its undoing tonight is me. So no, my dear aunt, there is no we—only me."

Sophie's bleak and grim expression fills the space between us. I know she wants to counter my claims, but she remains silent, observing me through tear-filled eyes.

Gregory bursts into the room, breaking the

awkward silence brewing between Sophie and me. He gazes back and forth at us as if he's trying to decide whether to engage. Thankfully, he doesn't let our dissonance distract him.

"Hey, Jack! We've got a ping on Dacari's Jeep. She was at Damina's place for a while and then headed home. She showed up alone, and then she and Delia rushed back out of the house. Shawn went to Delia's place and their housekeeper told him Dacari and Delia left out with the dog on an emergency."

"Oh, I guess that explains why she hasn't called me back," Sophie's tone is curt. I dart a glance of warning at her, but her stubborn exterior remains.

I don't have time to deal with Sophie tonight.

"We have every reason to think Damina is at her place—or at least she was over an hour ago."

"Thanks, Gregory. Let's go!" I reply.

"Jackson! I haven't finished removing the remaining shards! You can't go out there like that!" Sophie protests.

"She's right, Jack-O. I mean, but you could just wolf out and heal. You'd push the glass right through," Gregory suggests.

"I don't have time for phasing right now. I need to do this as a man, not a wolf. Have someone bring me a few pairs of socks and my Nike flops. They'll have to do until I can get myself cleaned up."

We're in the car in a beat and I can still hear my aunt calling my name from my front door. I know she's only worried about me. She has every right to be. Even with two pair of thick socks on both feet, tinges of blood still stain the rim of my heel. Sure, I could've taken Gregory's advice, but I don't trust my wolf right now.

He's probably just as pissed at me as Damina for my actions.

I can't face him right now. *But I know I'll have to soon.*

As Gregory speeds through the city like a banshee, I inwardly cringe at the tickets we're likely tallying from the speed cameras. There's truly no way to avoid them since there are cameras on almost every corner. I'm sure I can reach out to a few of my contacts to make enough of them go away, but it's still not the most pressing issue on my mind.

Damina is all I can think about, and we can't get to her place fast enough.

Every thought I have is of her. And now with her playlist blaring through my car's Bluetooth, I have no choice but to become enraptured in everything that is my beautiful lady. Tightening my hold of her phone in my hands is all I can do to feel her with me.

It's the last thing she touched—touching me—I'll take what I can get. For now.

"What's so funny?" Shawn asks, peering over my shoulder from the backseat. I can't help the light chuckle that escapes me when I think of how her phone always takes over in my car. It doesn't matter my settings. If Damina's phone is in proximity, the car automatically takes its cues from her. Funny—the car seems to be wiser than me when it comes to her.

"Nothing, just thinking," I quietly answer as glassy tears form when we pass the church where we were to marry. As we sit at the red light, I feel my skin tighten. Thoughts of our would-be nuptials race through my mind. Seeing the church today and picturing how lovely my bride would've been in the center aisle plagues my heart.

My body boils inside as my wolf gnaws at me, craving his release. But it's the sound of Chris Brown's song *Enemy* blaring through my radio that pierces my soul. I didn't even know Damina liked his music—but tonight—it's as though the song was meant for this moment.

It's the most appropriate melody of viciously scored retribution tailored just for me.

As Gregory pulls in front of Damina's building, I haven't the patience to wait for him to put the car in park before I jump out and sprint up the staircase. While I feel the remaining fragments of glass thrust deeper into my flesh, I dare not wince or blink. I must stay focused. I need to remain vigilant and prepare myself to reclaim my beloved.

Lunar speed carries me to Damina's door in what seems like less than a blink. I hardly recall using my key fob to enter. Yet, here I am again standing before her door as I did this afternoon. My sweaty palm glides its way to the imprint I left behind earlier today. Except now everything has changed, and I am confident upon opening this door nothing will ever be the same.

Dalcour

"DALCOUR! WHAT'S the meaning of this? Dalcour!" Jerrica's screams do little to quench the fiery rage brewing within me. I know storming into the mansion and tossing a wooden console across the foyer at my entrance is more than disturbing. But it is likely the rippling bolts of lightning I hurl up at the crystal chandelier, sending it crashing to the ground along with my deafening and rage-filled roar that truly alert both Jerrica and Braelyn to my distress.

"D! Calm down! Tell us what happened!" Braelyn shouts from between the parlor threshold with a watchful Jerrica at her side.

"Please, Dalcour tell me it isn't Brian. Is it? Has something happened to him?" Jerrica questions with a bleak yet hopeful expression. Yet, her hope-wrought eyes do nothing to disrupt my fury. Just the mention of Brian's name plagues me to my core.

"You dare ask me of that pompous, cross-bred mutt? I suppose you think it's all my fault too. Is that what you think, Jerrica?" I demand with my gaze locking with hers. I know I should back down—that it's not Jerrica's fault but it's too late. My rage is already set in.

"What happened, D?" Braelyn questions once more, this time in a slightly censuring tone.

"Where is Brian? What did you do?" Jerrica snaps, pulling away from Braelyn's side. Her eyes glow back at me and I see a glint of her fury forming with the bronzing of her skin.

"I did nothing to your little mongrel except teach him a lesson. I could've done much worse."

"Wait a minute! Will somebody explain what's going on here? You know us vile Scourge aren't blessed with your telepathic gifts," Braelyn adds coming between the rising stand-off between Jerrica and me.

I keep my sights on Jerrica and try to discern her next move, but she's still difficult to read. She's working hard to keep her thoughts from me, and I don't know why. I know I should press the matter, but I don't. Closing my eyes, I bite my lower lip and inhale deeply. I need to find a way to calm down. Even if I wanted to end Brian tonight---Jerrica is not my enemy.

"Abahana is dead," I answer gruffly. I had hoped to give the news more graciously, but the sweltering rage inside will not allow it.

Both Jerrica and Braelyn gasp at my revelation and hold each other tight at the waist.

"That's horrible, D!" Braelyn exclaims, her eyes glassy and tear laden.

"And Brian blames you?" Jerrica says with diffidence. I watch as her defenses fade, and her stiff posture softens.

"Why would he blame you? It was just a random Scourge attack, right?" Braelyn questions, her eyes still watchful of both Jerrica and me.

"It was Decaux," Jerrica answers before I can form a reply.

"Decaux?" Braelyn mutters softly.

"Yes, my wretched brother is exacting his vengeance

and innocent people have been caught in the crossfire!"

"It's not your fault, Dalcour. You must know this!" Jerrica exclaims.

"Well, you can try to sell that to your loyal canine, but I doubt he'll buy it."

"He's just upset Big D! Abahana was like his surrogate—the only family he's ever known," Braelyn responds.

"There were women, children—babies." My voice drifts as both Braelyn and Jerrica's voices grow mute as tonight's encounter replays in my mind.

"Dalcour!" Jerrica shouts, regaining my attention. "This isn't your fault," she states with stubborn resolution.

"She's right, D!"

"I should've put an end to my brother's schemes long ago!"

"And what? Kill your brother?" Jerrica counters.

"What other option is there? Decaux has proven time and again that his treachery knows no end! It's all one endless and deadly game of pursuit with him."

"Then let us end it, Dalcour—once and for all!"

"What would you propose? I'm doing everything I can to meet his wretched deadline."

"That is, everything except one—"

"Jerrica, no not again! Must we do this now?"

"C'mon D, at least consider this woman might be what you need to finally give you a reprieve!"

"I'm sorry but I don't see how me finding true love will solve anything—this isn't a fairytale!"

"No, it's no fairytale indeed. But even Decaux knows it has been foretold that only through the love of mates bearing the sacred oak will balance be reset—or even possible. Maybe in his own twisted way, he wishes to end his torment through you. It makes sense since of your lineage you are the only one who bears the mark." Jerrica exclaims. Her eyes dance once more with a hopeful gleam that would almost be convincing if I believed in such bedtime stories.

"I have no use of ancient and baseless prophecies of old fools, Jerrica! Nor have I the luxury of waiting to find someone who may not exist. Don't you think I've looked for her? Don't you think I want to find happiness? *To find love*. Well, I've never found her— she doesn't exist!" Jerrica's eyes fall at my admission and a flashing stream of her erratic thoughts flood my mind.

Of all the emotions coursing through her consciousness, caution swathes my being at the capturing of her most secret thought. "*If only my love were enough*," Jerrica confesses from the deepest part of her soul. Never before have I heard such thoughts revealed by her. Although Brian and Charlotte do a decent job of keeping her intimate thoughts safe, I'm accustomed to an occasional slip of consciousness from time to time. Yet, never anything like this.

This is different.

This changes everything.

With her canine attendants afar, Jerrica stands before me barren. One thought after another wreak havoc to my psyche, splitting my head in two. Now, I'm not only working to keep her thoughts out, but shoving my own aside just the same. It's obvious she never intended to divulge her affection nor have I the heart to bare my lack of reciprocity.

A fear grips me I never thought I would face. The fear of hurting my most trusted friend and ally. Never before has Jerrica appeared so vulnerable. Almost fragile. And while I know she is a formidable force all her own, tonight her most private thoughts are exposed to me. Jerrica's eyes dance once more, but she stares back at me, hesitant to reply. I spy a deep longing for me piercing through her gaze that is unfamiliar to me.

Who is this woman?

Beads of sweat form at my brow not due to my skirmish with Brian and the Scourge, but one brought on by the newfound knowledge of a secret never intended for release. To combat the tussle forming within me at her revelation, I do what comes easiest when matters of my would-be-heart brew at the surface: lash out.

"Like I said ladies, I don't have the luxury to sit around waiting for a happily ever after. It does not exist. So stop trying to play fairy godmother and know this there is no beauty in the world of men or the supernatural capable of taming this beast." As vehemently as I know how, I spew my words like a fire-breathing dragon, summoning the Altrinion force within to emanate through me with as much ferocity as possible. I take flight and rise to the top of the landing in a flash before either Jerrica or Braelyn can respond. Though gut-wrenching, I watch tears trail down the faces of both women. An eerie sense of satisfaction looms through my being and I know my actions had the outcome I intended.

For the first time tonight, the fogginess of my mind dissipates, and clarity takes over. Those around me have become too familiar. I've always been taught that familiarity is as much of a curse as the sun. At least that is what my father always said. Tonight I've been both challenged and wrongfully infatuated all due to familiarity.

This cannot continue.

Fear, not familiarity must return with the resonance of my name.

If I am to play the beast in the west wing, then it's high time for my beastly depravations to resume.

If we are to play Decaux's wicked games, the familiar must be pushed aside and only what is necessary will be released.

And if what is necessary is considered by some to be evil—then so be it.

Chapter 7

Jackson

With just the slight press of my palm on the door it opens, and a cold chill sends shivers up my spine as the sight of Damina's wedding gown hanging on the wall greets me at my entry. It's the most hauntingly beautiful thing I've ever seen and a damning reminder of the damage I've caused.

Quickly, my eyes scan the condo and I immediately know Damina is not here. Only a light trail of her scent remains. Yet, this time it's tinged with a fragrance I cannot detect. It smells like her—but doesn't.

Odd.

I have to wonder whether Gregory and Shawn got their facts straight. Looking around, I don't see her luggage, so I wonder whether she indeed left with her cousin. That would be the better of the outcomes because I know if nothing more, Delia will be my best ally.

I walk to the back bedroom just to be sure she isn't in her room, but to my dismay, she is not. I notice she cleaned up since I was here earlier. Boxes are neatly packed and prepped for the movers. Most are labeled but I inwardly chuckle that the majority are marked miscellaneous. She likely tossed a bunch of stuff in the boxes and bins and figured she'd go through it after our honeymoon.

Sounds like my baby, all right.

As I walk about, I hear a scraping sound under my flops, and I find a thin slice of glass near the couch. It's likely leftover from the picture frame of her parents that broke as we made out. Plopping down with the broken glass in my hand, I can't help recalling the passion we shared. If only I had stayed as she asked, none of this would be happening right now.

Instead of gazing at her mother's wedding gown adorned above me now through rueful eyes, I would only be staring at her perfectly naked body pressed against my own. She would be in my arms. Safe and protected.

Where she belongs. Not out God knows where!

Gnawing ire grows within me once more and my muscles stiffen as I work hard to stop my wolf from his eventual release. A loud snarl rumbles through my chest and I feel the walls around me shake.

Calm yourself, you fool.

"Jackson! Come quick!" I hear Gregory shout from outside, redirecting my rage.

Taking a deep breath, I try once more to settle down. I can't phase now. I must stay focused. Besides, I need to do my best not to bring too much attention to us so late at night. There's been enough of that already.

As I head toward the door, I notice a sticky note on the fridge from Damina to her aunt and cousin:

Aunt Delia and Dacari,

I'm safe but I have to go. I'll call you whenever I get to wherever I'm going.

Love, Damina

CRAP!

She's gone! She's not with her family! Where on earth could she be?

If she isn't with me *who* is she with?

Large pellets of water erupt from my eyes and my body warms all over. The thought of her gone from family—from me—is more painful than I can imagine. And without her phone, I can't track her.

"Jack-O!" Gregory shouts once more and I rush out the door, hopeful Damina is with him.

As I race down the stairs, my phone rings and Sophie's name is on the screen.

"What is it?" I snap.

"Delia just returned my call. Damina isn't with them. They were out—"

"Yes, because of the dog, I know but do they know where she is yet?"

"Well, it's a little more than that, but—no they

haven't heard from her. I just thought you should know," Sophie replies gently, obviously wary of my tone. I hate being so curt with her, but my patience is waning thin. I just want to know where Damina is.

"Call me back if you hear anything else," I demand and quickly hang up, shoving the phone back in my pocket.

"Don't worry dude, we'll find her." Gregory's voice is calmer than I'd expect as he rests his hand on my shoulder, but the thought of not knowing where she could be tears me up inside.

"Why did you call me out here?" My reply is brusque as I shove Gregory's gesture aside. He gazes back at me with a half-irritated smile, but I can tell he's doing his best to set aside his growing irritation with me.

"Check it out," Gregory answers, pointing to Tye's Mercedes pulling up curbside. I'm shocked when the window rolls down to see Shawn seated inside.

"What's going on? Why is Tye's car here? I don't understand."

"Do you remember when I asked you where Tye was earlier?" I hunch my shoulders at Gregory's reply, not sure of his point. "Why would Tye leave? At first, I didn't think too much of it, but then Brandon said he saw Tye jumping over your fence when we were all in the front yard. With Brandon being so wasted tonight; I didn't think anything of it—"

"You know I can hear you, right!" Brandon shouts from the other end of the block.

"I don't understand your point, Gregory," I reply,

both Gregory and I ignore Brandon's quip.

"What he's trying to say, Jackson is that Kyra took Tye's car, and we just found it two blocks from here!"

"I'm not sure what to make of all this chief, but it looks like these two were working together—against you."

"And I can bet they weren't working alone!" I bark as Sophie's warning of my brother's machinations earlier today replay in my mind.

Before I have an opportunity to dig deeper, I hear Damina's landline phone ring from inside her condo and I race back inside, hopeful that it is her. I'll even settle for her aunt or cousin if only they have more information.

"Hello!" My tone is grubby as both anger and grief form within me.

"Well, I was expecting the blushing bride, but I suppose you'll have to do just the same, brother."

"Keiron! What have you done with her?"

"Oh, whatever do you mean, my dear brother? Have you misplaced your lovely bride?"

"Keiron, I swear if you've done anything to harm her I—"

"You'll do what? Spare me your indignation. You've done more harm to Damina than I could possibly do in a lifetime."

"Where is she?" I demand through gritted teeth.

"Poor, Jackson. For someone who was once captain of his chess team, you haven't discerned there are far more players than just me. Still, I'm a mere rook on your board. Yet, because of your unwillingness to do what is necessary my dear king, I have the advantage on the board. I think you would call it castling—your move!" Keiron ends the call in a callous and slithering lilt.

A loud bellowing roar rumbles through me as I rip the phone from the wall and toss it across the condo into the next room.

"Jackson!" Gregory shouts my name once more. Racing out of her condo I see Gregory running toward a car. "It's her! It's Damina," Gregory yells, pointing at a dark BMW.

"Damina!" I scream. I try to run, but my momentum is hindered by a scraping piece of glass wedged between my toes. Glassy tears glaze my view, but not enough to block my sight of Damina peering at me over the backseat of the car.

Bending at my waist I try to catch my breath and Brandon and Gregory run past me. I wince when I look down and see blood pouring from my feet through my socks.

"I think I got the license plate!" Brandon calls back over his shoulder.

Gripping pain shoots through me as my muscles protrude and my stride lengthens. My phasing forces the remaining glass from my body in one fluid motion. The stinging sensation of my sharp canines tearing through my gums pinch my nerves, but it is the crippling sound of my bones breaking and contorting beneath my skin that sends a blaring growl from me which echoes through the empty city streets. Try hard as I might, the wolf has bided his time long enough.

He breaks through the caging of my bones, howling upward to the covered night sky. With the crescent moon as his only light he charges with speed until he reaches a nearby wood, releasing a yelping howl signaling the ache of our broken heart.

Dalcour

THE NIGHT has awakened. Overlooking the outline of New Orleans from my balcony, I watch as nocturnal creatures rise from their slumber. All manner of carnivora, both supernatural and mammal, slowly take their rotation in the order of night.

With my heightened hearing, the sound of racoons and skunks clearing paths through wooden lots on their nightly prowl meet my ears with more speed than the vermin employ. But they are not the only ones traipsing through the verge. Rogue Skull peer from their den holes just as bloodthirsty Scourge sleuth through the City seeking their nightly pound of flesh.

The wind howls incessantly, bringing with it the aromatic scent of freshly spilled blood. Although the smell wafts past me as a delicious invitation, I know better than to give in to the temptation it brings. Faint screams ring through my ears as Scourge make their murderous presence known. I grimace at the thought of life surrendered to the fate of such savagery, but I know what comes next.

Most Scourge will not live through the night. If their end doesn't come by the hand of the Guardians, it will come from their own kind—or that of the Skull.

Every night is a battleground; a turf war. Only one can be crowned victor. And while it is likely the most invisible and thankless of duties, the Guard marks a feat notably with each passing night.

But tonight, something is different. Something—some force is stirring on the horizon. Something is coming. I can feel it in my gut. I can smell it in the air.

Perhaps it's the nearing of the full moon in two days, I don't know. After all, it is typical for the nightlings to take extra precaution in preparation of the wolves in full bloom. Even rogue Scourge and Skull know better than to hunt on the night of the wolf.

It could be Decaux's lingering threat. Tonight was evidence that he intends to wreak havoc on the very balance he goads me to secure. Still, there feels like there's something else amiss. Every fabric of my Altrinion being tells me to prepare for what is coming next, but I feel ill-equipped to do so.

I wish I could put a finger on it. Sure, Jerrica's divulgement didn't help matters and I hate myself for lambasting she and Braelyn, but there's still something more. Even the current of the wind warns me of this growing threat. And for the might in me, I sense its looming power is something even I cannot fathom.

I take in a deep breath, wholly inhaling the fullness of night as it fills my lungs. The familiar and ever-growing sounds of the tussling of the Guardians against the demons of night bring me a solace in knowing Decaux hasn't bested me as much as he thinks. My chest swells with pride knowing it is the methods I alone employ giving balance between the supernatural and mortal world.

Despite tonight's misadventures I refuse to allow my brother's scheming to make me doubt the advances we've made so far.

"Well, I hope you've gotten some perspective while you're out there breathing in the night air." Hearing Braelyn's chiding comments are the last thing I want or need to hear right now.

And I was just coming along to a fairly good mood too.

I gulp in the late summer's muggy air lingering in my throat and swallow hard before turning around to meet her wary gaze.

"And just what type of perspective would you propose, young one?" I snide, leaning back against the terrace railing, staring at her through my French doors.

"Perhaps one that accompanies the huge apology you obviously owe Jerrica!"

"What should I be apologizing for this time, Braelyn? Do tell."

"Looks like somebody's still in a mood! I mean, really, I knew you and the B-man never really got along but you're totally letting all this stuff with your brother and Jerrica put you in a frigging funk!"

"Really? Well, I'll have you know I was actually starting to feel better until a little goth-faced girl from munchkin land decided to come upstairs for no other reason than to lay into me!"

Braelyn twists her nose, slightly irritated she can't find a snippy retort to match. She lives for our frequent feuds, but I can tell she's more serious than I suspected. She plucks her fingers through the lacing of her gloves and stares around the room, likely searching for the right response.

"Look Big D, I know you really don't want to hear about finding true love and all the stuff that goes with it—trust me—I get it more than I let on. More than you know. But this is bigger than you. If nothing else, Decaux has shown he intends to make good on his threats. I mean why else would he go after Abahana? He knew that going after Abahana could potentially reignite a turf war with the wolves. They're not just gonna sit idly by on this one. Like Brian, they will demand retribution."

"Don't you think I know that, Braelyn? I'm doing everything I can!"

"Except giving the people something—someone to believe in! Supernatural or not, if we're not fighting for love in its truest form, we're no better than the demons at our door! I know you can see them all from here rummaging through the night like the vile feigns that they are. And if we aren't careful, we'll be just like them!"

"So that's your grand answer? True love? Is that

what we're supposed to be fighting for?" My haughty laugh falls flat to the scowl marring Braelyn's normally bubbly persona.

"I don't know what's worse, the fact that you don't know the answer to your own question or the fact that you even have to ask." Braelyn's large, tear-pooled eyes stare back at me with almost the same vulnerability she had earlier, yet this time I also sense her disappointment piercing straight through me.

Words fail to form a response as her sentiment stings my soul, crushing my would-be heart. As much as I'd like to give in, I know I shouldn't. I can't. I must hold my ground—they need to fear me.

It's for their good. Or at least that's what I'll tell myself until this matter with Decaux is at an end.

Before Braelyn's tears have a chance to freefall or worse, she crosses the threshold of the terrace, I leap over the iron railing and land in the center of the overgrown maze garden. Sharp Greenbriar thistle and thorns tear through my shirt as I wrangle myself free of its vines, making my way to the street side.

Gazing at the mansion, I can feel both Jerrica and Braelyn's lament vibrate through me. Still, without returning to the monster they once knew, I know I must become the man they have long feared. Ripping the torn shirt from my body I toss it over the fence.

Racing through the streets with movement too quick for human eyes to detect, my body pulsates with the fury of the Altrinion force raging within me, propelling me in one fluid motion. Electricity fuels me as my body shimmers with blue lightning coursing through my veins and my reddened skin beams with a radiant glow. And while the curse prevents me from standing in the sun, the lingering semblance of its lifeforce pulsating through my being reminds me of the awesome power dwelling deep within me.

One screeching yelp followed by the harrowing cry of a Scourge's victim is all I need to stop me in my tracks. I dart through a narrow alleyway and find two Scourge's harping atop two young lovers. The smell of freshly spilled blood feathers my nose, causing my fangs to elongate and my tongue to slither at its invitation.

I leap onto the large green trash receptacle and pull one vampire from the young man, puncturing my hand through its chest as it combusts into flames. The lingering smell of pheromones lets me know the pair were likely caught off-guard during a make-out session. The young man was hardly able to put up a fight. He's ripped in two. There's no chance he'll survive the night. He reaches out toward me, calling for help through wispy breaths. But it is his last.

The young woman works hard, squirming and hitting the other Scourge with all her might but falls down when it scratches her body, releasing its debilitating venom into her pores. Just as it opens its mouth, I rip through its neck, severing the head from the body and toss its ashing corpse aside.

Unable to move, the woman lies still, whispering a small "Thank you," through bated breath. But the smell of both her bloody wound and the seduction it brings are too tempting to pass. Even more, she's seen my face—my true face. Truthfully, I don't even have the will to compel her to forget what she's seen tonight.

The fragrance of her blood calls to my carnality with wicked delight. Although her eyes plead with me to spare her this torment, alas I cannot. I am on her before the forming tears in their ducts can escape. Her young, lustful flesh brings me pleasure as her warm blood coats my throat as I savor every drop.

I feel her lifeforce leave her as I take in the second to last drop, just before her heart stops. Though she'll never know it, she should be thankful that I took her life instead. The torment the Scourge deliver is more than ruthless—it's savage. I palm her face to close her eyes as I stand to my feet, enjoying the endowment of power her blood brings as it fills my being.

Before I can loiter in the strength her blood brings, I hear low husky snarls echoing through the crevice of the alleyway.

Skull wolves.

I breathe in the haunting effervescence of spilled blood and belt out a ravenous roar. I'm still hungry and these wolves will be a welcome complement to my meal.

Or at least serve as a late-night snack.

Chapter 8

Jackson

A current of wind brings the delightful fragrance of her scent straight to my nostrils. Yet, there is something twangy in her pheromones that is unfamiliar to me. Fear. Sure, I've smelled it before but never from her. Ever. My tail stiffens at the thought of her frightened. Why is she afraid? Why can't I see her?

Where is she?

Sniffing along the meadow's ridge, I tip my paws through the newly laid leaves. My heart pounds within me and I fear something terrible has happened to her. The wind shifts and the mist of water freshly beaten at the cliff's edge tickles my nose, dampening my coat. The breezy gusts overtake me and the golden leaves swirl, *funneling around me like mini tornadoes.*

Kicking my hinds behind me, I try foolishly to combat the leafy monsoon surrounding me as an iridescent cloudy fog forms before me, blurring my view. The leaves rustle around like the sound of sandpaper scraping against rocks. I continue pushing my paws through the twister of golden leaves, each one sounding like shattered glass as my paw connects, breaking every leaf I touch.

The growing smell of her fear becomes more pronounced as the windy torrent bashes me with her scent, striking me blow after blow. Though I can't hear her screams, I know she needs me. I need to be with her.

While we were once allies, tonight nature preys upon me as the lion does the antelope. I am no one's prey. Especially not tonight. The wind forces me backward, sending its golden leaves like arrows but I've had my fill of this nature induced assault. A loud barking roar rushes through me and the blaring winds come to a screeching halt.

Instantly, the leaves fall to the ground, adorned like a pathway and I follow its leading. Damina's aroma blooms upon my nose as I near the Golden White Oak.

Finally, I see her.

Her grip is tight around the large bark and I watch with trepidation as she struggles to maintain her hold.

"Hold on!" I howl, but she doesn't understand. A small smile forms in the corners of her mouth and for a second I see that she is happy to see me. Oh, what I would give not to be in wolf form! I wish she knew it was me, her

Jackson, standing before her now.

She wiggles as her feet dangle, working hard to keep her small arms cradled around the bough. I howl once more. I know she doesn't understand or know it's me, but I want her to keep her eyes on me, if for nothing but her protection. The calmer she is the better.

With helplessness, I watch wondering how I can help her. As I ponder options, the wind-wrought feign returns. This time the blustery foe is not alone. Creeping snarls with threatening red eyes to match, embark around me as dark clouds fill the night sky. My tail stiffens once more, and I growl, warning the new predators to keep away. Their ravenous snarls continue, but they remain wary of me and rightfully so.

I will not allow them to harm even one strand upon her body.

I take a few steps toward her, but the wind creates a buffer between me and Damina, blocking my path forward, pushing me back. I growl again but this time my sound is made mute by the howling winds. Still powerless, I watch as Damina's eyes grow wide with fear. I know she wants me to help her, but I cannot.

There is nothing I can do.

Another force-filled wind howls through the meadow and the cackling snarls of the creatures around us grow louder. Though I feel their threat looming around me, I don't look back, I must keep my sights on her.

But the last gust is her undoing, and she falls from the cliffside as I watch, impotent with fear.

"Um, Jack-O, can I ask what in the hell is going on here?" Gregory whispers through the menacing snarls surrounding us.

"Quiet, Gregory. Stay very still," I quietly reply, motioning my hand for him to remain calm.

The pack of coywolf encircling us yip and howl in our direction. Some are noticeably defensive, others curious. Most have likely never seen a wolf transform into a man. Nestled in a sheet of leaves and twigs, Gregory had just found me asleep under a hollow tree. In his typical brusque fashion, he was so concerned about *not* seeing my naked body that he startled the already watchful beasts when he threw my clothes on my face.

I'm not sure how long they've been watching me. Nor do I know what they've seen thus far. It's been a while since I've phased in a public area like this. I've been such a stickler for only shifting in designated pack soil and dens that I'm just as surprised to find myself here as my canine kin gazing back at me.

There have been stories of coyote- timber wolf hybrid packs in the deepest wooded acreage of Rock Creek Park, but this is the first time I've ever seen them. While wolves have always been known to take necessary measures to ensure their survival, mating outside wolfen kin isn't customary. Why would a coyote integrate with a wolf? For what purpose? My instincts tell me they must have faced a predator that pushed them to such a brink.

Instantly, my heart aches and I wish I could

help them, but as a rule I know non-domestics are untrusting of others.

I can't say I blame them.

A larger coywolf snarls deeply and approaches me with its tail high and stiff.

"Be careful, Jackson!" The animal snarls once more, this time his sneering intended for Gregory. Gregory takes a step closer to my side, but the coy yelps in his direction but keeps his sights set on me.

"It's okay, Gregory. He just wants to check me out, make sure I can be trusted is all," I whisper over my shoulder, not allowing our eyes to part.

"You say that now. Let's see if you're so brave when he starts chomping on your man jewels!"

"You're okay, aren't you fella?" I answer as the coy takes a half-moon gallop around me, inhaling a great deal of my scent as he dawdles back and forth. He yips again, this time with a more distinct howl mingled in his cadence as he tips his paw down near my feet and sniffs around. I lower myself slightly to meet his golden eyes and blocky snout.

I offer him my hand and Gregory takes another step forward. I know he wants to stop me, but he only remains guarded. The coy whiffs my hand quickly and tips his paws back slowly and submits. Both Gregory and I stare in awe as the remaining pack follow suit.

"Whoa, Jack-o! I don't know what just happened here, but I've never seen anything like this before," Gregory says over my shoulder, his eyes ablaze with wonder.

"I think we just made a new friend," I laugh as I rub the lead coy's fur and watch as he and the rest trek around the wooded lot playfully.

"Well, heck man put on some clothes already before somebody sees us!"

"No worries, we should be fine. The park doesn't open for another few hours. Besides, I want to try back at Damina's or head to the church just in case she shows up." Snatching my shorts from the ground, I pull them up around my waist and tighten the drawstring while Gregory turns his back, giving me privacy.

"Um, Jack, I don't know how to tell you this, but I doubt you'll find her at the church or at her place."

"Oh, really? Did you find out where she went last night? I can't explain it, but my mind feels clearer than ever. I know it may take some convincing but I'm sure we can just talk it out." I yank my shirt over my shoulders and slide my feet into my tennis and turn Gregory around so that we are face to face. His glazed eyes and the quivering of his lips send an icy chill up my spine. "What Gregory? What's wrong?"

"Damina's not at the church. She's not even at her place. Delia's there now."

"Well, Delia can keep watch at Damina's place. I'll head to the church just in case Damina gets there ahead of schedule. We were supposed to take pictures early, so she might show up. I know she's probably still pissed at me but there's no way I'm not going down the aisle with her today—just as we planned!"

"That's just it, Jackson. *You didn't plan on going*

down the aisle today."

"Gregory, now you're not making any sense. I know I phased out of norm yesterday, but one night's run didn't make me forget that today is my wedding day."

"Jack, it's not your wedding day!"

"So what are you saying? Did she officially call off the wedding?"

"You had more than one night's run. You've been in form since that night. It's Sunday, Jackson."

"What! Wait! Are you trying to tell me that I shifted straight through my wedding day?"

"Yes, Jackson, that's exactly what I'm trying to say."

Dalcour

THE LOUD vibration of my phone in my pocket is a most wicked sound. Even the rattling of it knocking against my keys make the word nuisance seem innocent in comparison. While sometimes helpful, it's definitely my least favorite of the twenty-first century. More so, the fact I never get a reprieve because of this fascinating little invention vexes me to my core.

Maybe if I don't answer they will go away.

And just when I think the offender on the other end has given up—they call again!

"This better be important," I answer, my voice raspy with the morning and my eyes still closed.

"One hundred and forty-three," Braelyn replies coolly.

"Am I supposed to know what that means, Braelyn?"

"I just thought you should know your body count last night." Her matter-of-fact tone irritates me, but her statement sends my eyes wide open. The hexagon ceiling tiles above me create a dizzying effect as I work hard to get my bearings.

Crap! I'm at Razors. As I try to recall when and why I came to the club last night horrid images flood my mind. My bouncer, Crawley, had just rang the dinner bell and the feeding began as I arrived. While it's a normal practice to lure humans to the club in hopes of feeding on them, the goal is never to take life. Drink from the vein and compel them to go home and forget our faces. That's what we've done for centuries and it's worked.

But last night was different. I was in rare form. Filled with rage from my bouts with Decaux, Brian, and Jerrica's incessance, I became more than what was necessary—I became *him* again. The red beast. That is not what I wanted. I only needed to blow off a little steam. A flurry of panic swarms my mind as I think on the damage I've likely inflicted.

"Any humans?" My voice now just as cold as the marbled stone beneath me.

"Yep. Roughly thirty-eight from Titan and Cedric's count. The rest Skull and Scourge."

"Have they already begun clean up?"

"Well of course sunshine! They started working behind the scenes the minute you flew out of the mansion like a banshee on a tirade. I wouldn't worry though.

Tolu and Baron have already pushed the narrative to the community that it was all Decaux's handiwork. Meanwhile, the humans that can be compelled have been, and they're working on a spin for the press. Faulty gas leak or something like that."

"That all sounds good, but I don't want people thinking it happened at Razors. Be sure they point it in the direction of the abandoned warehouse down the street. College kids have been partying there a lot lately. I want all suspicion off me!"

"Dude! You know I have your back! I'll make certain to redirect traffic where necessary. I mean really, that should go without saying by now. Come on, D, what gives? What's gotten into you?"

"Look Braelyn, I'm not really in the mood for your chastising right now!"

"Well lucky for you that's not why I called."

"Oh?" I reply surprised. It's not normal for her to give up so easily.

"Nope. I'm just calling on behalf of Jerrica."

"Now Braelyn, if you've called to talk about my heart and true love again—"

"No, no. Stop right there, death stroke—"

Death stroke?

"Listen, D, I learned my lesson. I'm staying as far from that track as I possibly can. Jerrica just asked me to tell you not to come back to the mansion."

"What! You both understand that place is technically mine, right?"

"Duh! No one has forgotten that I assure you. It's just

that Jerrica told Brian and Charlotte they could host the vigil for Abahana and the other fallen ones there tonight," Braelyn's tone is cool but cautious.

"Oh did she?" The fact that Jerrica didn't call herself lets me know she's pretty upset with me. Still.

Braelyn breathes out a huge sigh, refusing to allow silence to part us. "Look, it's the least you can do, D!"

"Braelyn, are you blaming me for what happened in the Tremé?"

"No, I'm not blaming you at all. It's just that with everything going on, just the gesture could help soften the air a bit, don't you think?" Braelyn thrusts her request forward, but her parting words trail. She's worried.

"I suppose. How is she?" We both know if I allow this, it's only for Jerrica's benefit. Not Brian.

"She's Jerrica. Just peachy. All about business with her mind set on all things mansion revitalization."

"Good. Throwing herself into work has always made her happy."

"Well, I didn't say she was happy."

"What does that mean?"

"Look, I know I said I wouldn't bring it up—least of all to you of all people but—"

"But what?"

"Apparently even though she got confirmation that the woman she wanted you to meet signed for the letter, she hasn't gotten a reply on whether she'll accept. Jerrica's pretty ticked about it though she's not trying to let on that she is."

"Hmm...sounds familiar. You know the whole getting your hopes up on true love thing."

"Whatever dude!"

"I won't say I told you so."

"And you've just said it."

"Oh, that I did!"

"Whatever, D, just make sure you don't come back anytime soon tonight."

"No worries, I'll keep my distance." Until I get my rage in control it's not a good idea to be around Brian.

Silence spans the space of the time and I start getting twitchy. Quiet is never a good sign with Braelyn.

"Well is that everything, Braelyn?" I need to find a way to end this call. I can still feel the beast churning within me.

"Dalcour, are you sure you're okay?"

"Wow, you're being more formal than usual. No Big D or anything."

"I'm trying to be genuinely serious here, Mr. Darkside!"

"There she goes!" Good. Braelyn's cynical snarkiness is part of her charm.

"Death stroke. Darkside. It's all the same. Just tell me the truth, are you okay?" Braelyn snaps back.

"Look, I know I spent the last twenty-four hours in a bit of a tailspin. And I know I've got a lot to answer for because of it. But I assure you, I'm just fine," I respond in a low soft tone hoping to assure her.

"Good!" Braelyn's bubbly tone returns and I'm not sure this is necessarily a good sign. "Well, to show you how good a sport I am—and because you didn't outright say I told you so, I'm doing you a solid. But listen here, this is just a one-time thing—don't go getting any ideas that I'm your goth-pimp or anything."

"What? You're not making any sense."

"I've arranged for those grizzlies I saw with Titan the other day to come and um, keep you company at the club. Now, however you choose to entertain yourself is completely up to you."

"Why Braelyn, you shouldn't have."

"Oh I know I'll probably pay for it later. Just because true love is off the table for us doesn't mean we can't have a good time, right D?"

"Or is it perhaps you'd rather these grizzlies spend their time with me instead of Titan?"

"I could care less who Titan spends his time with! I just figured you could find better ways to redirect all that pinned up energy instead of a slaughter fest. They should arrive just after sunset. So, go clean yourself up and be on your best behavior."

"Thank you, Braelyn. And not to worry, I have every intention on being my absolute best. I have a good feeling about tonight."

Chapter 9

Jackson

Horror and disbelief fill my soul as Gregory recounts the last twenty-four hours back to me. Learning that I was in wolfen form since Friday is beyond puzzling. That has never happened to me or any of our kind before. I almost don't know what's more heart-wrenching, the fact that I phased straight through my wedding day or that Damina has left and no one knows where.

I'm sure it's the latter.

"There's more," Gregory says in a throaty tone, as if he gulped in too much air. I gaze back at him, eyes glowing, fearful of his next words. What could be worse than Damina missing? I'm not sure how much more bad news I can take in one sitting.

Gregory keeps his eyes on the road before us as he drives, inching cautiously to the yellow light preparing to stop just before it turns red. He takes in a deep breath, swallowing the hard air in his throat as he leans toward me.

"You were different, Jack."

"What do you mean? Different?"

"Well when you first phased in the street in front of her place you looked like your normal wolf. I followed you to the edge of the woods and Shawn took your things back to your place. When I got there you started howling and growling like you were in some sort of pain. Then you started."

"Started what?"

"Phasing again."

"That's impossible, Gregory!"

"I swear if I didn't see it with my own eyes, I wouldn't have believed it. The silver of your coat shed to the ground and your fur became a thick and creamy white."

"Maybe you saw another wolf. There's no way we can just change like that!"

"I'm telling you what I saw, Jackson! The only thing that stayed the same were your eyes and your howl. Except your howl was deeper and seemed to reverberate off the trees. But more than all of that was your size. If I didn't see it happen in front of me, I would have thought I was imagining things. You looked like the Dire Wolf of old."

"The Dire? Now you're just exaggerating! Gregory, please, they've been extinct well since the ice-age!"

Gregory keeps his eyes fixed on me and I see there

is no pretense to his tone. He means every word. Only the sound of a honking horn behind us breaks his gaze as the light turns green.

"Didn't you say that Delia was at Damina's place?" I say breaking the forming silence between us, shrugging off Gregory's grisly depiction of my wolfen form.

Gregory parts his lips and pauses before speaking and only nods in affirmation. I can tell he wants to continue our discussion but knows to back off.

"Good, take me there."

I am thankful the remainder of our ride is quiet as we drive to Damina's condo. Gregory stares back and forth at me often, likely wanting to say more, but keeps his budding thoughts to himself. While I'm glad he's holding back, I also know this won't last long.

As soon as he parks the car, I race up the steps, grimly hopeful Damina has returned. Although I know better.

Bursting through the door, my heart falls when Delia's sorrow-filled face is the first I see. Tears immediately erupt from her eyes at my entrance, and she runs to me, throwing herself on my shoulder and sobs. To date I've never seen Delia display emotions like this. The only time I've ever seen her cry was when I proposed to Damina and those were happy tears.

Seeing her lose it like this in my arms is new territory for me. I've never been one for public hugs. It just makes me feel awkward.

I try wrapping my hands around her, patting her arms softly.

"It's okay, Delia, we'll get her back. If it's the last thing I do, I'll get her back." I whisper in her ear.

Delia pulls away from me, wiping her cheeks with a wad of tissue crumbled in her hands. She sniffles a little, narrowing her eyes as she takes a few steps back.

"How could you let it come to this, Jackson? You promised me you'd keep her safe. You promised her father—the Order!" She snaps. Her voice is hoarse, likely from continuous crying. But it is the Jekyll and Hyde vibe emitting from her that is throwing me off.

"You're not seriously blaming me! Sophie said she told you everything. You know I would never do anything to harm Damina!" I shout back.

"And the woman, Jackson? Who was she?"

"She is my ex. But she's inconsequential. They used a changeling, Delia! A changeling! It could've been anyone and I wouldn't have known the difference!"

"But you promised! You had one job! Keep Damina safe!"

"How dare you! You're as much to blame as me! I'm not the only one who kept things from her! If you had told her the truth of her lineage—I would be married to her right now."

"Hey now! Everyone calm down!" Gregory says, positioned between me and Delia. "I'm sure there's more than enough blame to go around. None of it will help get Damina back."

Delia continues her venomous glare, squaring her shoulders. Her alpha is showing. She's not backing down. Neither am I. Although I want to relent and assure her we are on the same side, I keep my stance strong as the will of my wolf keeps my feet bolted in place.

Gregory shifts his posture between Delia and I, relaxing his shoulders. I am equally surprised and impressed he is keeping his wits about him. He's never let up on a fight before, but this time something's different.

He's different.

"What we need to do is find Kyra and Tye. We've got to understand why they teamed together to break up you and Damina," Gregory says, pressing through the awkward silence.

"Well that answer is clear." Sophie's sullen, yet crisp voice whispers at the entry of Damina's bedroom. I didn't know she was here. Her tear-filled eyes are puffy, but it's her unkempt appearance that's more disturbing. With a messy bun, untucked blouse, and jeans she barely resembles my typically posh aunt. "It's Keiron. This whole situation wreaks of his involvement," Sophie adds.

"What? So your brother *is* behind this?" Delia lashes.

"We don't know that for sure, Delia," Gregory calmly replies.

"No, Gregory. Sophie's right. This has my brother written all over it," I answer.

"Jack, how can you be certain? I mean, your brother is a lot of things—but he's still *your brother*." Gregory's eyes are wide with disbelief as he watches Sophie and

I exchange knowing glances.

"He called here, Gregory!" I shout, reluctant to reveal the truth. A sharp pain rivets through me. It burns me inside to think of not only my brother's involvement, but his betrayal.

"What?" Gregory whispers back, lowering his shoulders stunned by my admission.

"Yes, he called when we came looking for Damina. He called her home phone—so that means he was close enough to see we were here. He just wanted to taunt me—telling me there's more going on than even I understand. Said there were more players on the board." My voice trails as I recount the callous, unforgivable manner by which he spoke to me. He didn't seem like my brother at all.

He was someone else.

"Then hear me well when I tell you this, Jackie," Sophie begins, her strengthening demeanor returning. "You do whatever you must to see to it that Damina is found well. It is not just your responsibility as her fiancé, but as Prime Alpha."

"Of course, dear aunt. I'll go to whatever end to bring her back where she belongs."

"Good then. Do what you must nephew. Even if it means putting an end to your brother's schemes. Even if it means taking his life."

Dalcour

BRAELYN DID good for a change. The girls aren't as *grisly* as she made them out to be either. Though I'm sure Braelyn's sentiment was more aimed at Titan and his unquenchable desire for new partners night after night. Her strategy of keeping these three lovelies far from Titan's lure isn't lost on me.

So I suppose I should do my best to be a good sport.

All three of the ladies are easy on the eyes. But it's the sound of their cringy, whining voices that is driving me crazy! I tried turning the music up at Razors as they danced around on the stage entertaining me from the poles and it's still not enough to drown their nasally tones. While it's tempting to just compel them to quietness, I fear the red beast's return should my lust take over. I'd surely hate for these women to succumb to such a fate. They're far too young.

Thankfully, Braelyn knew I needed a distraction and that's exactly what they are.

Nothing more.

As I spy the last of the sun's light pass beneath the doors of the club, I immediately rush the girls out of the building. My staff will arrive soon and the last thing I need is to entice them with the smell of youthful blood. It's almost too much for me to bear. Besides its Sunday or what we like to call *rehab night* at Razors. We only open the club to vampires who have been rehabilitated from their Scourge-like state to come here after they survive the taming wells of the Civility Center. It's their first test to see if they can be out in a public setting.

They have one goal. Feed and release. We keep the mature vampires or Altrinion vampires around to compel the humans as they exit or stop one of the rehabs from going too far. And now that Jerrica is using the mansion for Abahana's memorial service, I have nothing else to do but keep my mind off my wicked brother.

"So Mr. Merchant, where are you taking us?" I keep my eyes on the dangling cleavage of the bubble gum-popping, strawberry blonde in front of me. It's better I keep my eyes lowered, lest the glowing hue of my irises betray my dislike of her voice and the mispronunciation of my name.

Names are sacred for Altrinions. Hearing it pronounced incorrectly stings like a hornet's nest in my ear. Thankfully, her bouncing boobs are far more interesting than anything coming out of her mouth.

"It's Marchand," I answer gruffly, tugging the least nasally brunette closer to my side. I let out a faux chuckle. I need to let them think they are entertaining me.

"To Bossier's," I say to the Hitch driver. Taking them to the one place that's sure to mask their pitch enough for me to just enjoy their company is the best thing I can think of. It is also the safest.

Everyone, human or otherwise, is welcome at Bossier's Tavern. *Even me.* Melvina took me off the naughty list years ago. Sure, Calvin will likely never forgive me for taking his leg before he and Bessie were married, but he knows he provoked matters. It's not my fault he couldn't control his lady. Bessie and I had our *mutually satisfying relationship* long before he came on the scene. But even when she chose her lycanthropy over her Altrinion lineage, it didn't stop her advances toward me.

I think she actually enjoyed surrendering to the Altrinion force within her, but her wolf-borne father wouldn't have his daughter be reckoned with an Altrinion's curse. As a hybrid, she wouldn't have the vice of a Dune's curse, and she could phase at will; unlike most wolves. Her father, Alonso, watched in horror as his wife was given over to a Scourge's fate when she took the life of the man who tried to rape her.

She changed right before his eyes.

As unfair as it may be, Altrinions are to honor human life above all—even to our own detriment. Double-dealing is what it is. What did the Elders of the Order expect her to do? Allow the assault? Hypocrites!

I don't blame Alonso for wanting to keep his children far from their mother's fate. But Calvin blames me for seducing his fiancé. Well, I suppose I did a little. Okay, maybe a lot. Nevertheless, Bessie was free to go as she pleased. So it's no shocker that when he found his fiancé and I sharing a farewell kiss he went mad! He flung the window shades open and attacked me as the burning light of the sun scorched my body like fire. So I ripped his calf in two and threw him against the window to blot out the sun.

I could've done far worse.

Bessie's been indifferent since that day. She acts like she hates the sight of me, but I know better. I'm sure she wishes I would come around the Tavern more often.

Tonight, however, is not about either Bessie or Calvin. Apart from drowning the sound of the cheerleader's voices, I feel a momentum within me almost pushing me to the Tavern. Perhaps knowing Melvina is here is my driving force. A strong bulwark such as she can keep my beast at bay. If the wretched, beastly part of me seeks his escape even once, Melvina will send him barreling back to his hell hole. That's exactly what I need.

Or at least that's what I tell myself.

It's as busy as I had hoped when we arrive. A live band is paying homage to one of the greats, Stevie Wonder, and many of the patrons are throwing caution to the wind and surrendering to the dance floor. It's almost standing room only, but we are quickly seated at a booth in the center of it all. The atmosphere is as relaxing as I had hoped. I see the girl's mouths moving, but I can hardly make out their words, nor am I working hard to summon the force within me to do so.

I exhale, blowing out my annoyance with my companions only to inhale deeply and be surprised by a strangely enchanting scent wafting past my nostrils. I take another deep breath and smile. The fragrance is pure but potent.

What is it? Who is it? My eyes search the room but

nothing and no one catches my eye. It could just be my senses playing with me. I don't know.

"C'mon don't you want to dance with us?" The lovely brunette questions me. "Don't tell me you don't want to dance with me," she says softer as she grinds on my lap with her hand trailing my cheekbone. Her body feels warm and as interested as I should be, the scent has me distracted.

"Make room for me, Lisa! I'm sure *Mr. Merchis* can handle two of us at a time," the irritating blonde says perched on the side bench with her boobs meeting my eyes. This time her mispronunciation is almost forgiving.

"Two's a party, but three is company, girls!" The mousy-voice, curly-coifed cheerleader is the loudest of them all. She dances in front of the table in ways that would make a weaker man faint. I am not that man. *More than my interest is beginning to pique.*

"I'm afraid you've mistaken my establishment for your club, Mr. Marchand." As much as I try to enjoy the titillating lap dance and grind the girls are giving me, Bessie's sharp, spite-filled tone breaks my muse.

Still, I'm not ready to let up just yet. With my heady lure freshly seeping through my pores, I enjoy watching the ladies succumb to my trance without their knowledge. I can't help it, the more I get turned on, the more my lust-filled pheromones fill the air. As I stare around the Tavern, I notice all the patrons fall prey to their own abandon. I even sense a sultrier mood form from the band and the dance floor shifts from hand-dancing to body-touching hip rotation.

While the strength of most of my kind rests in earthly nature, some of us have been known for mood setting. Whether it be stirring the type of unrest that starts bar brawls or the kind to weaken magistrates to take the heads of the greatest prophet to ever live— our panache for disrupting atmospheres either by nature or the flesh is renown.

"Oh Bésame!" I answer rising to my feet to meet her eyes, taking her hand. I know no matter my impasse, my charms can still sway her to my side. "I'm just here, letting off a little steam. You know how it goes!"

"Yes, I know exactly how it goes, Mr. Marchand. Rumors have spread about how it's gone for the last forty-eight hours."

"Now Bessie, I know you don't believe everything you hear."

"No, only what I see."

A chill rips up my spine and I wonder whether Bessie saw my otherworldly self. Though she's seen it before, I'd hate for her to see me like that. Nor do I wish for her to be in my path during such a time. No matter our history, I'd never intentionally bring harm to one I've shared a bed with.

I stare up at the fixtures along the walls and ceiling and try hard to push aside any thoughts of my wretchedness.

"So I see you've made some improvements since I was here last," I say, attempting to change the mood.

"Oh, you like them?" Bessie says with a bashful hue

glowing through her cheeks. Good it's working.

As she begins to share the background about how she acquired each piece, her voice dims and a warmth like I've never felt before envelops me and the room seems to darken with nothing but the most beautiful sight I've ever seen gazing at me.

Our eyes lock from across the Tavern and sweltering heat fills my being. This time it's not the red beast. It's something different. Stronger. Something I haven't felt in almost five hundred years.

My beating heart.

Chapter 10

Jackson

My heart drops to the floor. As if losing Damina wasn't enough, now my aunt wants me to kill my brother. Sure, Keiron's treachery must be dealt with, but the thought of taking his life is beyond unbearable.

"Jackson, there's something else," Gregory says, forcing his way through Sophie's hard stare. He squeezes my shoulder gently to keep my attention, ignoring the rumbling roar rising within me at Sophie's declaration.

"What?" I snap and try to keep my eyes set on the only ally I have in the room.

"Shawn said Allyson was in the car with Damina when they left. We've tried to get a beat on the tags of the driver but seems like they were fake."

"Well, why are we standing around here, we need to go to Allyson's place and see what she knows."

"That's why I'm telling you. She hadn't been back since that night, but Shawn just called me when we arrived and said her lights came on just a little while ago."

"Then why are we standing around here? Let's go!"

"Jackie! You should be trying to find your brother! Besides, what makes you think this woman will tell you anything?" Sophie hollers, tugging my arm, preventing my exit.

"Sophie, let me go! I'll get to Keiron soon, but now I need to find Damina. Allyson was the last person to see her. I need to know where she is!"

"But Jackie, what if she's working with your brother? This could be a trap!" Sophie yells as remaining tears break through her lids. Her hold on me is still tight but her hands are shaking.

"I highly doubt it. Allyson is only working for Allyson. She's an opportunist at best. She finally saw an opportunity to meddle, and so she did."

"Do what you must," Delia says coolly, hardly above a whisper. The hurt in her eyes is inexplicable and the grief emanating through her pierces my heart. But it's the sheer look of disappointment marred across her face that rips my soul in two.

She trusted me with her niece and as much as I hate to admit it, I let her down.

"Come on, Jackson, let's go." Gregory pulls me from Sophie's grip, and we are out the door. I can faintly hear Delia crying at our departure and my heart aches for her. Even though we've never seen eye to eye where Damina's concerned over the years, she's always believed in our relationship. She's been my number one supporter from the beginning, and I have to make good on my promises.

And like my aunt said, I have to do whatever's necessary to make that happen.

We make it to Allyson's building just as another resident opens the door. Thankfully, it's a guy named Aiden and his partner, John. Damina and I have seen them in the deli often. He doesn't seem to wonder why I'm coming in this building, and I keep my movements quick before any questions are asked. They both smile and offer a quick congrats as they hold the door for us. When he tells me to give the lovely bride his well wishes, my heart nearly falls out my chest and I press my eyes tight to fight back my tears.

Great! Is this how it's going to be? I hadn't thought about how awkward it will be when people see me *without* Damina.

I don't know how I'll manage.

We bang on Allyson's door, but no one answers.

"Wait a minute, Gregory," I say quietly. My hearing feels more acute than usual. I listen for breathing or heartbeats, but still, nothing. Moving Gregory out of the way, I press my face against the door and try to gauge any scent.

Although faint, there's still a trace amount of Damina's lingering presence along the doorpost and even against the welcome mat; perhaps even more along the floor's edge. A stinging ache ripples through me as I try to imagine why she may have been on the floor. I can't help wondering if somehow, she was taken against her will. Allyson's recent strange behavior makes me think it's possible.

I also detect another fragrance seeping past the threshold, and it's not human.

It's wolf!

"Gregory!" I yell, quickly turning to meet his face. "Do you smell that?"

"Yup, I do. There's been another wolf here. It's a rather doggish odor too—must be a Dune!"

"Why would a *Dune* be here with Allyson?" I whisper to myself.

"Jack-O, I hate to say this, but man something doesn't smell good about this entire situation." Gregory's dark tone exposes the hint of fear pouring from his pores.

"I guess Keiron was right after all. There are more pieces on this chessboard after all."

Gregory stares at me with fear-wrought eyes as his concern for me grows. "What does that even mean, Jackson?"

"Jackson! Gregory! Come Quick!" We hear Shawn shout from outside the building.

Both Gregory and I bolt out of the doors in a flash. We nearly trip over one another when we find Shawn standing in front of the steps with his arms locked tight with Kyra.

"Kyra!" Gregory yells as he jumps in front of me.

117

I know he's afraid of what I'll do to her, but I stand still. Frozen. I hadn't expected to see her so soon.

"I'm fine, Gregory," I reply, pushing him aside. Shawn's face is tight and his expression pensive. There are still people walking down the city streets this time of day, and he's trying his best not to cause a scene.

"I found her watching us from the market across the street," Shawn states, tugging her in close as she wiggles slightly in his grip.

Kyra looks awful. I've never seen her unkempt even once. With mascara running down her face, smeared lipstick, and matted hair she looks like she slept on the street or worse.

"What are you doing here?" I say through gritted teeth. While she's noticeably not in a good place, I don't care. All I see is the woman responsible for ruining my life.

"Jackson, I'm so sorry. I—I only did it because he—" Kyra's words veer as her sorrowful state overtakes her, and she buckles at her knees. Shawn pulls her so that she's leaning on his shoulder, holding her firm at the waist.

"Jack-O, I know you couldn't care less right now, but she doesn't look good. We need to get Kyra out of here before either Delia or Sophie see her. They'll show her no mercy," Gregory says with a watchful glare along the sidewalk, likely hoping no one notices anything untoward.

Kyra continues sobbing, but I can tell she's trying to say something. I need to know as much as I can right now.

"Finish it!" I demand of Kyra, pushing aside Gregory's plea for me to table it for now. "Why did you do this to me, Kyra? Why are you here at Damina's place?"

"They eschewed me, Jackson," Kyra's muffled words barely escape her lips as she watches me through her puffy, tear-filled eyes. "Shunned me like I never existed! Keiron said he'd protect us—but he's a liar! I'm so—so sorry!" Kyra cries once more, folding into Shawn's shoulder as he maintains a tight hold at her waist.

"Get her out of my sight." Even though I'm rightfully upset, the brazen tone seething through my speech is uncommon for me. Both Gregory and Shawn stare at me, likely unsure if I meant what I said. "NOW!" I shout.

I meant every word.

Gregory taps Shawn's shoulder and nods his head toward Shawn's car after he takes one final glance at me and sees my posture unmoved. Heat rises from my fists and a growl deeper than I've ever heard rattles through me as I try hard to stifle my rage.

Everything in me is screaming for me to phase here and now. But I cannot. I can't afford to lose another day.

As Shawn and Gregory aid a tearful Kyra to the car, I think on her mention of my brother and decide to call him.

He accepts the call immediately but remains silent.

"Keiron, I know you can hear me. I have no idea

what kind of games you are playing but I'll warn you once and once only: if any harm comes to Damina—if she gets just a scratch, not even the gates of hell will keep you from my reach. You better pray I find her alive and well before I find you."

"Well then, dear brother, let the games begin."

Dalcour

I CAN still remember the day I felt the rhythmic pattern of static electricity leave my heart when I first took human life at my father's command. My body felt numb all over and my insides like an acorn shaking in its shell.

Tonight, however, is something different entirely.

Gazing at the most beautiful creature I've ever seen in my life makes my body warm like a volcanic tidal wave. Even with a hoodie, shades, and an ill-fitted wig, I see her soul for the beautiful creature she is both inside and out. Her sensually sweet aromatic scent calls to me from across the room. I inhale deeply, trying to take in her essence wholly.

While I know the Tavern is full, it feels like there's no one here but just us two. Her caramel and flame-filled eyes set into mine with a deep longing meant just for me. Everything inside me is screaming to rapture her in my embrace and never let her go.

I don't know if it's the shape of her perfectly plump berry-hued lips or the radiance of her honey-coated skin that sends me into such a frenzy, but there's a magnetic lure in her being beckoning me to her side. Despite her oversized and baggy sweat suit, her luscious frame kindles a fire in my loins I've never felt before. This is beyond lust.

How can this be?

Her beauty is beyond description. Only heaven itself can rival the purity of her presence. Everything about her exudes passion, love, and a freedom in my spirit I've never felt before. I watch as her lips part slightly, and it's the sexiest movement I've ever seen in my life. I try hard to restrain the fervor and desire for her building within me. If it weren't for the tethering of my feet to the ground, she'd be in my arms right now, but I can't move.

The thumping of my heart knocks through my being like a caged lion begging to be loosed. Oh, if she would loosen me to love her! I'd be whatever and whoever she needed. For her, I'd work a thousand lifetimes if only to meet her expectations. Just her presence alone makes me want to be better.

How can this nameless woman restore a cadence to my desolate soul?

I wonder if she knows what she's doing to me.

Still, there's something off. Why is she here? By the way she's dressed I can tell she's running from something or someone. I know Bessie gives shelter to women of domestic abuse. The thought alone sends a stirring flame through my core. Without knowing her name, I know I'd gladly end anyone who'd cause her just an ounce of pain. Why I feel the need to protect someone I don't know is strange, but I know I'd do it just as sure as my heart beats in my chest.

Closing my eyes, I take in another gulp of air, hoping to fill my insides with as much of her as I can handle.

Just then our moment of enchantment is broken when an aluminum pan falls from her table, restoring the bustling sounds of the Tavern.

"Dalcour, you need to leave!" Bessie demands, yanking my arm. I glance over my shoulder and see her adjutants leading my company out the front door.

I forgot they were here.

"Now, Dalcour!" Bessie exclaims once more. I pull myself from her grip. Looking into her eyes, her thoughts are exposed before me and I know her truth. Bessie is jealous. She only wants me gone to get away from the beautiful woman whose soul calls to me.

Quickly, I turn my attention back to the woman and I instantly feel the beast within me arise as I now see Javier, Bessie's duplicitous brother, with his hand on the shoulder of my heart's siren. Seeing him touching her tempts the wretchedness inside me to awaken.

I can't do this tonight. Not here. Not in front of her.

Although it pains me to do so, I must leave. I can't risk unleashing the depraved and wicked thing that I am before her. I take one last glance and see Javier talking with her and a low snarl seethes through me as I watch his hands trail her shoulder. A small smile breaks my forming rage when I spy her retract at his touch, obviously annoyed.

Good.

Perhaps she already knows she'd rather it be my touch instead.

I take one last deep breath, hoping to catch just another ounce of her scent before taking my exit.

A warm euphoric sensation comes over me at just the thought of her. And while I feel the darkness within longing for release, the thumping of my heart pounds the vile creature beneath my skin into submission. A glint of hope arises at the possibility that perhaps the beast may have met his match in this nameless woman.

Just as I cross the threshold of the Tavern, a stinging pain shoots through me and my euphoria is lifted. I turn behind me and see a bright, golden light shining across the borders of the Tavern. Looking up, I see Melvina standing along the upper-level terrace and I know she's shielded the building from me. An iridescent fog shimmers all around, but its brilliance is too bright for human eyes to detect. Melvina shakes her head in warning and walks back into the building.

Bessie and her team are quickly at my heel before I have a chance to cross the promenade. They encircle me and the tipsy company at my sides and I'm almost impressed by their efforts until one of Bessie's men grabs my wrists and threatens me.

I barely have time to ponder his poorly executed motion when the feathering fragrance of the beautiful woman pulls me back into her trance. I gaze around the street and wonder if she's outside, but her scent is just beyond the stronghold of the Tavern. The shield

Melvina constructed glows brighter as Bessie rushes to the threshold and closes the door, causing the Tavern to fade from my view.

It's okay. Somehow, I know this will not be our last meeting. Much like a child counting the days to Christmas, I know my gift is just beyond my reach. And I will wait, with joyous expectation to open such a present designed just for me.

"Hey Big D! What's going on? Who moved the party outside?" I hear Braelyn call behind me.

"Braelyn, what are you doing here?" I question, pleasantly surprised to see her as she rounds the corner to meet me.

Bessie stares at her with indifference. The two have never been fond of one another. Perhaps Braelyn voiced her dislike of Bessie one times too many, but in any case, there is no love lost between them.

"Looks like you're too little too late Ms. Dortches," Bessie says flippantly.

Braelyn ignores Bessie's lingering sentiment from behind her and keeps her sights on me and the giggling companions surrounding us.

"So I see you and *Mrs.* Bossier are still fast friends," Braelyn replies with a haughty laugh. She turns only to see Bessie's lethal-eyed glare aimed at her.

Bessie rolls her eyes and waves her adjutants aside. I hardly notice the man is still grasping my wrist when Bessie tosses her hand over her shoulders, dismissing him. He realizes his mistake when I flash my eyes brightly in warning as his hold lingers, and he backs away quickly with a baleful glare.

"Well then, I suppose you know you're no longer welcome. Now, why don't you and your drunken playthings take your party elsewhere," Bessie barks as she quickly lights a cigarette and blows smoke toward the girls.

"Watch the second hand!" Braelyn teases while fanning the smoking cloud around us.

"Bessie, you and I both know Melvina's little marker will not keep me away from her. Now tell me, who is she?"

"Who she is, Dalcour is off limits!" Bessie snaps, turning abruptly to reenter the Tavern.

"What is she talking about, D?" Braelyn asks, her curiosity chomping at the bit.

"Look, I'll tell you all about it later. First, I need you to do me a favor."

"Sure, D? Anything, what's up?"

"Get a hitch or taxi for these ladies and send them home. They're too drunk to go back to Titan."

"Okay, I can do that but where are you going? I came looking for you at Razors and Crawley said he heard you tell the driver to bring you here. I was hoping we could hang out. I can't stand to be at the mansion for long. That place had too much gloom even for me!"

"Look, Braelyn, I'll tell you everything soon, but I've got to get out of here," I answer as nervous energy builds inside me. The thumping of my heart beats fast like a snare drum and I feel my pulse picking up speed. I'm not sure what's happening to me, but whatever it is I don't need it happening in front of these people. Not now.

Just as I turn away, Braelyn grabs my forearm before I'm able to speed off.

"No, D, I'm not letting you just walk away like that—what's gotten into you?"

"THIS!" I shout and place her tiny hands over my chest, allowing her to feel the thumping inside me.

Braelyn gasps and steps back, her eyes wide with both amazement and fear.

Chapter 11

Jackson

Whoever said pain is an indicator of growth has never been in my situation. With every passing day, I feel my grasp on reality slipping. It's Monday and Damina has been missing since the eve of our wedding. We've never been apart without speaking to one another this long in all of our five years together. Even when I went away during the full moon, I was always eager to be at her side.

There have been no signs of her. No receipts from credit card purchases or tickets from trains or planes—no paper trail whatsoever.

It's like she's a ghost. A ghost of my own making. But I know better. Damina has done this deliberately. She doesn't *want* me to find her. And why would she?

I broke her heart in the worst way possible.

Still, she didn't do this alone. That meddlesome Allyson has long waited for my mammoth-sized screw-up, and she finally got her wish. I'm sure Allyson couldn't wait to get her away from me. She's even covered her tracks as well. She's never at her condo—or at least not when we're looking.

I've slept in Damina's place ever since I returned from my last phasing. I want to be here when and if she returns. Though her place is almost barren of any trace of her, being here is the only thing I have keeping me close to her. As I lay on her couch and stare up at the ceiling my mind wanders to fonder memories of me holding her in my arms, kissing her, touching her, and her body pressed against mine.

Today would've been our third full day married—if I weren't such a colossal screw-up. She would be Mrs. Nash, and she would've known the real me.

Try as I might, I work hard to push away my longing thoughts of her. My body aches with painful desire as I think of just how pleasurable our honeymoon should be right now. We waited so long to finally come together—trying to do it the right way, only to wind up here. Alone and miserable. A low snarl pangs through me as I recount how she wanted me to stay and make love to her. Once again, by trying to do the right thing, I set this course in motion.

If only I had stayed as she requested, neither Kyra, Tye or Keiron would have been able to interfere. That's just it! They were all counting on me to do what

I always do—the right thing. Now it seems the right thing would have been to behold my beloved as she requested.

Now, she is gone from me and I feel helpless.

This is a new feeling for me. I don't like it.

I've even asked the guys to keep an eye out for any strange storms or outbreaks in nature. Just as the sky roared in response to her pain on the eve of our wedding, I'm sure the heavens will once again tell of her outcry. But so far, nothing.

Shawn is tracking a few storms in the Gulf, but none of it appears to be out of the ordinary for this time of year. It is hurricane season after all. And without any airline or train tickets pointing in her direction, we are at a loss. We're still waiting for camera footage from my security team in the District, but since its Labor Day weekend, it's been a slow start to say the least.

To make matters worse, the air in her condo is off. I forgot she probably called the power company to service disconnected service. Not that I care for any light, but the lingering summer heat makes this place thick with humidity.

Thankfully, Gregory got me a cooler of ice and drinks and a few things to eat. Normally, I don't eat much after a phase since the wolf usually stocks up on enough deer and woodland creatures to last me a good while. But this time something is different. I'm ravenous. It could be the full moon approaching that has my body in a tailspin or just Damina's disappearance that has my body driving with hunger. I don't know.

As I make my way to the fridge, my eyes spy a large envelope lying in the trash. It's from JJ Properties in New Orleans. JJ Properties is extending an offer for her to attend an apprenticeship program designing and restoring mansions in the Garden District. Sounds like something my baby would love to do. I even notice she was recommended by Harrold Emmerson. Which is very strange since he died some time ago. Perhaps, he put in an application on her behalf before he passed away.

While I'm happy to see the offer in the trash, something about it disturbs me. The name of the company sounds familiar, so I contact my assistant Nicolaus and ask him to look into their operations and get back to me.

Argh! A loud shout bellows through me and I pound my fist against the wall as I toss the letter on the kitchen counter. Yet another thing trying to take my baby from me! I can't catch a break. Everything is just a reminder that she is not here with me.

Keiron's warning that there are more players on the board than I am aware replays over and again in my mind and my palms sweat as my fury begins to rise in me.

The wolf wants to be free.

I've got to get out of here!

Once more, I pound my fist, this time on the fridge and the sticky note Damina wrote to her aunt and cousin falls to the ground. And it hits me.

If there's anyone Damina would tell of her

whereabouts its Dacari. There's no way Dacari will allow Damina to ever truly escape her grasp! I mean the girl even asked me for the travel itinerary of our honeymoon! Why wouldn't she do the same in this instance?

I snatch my keys off the counter, race to my car, and leave for Delia's place.

Luckily for me, it's a holiday weekend and the roads are fairly open despite it being the evening rush hour. Just as I lift my hand to bang on the door, Delia opens.

"I could hear you skidding up my driveway all the way from upstairs." Delia's short and brash tone lets me know she's still not happy with me.

"Hi to you too, Delia. Can I come in?"

"What do you want, Jackson? It's late."

"Have you heard from Damina yet?"

"No, I haven't. Don't you think I'd tell you if I had?"

"What about Dacari?" I ask squeezing through the narrow gap in the door. I look around, hopeful for some sign of Damina.

"Neither me nor Dacari has heard from her. Besides, didn't Sophie tell you?"

"Tell me what?"

"Dacari's dog died. So in addition to not knowing where Damina went, she's grieving her dog!"

"I'm sorry to hear that, Delia. Truly I am. But perhaps I could just talk with Dacari. I can't imagine Damina leaving without at least reaching out to Dacari in some fashion. It's just not like her."

"Well, Jackson you of all people should understand

that perhaps Damina isn't herself right now. She has no idea that Doodle passed away. And I know if she did, she'd be right here for her cousin. She would be right here with all of us. But she's not and it's all your fault!"

"Delia, I'm sorry and I'll apologize as many times as I must until you forgive me but I'm just trying to find her."

"Then shouldn't you be talking to that wolf *girlfriend* of yours? Sophie told me that you have her at your place!"

"It's not like that, Delia and you know it. And she's not my girlfriend! I've been at Damina's ever since I got back from phasing. Kyra was eschewed by her pack— she's rankless. This is all my brother's doing." Delia gasps at my admission. She's never had to strive for ranking since she's a hybrid, but even she understands that for our kind it's a fate almost equivocal to death.

As Delia's defenses drop, she begins to tell me how Doodle died and Dacari's miserable state as a result. While I do my best to take interest as she confides how she's worried about Dacari and some muttering about Dacari's biological father, my newly acute hearing picks up on Dacari's voice down the hall. She's speaking in a muffled tone and I can tell her hand is cupping her mouth. Noticing my disinterest, Delia quiets enough for me to pick up on another voice coming through Dacari's phone.

My heart races as I hear Damina's sweet tone whisper through the phone. *"I'm so sorry Dacari. I wish you weren't in the middle of my drama,"* Damina says, apologizing to her cousin.

I race to the other end of the hall and rip the phone from Dacari's hand as she struggles to get it back from me. She grabs my arm and I wiggle out of her loose grip, and she falls onto her bed. "Jackson, no!" Dacari shouts at me. Delia rushes to Dacari's aid, obviously confused. She seems genuinely surprised to know that Dacari and Damina are communicating. But that is not my concern.

Just knowing Damina's safe on the other end brings me both comfort and sadness—she's safe without me.

"Damina," I say as soft as my voice will allow. I don't want to scare her off. She remains quiet but I can hear her breathing through the phone. I repeat her name once more and she remains silent. It doesn't matter. The only thing that matters is that I know my baby is well. I will seek her forgiveness for my whole life if it means I'd have another opportunity to make her mine.

Dalcour

"So Trieu, what do you think?" Trieu's strangely calm and bleak expression is disturbing. I can't tell whether she's being contemplative or if she doesn't believe me. What's worse is that I can't read her—at all. Coupled with Dranoel and the other wolves cloaking her, she's worked hard to keep her inner thoughts hidden from Altrinions and vampires such as myself.

Slowly, Trieu stands from her rocker and with a gliding motion, paces the floor. I get up too. Even with my six-foot-plus height and broad frame, Trieu makes me feel petite with her seven-foot stature. I watch in admiration as she moves, her almost translucent skin shimmers, leaving behind stardust-like waves with each movement. Trieu is one of the most beautiful and enigmatic Altrinions I've ever met. Most Altrinions can blend in with humans seamlessly, but she cannot. That's why she's lived in seclusion with the last of the Beta Primes.

"Please, Trieu I need to know. I mean, perhaps I could've been imagining things. But I know what I felt. I felt my heartbeat!"

"Lord Marchand, please sit." Trieu's delicate tone sounds like whispers made through seashells. As I sit back down, she grabs a small book from her shelf and returns to her chair. "I had to think about it for a moment, but I finally recalled the oracles about your lineage. I thought they could help us."

"Oracles? Please Trieu, you know I don't go much for the powers-that-be bullsh—"

"Lord Marchand!"

"Look, I'm sorry. Maybe I shouldn't have come here. I just thought you could help me," I say rising back to my feet. "The last thing I want to hear about is some ancient mumbo-jumbo about my lineage."

"Sit. Please," Trieu says in a commanding voice stronger than I've heard from her before. She's never raised her voice at me until now. And I suspect she'd only do so if she thought it was important, so I take my seat.

"Listen, Trieu all I know is when I saw her my heart was beating like a mad drum in my chest. It was almost violent. In all my five hundred years I've never felt what I felt last night. After I left the Tavern, I moved as fast as I could, soaring around Louisiana almost a hundred times until the electric energy pulsating through me was relieved. But the worst part was, the further I got from her the more it hurt. It was like my heart was aching to be near her."

"I see. Did you tell anyone else?"

"Only Braelyn, but she won't tell a soul."

"Good."

"Why?"

"For starters, I'm not sure whether it would be safe for either of you."

"Okay, now you're not making sense."

"Now, I don't know whether it was caused by the energy you described or not, but last night there was quite a torrent that swept through the City unlike any I've ever seen. The Tavern was at the epicenter of that storm. If the oracles contained in this book are correct, you may have found your mate. And if indeed you have, you two may be in grave danger."

"Danger? What! All because I felt my heartbeat. I don't even know her name."

"Tell me, did she have the same crest of the Great Oak on her body?"

"No. Well—I don't know I didn't get to see her

that close. Why?"

"Lord Marchand, you are aware that as a carrier of the sacred crest you are destined for one fated mate?"

"You mean Anuel's curse?"

"It's not a curse, my lord."

"Yes, it is, Trieu! He went mad when he lost his true love! It was his madness that caused us to become the progenitors of the scourged vampire race!"

"No, my lord. That was all Nuhtlus' doing! He began the Strigoi strain. Anuel's only downfall was a broken heart."

"Yes, and now you're telling me I'm due his same fate?"

"No, I'm telling you that your heart was destined to have one great love. So my lord if that is the one great love to awaken your heart, you may have indeed found your soul mate. The one who can break your curse and set your soul free."

"Yes, a love that's so fated—that it's doomed!"

"It doesn't have to be that way. If she bears the sacred crest, she is bound to you and you to her."

"Well, there's no true way of knowing whether the one from last night is the one. I just know I've never felt anything like that before."

"Then, my lord, you should trust your heart."

"It no longer beats. Besides, the woman from last night could've just been another woman. And I am sure a woman like that already has someone else."

How could anyone ever leave a woman like that alone?

"The oracles are clear, my lord. Your one true love is fated to be with you as well. There is no escaping it."

"What does that mean?"

"What it means is that she cannot be with another no matter how much she tries. Or no matter what comes against you. You are destined to be the ones to bridge the gap of the supernatural world and return a finality to the balance to its fallen state. The oracles are clear: the branches that were broken by the House of Anuel shall be restored by the fates of love bearing the *Ramus Otium*."

"The Branches of Peace?"

"Yes, my lord. You are bound with the sacred crest of the Great Oak. You bear the Ramus Otium. If this woman bears the same—she is fated as are you. Fated to bring about a peace!"

"That's impossible! My brother bears the same crest, and he is no more peaceful than a herd of wild boars."

"No, Lord Marchand you are incorrect. While his crest is similar it is not the same. He bears the markings of the tree in full bloom. Look in this book. As you'll see the Branches of Peace are without leaves. They are barren to denote the stripping away of all that once was in preparation for the better to come. Just like the barrenness of winter brings about a bountiful spring. You and your beloved are that better."

"How can that be when there's still so much darkness in me?"

"Only the love of the one can restore the light to

your soul as you will bring love to hers."

"Trieu, I know you've heard of the atrocities I caused just the other night. There's no way I am a bearer of peace!"

"Yes, my lord. I am aware of your downfall, but all is not lost."

"How can you say that? After everything I've done."

"Because I yet see hope in your eyes." Trieu's mild and calming tone sends a rippling warmth throughout my soul like a small fire embracing winter's chill. As much as I want to dismiss it, I don't.

"And it is that hope, my lord that you must protect. You must protect it like your life depended on it."

"What do you mean, Trieu?"

"Know this, Lord Marchand there are others who will not be receptive to the peace your love shall bring. Many, like your brother, would rather chaos and anarchy rule while others would seek to use your powers for their own corruption."

"And you speak of me and the woman?"

"Yes, my lord. Many will not want you two together out of fear. Make no mistake there are plots working against the very Order of Altrinion with one purpose—to never see these oracles fulfilled. If indeed this woman brought about rhythm and beating to your heart, you must find her and protect her. For if she is fated, as I believe she is, her very life is in danger."

A low, sneering growl rumbles through my chest at the thought of anyone inflicting pain on the beautiful woman I saw at Bessie's place last night. The thought alone is unconscionable! Not only do I feel protective of her, I fear for her. And while I do not yet know her name, I know that I will give my very life to see that she is protected.

"Then know this, Lady Trieu, our dutiful keeper of the Order, I shall remember your words. And by the Order of Altrinion I swear to you this day, no malice shall come upon her. I will shake the foundations of Earth and hurl stars like fire through the sky before I'd allow harm to come at her feet."

Chapter 12

Jackson

Everything feels different. I feel different. Here she lays at feet, her small fingers tracing the golden pawprints etched in the ground beneath me. She seems more curious than fearful and it warms my heart. I never want her to fear me. I just want to protect her. Love her. Keep her safe.

Lowering myself to meet her eyes, she gazes back at me as though she wanted to uncover the man behind the eyes of the beast. If only she'd just touch me, perhaps she would know that it's me beneath this furry exterior. Just as her fingertips attempt to trail my crown, a loud roar from the wolfpack pulls my attention, breaking our exchange.

Danger lurks in the shadows and a growing threat

amasses us round about. Duty calls to me, but my desire for her holds me still. With reluctance, I pull away, giving my attention to the cries of the wolfpack. Still, I can't leave without letting her know I'll return. I issue a low growl, and she nods in affirmation as if she understands I must go. Walking toward the pack I turn back quickly to see her just once before resuming my duty.

The glimmering shield that has protected us is beginning to fade and the wolves cry out, hopeful to give aid to waning power of the Order. Darkness sets in the meadow and menacing red eyes pierce through the shadows as slithering, screeching sounds like claws on chalkboards wreak with echoes through the night sky.

Only the power of the moon aids our plight, strengthening the pack as the pounding beneath our feet girds the earth below. My muscles retract and pulsate as if I were about to phase again, and I marvel at how my stature towers the surrounding wolves.

A strong, pulsating roar emits through my entire being and the looming darkness gives way to slithers of light around us. I roar again and the iridescent walls around us strengthen and the meadow brightens around us and the threat retracts its lure, and the wolves follow my lead, echoing my howl.

Pride swells within me and I gaze about the meadow, pleased with our results.

But my joy is short-lived as I feel the ground beneath me rattle and I turn to see a glowering figure enticing my beloved, leading her with his enchantment. I also notice the shield behind us failing, giving this figure just enough space to invade.

Fear pierces my heart and I issue a loud cry that sends the enticer back away from her, and she buckles beneath me, fearful and afraid.

I try to soften my stance, lowering myself as before to recapture her gaze, but she is too afraid. A low rumble scores through me as I bay her name, and she looks up at me, her eyes filled with wonder and fear. I bay once more and a small smile forms in the corners of her mouth, and I am thankful. I need her to see me not fear me.

I love her.

Slowly, I lower my hinds and tilt my paws downward, submitting to her. She smiles once more; this time her smile meets her eyes and I know she is finally beginning to see. I know if she touches me, all will be revealed, and we will be made whole.

My loins ache and my heart races at both the thought of her touch and her revelation. I feel like a toy on Christmas morning yearning to be opened by a child. I am just as eager for her touch as she is to touch me. I no longer wish to hold this secret. I only wish to give it to her. My secret. My love. All of me. I want to give everything that I am—that I even hope to become to her.

Just as the tips of her fingers feather my coat, a distinct floral and lavender scent invades our space, and she is stripped away from me.

A painful cry roars through me and rage swells my being as I watch my beautiful beloved swept away.

"Jack-O! Hey buddy, it's me, Gregory! It's just me!" Gregory shouts as he leaps backward, landing atop Damina's kitchen counter. Fear wreaks through his pores and his eyes are wide in shock as he gazes at me with awe.

I sit up on the couch, dripping wet with sweat. My skin feels like a furnace and my heart pounds within me. A light creamy coating of fur outlines my forearms up through my shoulders and I feel my canines protruding from my mouth.

Strange.

I'm in mid-phase. I feel stuck.

I jump to my feet, growling and turning about, trying to force my phasing away. I need to return to me.

"Just steady yourself, Jack," Gregory says in a low tone, hopping down from the counter. I know he wants to come closer, but he keeps his distance watching me with an intense glare. "Focus on your breathing," he says calmly.

My phone falls out of my pocket and my favorite picture of Damina pops up on my screen. As I stare at her, my breathing settles and the pacing of my heart slows its beat. Slowly, the hairline along my forearm recedes and my sharp teeth retract to normalcy.

I turn back to Gregory and am surprised to now see a large gash beneath his torn shirt. Looking down at my hands I watch my claws draw back under my nailbed.

"Don't worry about it. The full moon is tomorrow,

I'll heal," Gregory offers with a raised hand, relaxing his shoulders.

"Gregory, I'm sorry. I was just—dreaming."

"Must've been some dream," Gregory says, holding up his phone and pointing to the date.

"The thing is, I don't think I realized I fell asleep." I look at my phone and see it's Wednesday!

Crap I lost another day!

"Well, you were growling pretty gruff. I had to break the doorposts in a bit to get in. I knocked for a while and I got worried something was wrong."

"Last thing I recall is talking with Damina and texting her earlier. I think I paced around for a bit after I left Delia's place. I texted her so many times before I finally heard back from her."

"That's great news. Isn't it?" Gregory looks at me with an awkward grin, likely uncertain whether to celebrate. I can tell he is concerned about me falling into yet another deep sleep, losing time.

"It's a start," I answer flatly, staring at her wedding gown. The sight of it alone torments me, a constant reminder of how far we've come from our wedding day. While I'm glad Damina is at least talking to me, I'm irritated that she's remained elusive. I know I hurt her, but her behavior is uncharacteristic. I can literally feel her slipping away from me.

Gregory clears his throat, placing himself in front of my view of her gown. "Did you two work *anything* out?"

Turning quickly on my heel, hopeful Gregory hasn't

spied the tears forming in the corners of my eyes, I bend down and grab my duffle bag and pull out two tee shirts. Flinging one over my shoulder to Gregory, I reply, "No she's not ready to talk, so I just let her know I'm here for her. She did ask me to leave her family and friends alone. So I'll ask you that we keep our distance from her family for a while."

"Thanks!" Gregory answers as he snatches the shirt out of the air. "No problem, here. Do you at least know where she is?"

Picking my phone up from the floor, a small smile tries to escape but it's quickly pushed aside when I think about how hard Damina is working to evade me. "Nope. Damina made a point not to give up her location. Besides, Dacari was too busy screaming in my ear for me to hear anything in the background."

"That sucks." Gregory grimaces as he watches me shove my phone back in my pocket. His face softens and his eyes lift as he continues, "But I've got good news."

"What's up?" I respond dryly, plopping back down on the couch gazing up at her gown.

"Well, someone spotted Tye not far from here. No takes on your brother just yet." Gregory's eyes are hopeful. He's working hard to lighten the mood. *He's a better friend than I deserve.*

Jumping up from the couch, I smile and do my best to match his mood. I pat him on the shoulders and walk over to Damina's gown and zip the garment bag. The gown has haunted me long enough.

Turning to Gregory I smile once more, working desperately to shake off my soured state. "Good, at least we can finally get some answers from Tye. What about Kyra? Has she said anything?"

"Nothing that we don't already know, and I suspect she'll say no more until she sees you again. Do you think you can manage?" Gregory questions, still searching my face for hope.

"I don't know if I'll ever be ready to see her after what she's done, but if it means getting closer to the truth, I'll do it."

My time of sulking and wallowing in the mess I've made now ends and my time for redemption awaits.

Dalcour

"DUDE! WHERE have you been? I mean really, D, what gives?" Usually, Braelyn's snarky, little sister-like tone is a part of her charm but today I'm not in the mood. I also didn't expect to see her. She's been wrapped up in Jerrica's world since I took off a few days ago.

"What are you talking about, Braelyn?" I respond annoyed. I've done my best to avoid the mansion these last few days. After my meeting with Trieu in the Bayou, I've only come here to grab a few blood bags from my stash in my suite. Ever since Jerrica's began hosting her La Salle de Jeu, I haven't been in the mood to run into any of the contestants. Especially Colin's daughter. All my energy is fixed on finding the woman from Bessie's place.

"Look, D, I know you had a little scare back at Bessie's place when she put the borders up. The little pulsating you had would've driven anyone stir crazy, but you've been incognito!"

"I've just been busy, Braelyn. Besides, I'm sure you don't miss me with all your hosting duties with Jerrica."

"That's what I've come to talk to you about."

"What about it? You've got all the paperwork, right? And if you're sure Abraham's boy can pull it off, I don't see what else is needed."

"Sure, Mark and his cronies will be fine. That is if Dauphine and Claudia keep their hooks from him!"

"Do I detect some jealousy, Braelyn? Look, you and I both know Mark has a monumental task before him if he is to alpha his pack. If he decides to be with Dauphine or Claudia it's only his duty to his pack that prevails—but if you're worried about it, perhaps you should tell him how you feel."

"Oh no! This isn't about me and that boy and you know it! I wanted to tell you that the woman that Jerrica's wanted to introduce you to *is here* and I really think you should meet her."

"Don't have time—"

"Why? What is up with you? Dalcour, come on this is me you're talking to!"

"Look, Braelyn, I don't have time to explain. All I can tell you is what I'm working on has possible life and death consequences."

"*Life and death?*" Braelyn's muted and exasperated

tone doesn't go unnoticed. I'm sure she thinks I'm referring to Decaux and his schemes, but I don't have the time nor the heart to fill her in on my discussion with Trieu. And if she thinks the pulsating was only my reaction to Melvina's protection border, it's best to leave well enough alone.

I push past Braelyn to look for the two new Mercy Blades I got from Titan a few months back. If there are indeed forces working against me and my mystery woman, it's best that I be prepared. I don't care whether I have to face Skull, Scourge, or Altrinion-vampires, these blades will take out any creature; supernatural or otherwise.

"Yes. Now please, Braelyn, I must go—wait what's that smell?"

Just as she turns, a strong wind blows through the French doors and a familiar enticing fragrance brings me to a halt. My knees buckle at its entreat and energy rivets through my being, sending bolts of electricity through me all at once.

"Huh? What smell?" Braelyn responds, twitching her nose as if she smells nothing out of the norm.

I know I'm not going crazy.

"That scent—I've smelled it before," I say as the aroma pulls me to the threshold of my door. I lunge forward into the hallway, still holding onto the doorposts as I inhale deeply, allowing the fragrance to fill my lungs completely.

The aroma is so calming and sweet, it sings to me like a siren, luring me into its reach.

"Um, D, are you okay?" Braelyn says pushing me from behind.

As I turn back toward her, she gazes at me with her wide-eyed half-grin. *She must know something.*

"Braelyn, tell me you smell it? Tell me I'm not crazy."

"Well, I'll never be the one to outright lie to you. But yes, I smell something sweet," she answers while poking her fingers through the fishnet holes of her gloves with her nose scrunched.

"Braelyn!" I shout grabbing both her shoulders. She feigns a faux startled expression and then breaks her pretense with a snort and cackle. Her laughing is so unbecoming. I repeat her name once more when she loosens from my grip and continues laughing as she turns away from me trying to catch her breath.

Clearing her throat, she holds her hand over her mouth and looks at me once before giggling again and plops down onto the wingback chair in the corner of my suite. Once more, the enticing scent pulls me back toward the door and I turn back around toward the hall and take in another deep breath but this time something is different.

I know this smell.

"Okay, okay, before you go Flintstone and run down the steps like a caveman, maybe you'd like to hear about the woman Jerrica wanted you to meet."

"What is her name?" I question with my face still pressed against the drifts of wind carrying her essence to my door.

"Firstly, her name is Damina Nicaud."

"Nicaud. Unusual last name."

"Yeah, we thought so too. But that's her name. She's definitely Altrinion but Jerrica doesn't think she knows it."

"What do you mean?"

"Well, from what I hear her parents died when she was young, so I don't think they ever got around to spilling the news. Anyway, she's here now. Do you want to come down and meet her? She just asked me to round up the finalists for the project. This would be a good time for our illustrious benefactor to make an entrance. Don't you think?"

"Come down? Now?" I question as passionate heat boils within me. I want to see her. I need to see her. But I can't go down yet. Not like this. Especially if she doesn't know what and who she is, this would be too much too soon.

"Yeah, come on, D. I'm sure she'd love to meet you. As it turns out she's just overcoming a major heartbreak, so meeting you would surely help her get over the hump!"

"A heartbreak you say?" The thought of anyone hurting her fills me with rage.

Braelyn tugs my arm, turning me back around toward her.

"Yes, a heartbreak. But I think that's just an open invitation, don't you?"

"Well, I guess it depends."

"On what? I mean, look at you! You look like you're about to sprint out the door all because of her smell and now you're hesitant?"

"Well, sure she smells nice Braelyn, and I'm obviously intrigued—"

"Intrigued?"

"Yes, intrigued. But while she smells like the girl from Bessie's it may not be her. And that's the girl I need to find. She's the one."

"How can you be so sure?"

"I just know—okay."

"Okay, if you say so. Then that's even more reason why you should come meet her yourself. If she isn't the one, you can try to find the girl again."

Suddenly, Jerrica's loud chuckle breaks through the forming silence as I ponder Braelyn's request. She's outside and I hear another voice with her. A woman.

I race to the balcony and look below to see Jerrica walking alongside the most beautiful creature I've ever seen—but this isn't the first time I've seen her. It is the woman from Bessie's place!

Just then, my heart thumps like a caged lion in my chest and blue embers of electricity rivet through me. And it hits me, the woman I've been searching for has been under my nose this entire time! In my house! But I want her closer. I need her closer. In my arms. In my bed. All I know is I need her, and I need her now.

My mystery woman laughs as she and Jerrica walk back into the mansion from the garden. *Even her laugh is beautiful.* In fact, it's the sweetest and harmonious sound I've ever heard. Seeing her smile makes my soul leap. Knowing she is happy warms me all over. Everything inside me wants to race down the stairs and bury her in my embrace, but I know I need to take my time and do this right.

And I have every intention of doing so.

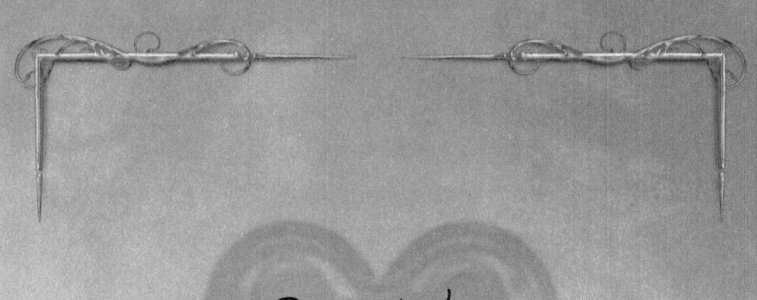

Chapter 13

Jackson

"I didn't think you wanted to see me," Kyra says just above a whisper. I knew seeing her again would be rough but the sight of her curled up in Damina's favorite spot—the very spot where I broke her heart—fuels a fiery rage within me.

"Move over," I quickly command, motioning for her to slide over to the sectional adjacent to the chaise. Kyra moves quickly, wiping the freefalling tears from her face and sweeping her hair to the side. While faint and marred by her treachery, there was a time when her swept hair stirred the very core of me.

But not today. Today, I only see someone who ripped my one true love from me.

Taking a deep breath, I work hard to rein in my

anger and remember that my brother is at the root of it all.

"Jackson, first I want to say—"

"No, Kyra. I don't want your apology. There is no apology you can give to reconcile what I've lost—what you've taken from me. I hardly care to know the why behind it all. I'm more interested in the who—my brother. I want to know why you teamed up with my brother to betray me!"

"Look, Jackson, I take no pleasure in this, you must believe me!"

"Why should I? How could I?"

"That's what I was going to say. I wanted to say, I know there's nothing I can say to make you forgive me, but I wanted you to understand why I felt it was my only option."

"Because you were eschewed? You want me to believe that since your pack abjured you from ranking that you had no other choice? Please! If you needed money, resources—you could've come to me, Kyra! I would've helped—"

"But I did come to you. I called you and you never had time for me. Once you got with your precious Damina you barely cared for the packs—much less leading them! You've been ghost in the last few years. Many have wondered if you even bother to look around—to see what's happening to us all!"

"I can't believe you! You're so narcissistic! Even now, you're finding a way to turn it around on me—make it my fault! Now I remember why we didn't work!

Thanks for the reminder!" I growl jumping up from my seat. Grabbing hold of the bar, I try hard to quench the raging wolf inside, pleading for his release.

"No, Jackson. We broke up because you didn't care much for wolf business."

I sigh and turn around to see her now standing with golden-hued eyes glowing back at me. I'm not surprised her haughty wolf is rising too.

"And what does that supposed to mean, Kyra? How do I not care for wolf business as you put it? I'm an alpha for crying out loud! Aren't I? Somehow I've managed to maintain ranking—so how pray tell could I have done so unless I cared for some part of wolf business."

"Okay, sure you're an alpha. A Prime Alpha, in fact. All that means is that no one other than another Prime can challenge your ranking. It doesn't mean there isn't dissension in the ranks. You barely come to den meetings and all you do is pass down your commands—but you've yet to be the alpha the packs need—the alpha they deserve."

While some of what she says hits below the belt. I refuse to allow this to distract me from the fact she worked against me with my brother to break up me and Damina.

"Kyra be honest now. What does any of this have to do with us? With me and Damina?"

"It has everything to do with it!"

"Why? Is it because after you dumped me for being, what did you call me before, a shell of an alpha-not fitting to be lord, you saw me happy, very happy in fact, and moving on with my life? Not only was I moving on, but I was getting married to someone who wasn't you!"

"How dare you?"

"How dare I? *How dare you?* You lay up in *my* house for days, and on the very chair where you brought me to ruin, no less, refusing to speak of your treachery and when you do—there's only accusation from you! So tell me, Kyra didn't it truly burn you to your core to see me moving on without you?"

"Well said, my Lord. Well said," Kyra sneers with a callous clap to match. "And while you're standing here intent on making me the villain of all your pain your brother Keiron has his mouth to the ear of every wolf and den looking for a leader."

"They already have a leader, Kyra," I reply with folded arms at my chest.

"Do they?" With a dark glare, Kyra's spite shoots at me like an arrow; just as she intended.

"Tread carefully." My brusque and sharp tone more than mirror Kyra's sentiment; it's deadly.

"Then let me speak plainly. If you'd bother to come up from the air that is Damina you'd see you're losing your grip. Keiron has been working the circuit, playing the background—working against you. He has everyone convinced that you aren't fit to lead."

"Why? Why would anyone give my brother a second thought? Is it because I don't go to den meetings, pack parties, or make myself more accessible? What reasons could they have to align with him? What need have they to outright defy me?"

"You say I'm jealous. Perhaps there is some truth in that sentiment. You turned from your own kind to wed an Altrinion—a pure line one at that! Some even say she is a Fated One! And we both know what that means!"

"That's ridiculous! The myth of the Fated Ones is as old as time! Not since before the dark ages has the world come against such a force! Besides, if Damina were Fated I'd know it."

"But what if she is? Are you prepared for what is to come? Can you honestly say that you are?"

"Enough of this, Kyra! You're stalling and you know it!"

"You asked me why I aligned with Keiron, so allow me to tell you. What you do know is that yes, my pack eschewed me. They abjured me and my mother because we fell from ranking—never met our obligations by securing a future for the pack. Keiron promised if he was able to show the Altrinion Elders that you weren't holding to whatever vows you made to protect Damina that you would be pulled from ranking. Naturally, the ranking would fall to him and he would marry me, thus allowing me to reclaim my status among my pack."

"Because you would be married to a Prime," I reply with a gritty tone. The thought that Kyra would marry my brother isn't lost on me. She knows the thought is revolting to me, but I refuse to give her the jealous response she obviously desires. Kyra gazes at me for a moment before walking to the mirror to finger through her hair.

"Exactly. But what you don't know is that there are others like me and Tye who was are willing to see this plan through."

"What do you mean *others*?" Once more, the chess pieces my brother alluded to come into play.

"Others who wanted more than to pull your ranking—they wanted to end Damina!"

"What do you mean, *end Damina*?" I shout pushing back the two barstools at my sides.

"Please, Jackson just hear me out," Kyra counters, her voice trembling. "Now I wasn't privy to all of the details. But as I've said before many believe her to be fated and as such would see her life forfeit."

"What! Why would anyone wish her harm? If I have to choose between Damina's life and my alpha status, I'd choose her life without hesitation," I declare as I work hard to stifle my growing rage.

"And it is that, my lord, why the others came into play. Your love and need for this—for her, impairs your vision. Can you not see how your love for her endangers not only your status but her as well?"

"That's ridiculous!" I chuckle, I can't help laughing. My patience for Kyra is waning and she knows it. Kyra stance is guarded as she watches me as she walks back to the sectional and takes a seat on its edge.

"Look, I know I don't have to recount your history to you about the Primes. It was the strength of the Primes who ended the curse of the last Fated Ones.

The Primes were the ones who ended Nuhtlus and Anuel's reign. Legend even states it was the Primes who ended the legend of Drac—"

"Enough, Kyra! You're not telling me anything that I don't already know!"

"Then if you know that—know this," Kyra yells, rising back to her feet, "no one is convinced that should the time arise for you to stand against the Fated Ones, be it Damina or otherwise, that you would uphold your oath and do what is necessary."

"Well if that were true and you were all so worried about Damina succumbing to this mythology, perhaps you should have left well enough alone, and not interfered in our wedding and maybe she would never have to endure such a fate."

"And if you truly believed that to be so, my lord, you wouldn't stand here as you do before me now—with fear in your eyes."

Shivering pain shoots up my spine as Kyra's lashing scores through me like a haunting tune.

Dalcour

"RAZORS!" I shout to Braelyn as I rush back into my suite from the terrace.

"Razors? Huh, I don't understand," Braelyn replies with hunched shoulders and a blank expression.

"Bring her to Razors!"

"Okay, now I'm confused. Just a minute ago you

didn't want to see her. Now after one whiff you're hooked! I thought you were going to find the girl from Bessie's place, D?"

"I think she's the one."

"Are you frigging serious? You mean like the one— the one?"

"Yes, I mean it exactly the way you said it. How was I supposed to know she was the one from the Tavern? But despite that ridiculous get-up she was wearing; I'd recognize her from miles away."

"D, this is unreal. Are you sure?"

"Yes, I'm sure, Braelyn. Now please, find a way to get her to Razors!"

"Okay, well nothing like a little time of celebration. Besides Lady J has a conference with Sue tonight so—"

"So why are you still standing here? Go now!"

"Okay! Okay! But before I go, be sure you have your phone with you. I'll text when we leave."

"Sounds like a plan. No worries, I have my phone," I answer quickly, holding the phone in one hand and shoving Braelyn out with the other.

"Oh, one more thing!" Braelyn says, tugging on my arm and digging her feet in the floor, preventing me from pushing her further.

"Now you're stalling."

"No, really I'm not. I mean I'm kinda geeked to see you all up in arms over a girl. But are you sure you want me to take her to Razors? What if some of our folks are there—or worse?"

Dread fills me as I think on Braelyn's notion. She's right. After my slaughter-fest days ago, it will be hard to keep Scourges from roaming about not to mention bloodthirsty Altrinion-vampires.

"You bring up a good point. I'll reach out to Crawley and tell him to send our folks to the CC. Only humans and our VIPs will be allowed inside. We'll make it glow-stick night or something—just be sure to get her there! Now go!"

"Aye-aye, Captain!" Braelyn responds with a lilting chuckle and takes her flight down the hall in a flash.

As she leaves, thoughts of having my mystery woman in my arms become more than a beautiful dream, but an attainable desire. And with that desire, the urge to protect her from the danger Trieu described, grows stronger.

Immediately, I call Crawley and inform him of my plans to go to the club and give instructions for it to be a mostly supernatural free zone, save the ones who will join Braelyn and those on our VIP list. I also reach out to Titan and ask him to beef up the presence of the Guardians near the area and request that he sends Lux to keep watch of any rogue Skull or other wolves nearby. The last thing I need is to put my mystery woman in any danger. Thankfully, neither Crawley nor Titan pry or question my requests, and I am confident they will carry my orders out in the manner they were given.

Not long after my calls end, I get a text from Braelyn that everything is a go. But when I hear the loud merriment and celebration of the team exiting the mansion, I know my plan is fully in motion. A broad smile covers my face from ear to ear as my excitement grows. Ripping off my tee and tossing it in the bin, I rummage through my closet searching for something to wear as I prepare to shower.

I can't get there quick enough.

I am surprised to find Jerrica now in my doorway when I come out of my closet. Standing shirtless before her, awkwardness swarms over me. Sure, she's seen me like this plenty of times, but knowing how she really feels makes me uncomfortable.

"Going somewhere?" Jerrica says in a soft tone, working hard to avert her eyes from my chest.

"Yup, just came back for a quick shower and change." I say quickly, pulling a towel from the drawer and draping it over my neck. At least it will cover me just a tad.

"Ah! I see! Well, you've been such a disappearing act the past few days I thought you'd forgotten about us and about the revitalization project."

"Of course not. No worries, Braelyn has kept me apprised." I lie. I don't want this discussion to go on much longer. I'm not sure if Braelyn told her of my plans, but I don't want her to linger either.

"Did Ms. Dortches also inform you we've selected the finalists?" Jerrica questions, obviously hopeful.

"Yes she did," I reply gently. This time my need to sound interested comes easier than before.

"I'm happy to hear. Do tell me you'll be able to greet them tomorrow? Besides, I have *someone* I'd like for you to meet," Jerrica's overly excited tone betrays her.

She wants to talk about my mystery woman.

"I'll be more than happy to greet the team. Tomorrow. But now, my friend, I must tend to other matters."

"Oh, but I didn't get an opportunity to tell you who—"

"Madame Jeffers," Ms. Zamora's dark gritty tone reaches from behind Jerrica. Jerrica frowns, rolling her eyes over her shoulders. "Your call with Ms. Burgin is set up in the office. She and the rest of the City panel are on the line."

For once, I'm happy to see Zamora. Normally, her grim and sulking presence disgusts me. "Go, Jerrica. Take your call. I'll see you tomorrow and I promise I'll greet your team."

"Splendid!" Jerrica's eyes sparkle and dance. She turns quickly on her heel and goes down the hall with Zamora.

In no time I'm standing near DJ Mack on the platform watching the most beautiful creature I've ever seen stride across the dance floor. The flash-of-lightning-like shower I took was well spent. I'm sure I put on my clothes while in flight to Razors. I made it just in time to make eye contact with Braelyn while they had fun on the karaoke stage.

Crawley told me he gave a discount to some of the group tour companies we work with which helped fill the club up rather fast. Yet despite the full, fun, and festive atmosphere of the glow-in-the-dark night at Razors, it's only her scent pulling me into

163

a trance. As Sia's *"Move Your Body"* chimes through the speakers, I make my way down to the dance floor, pushing past any takers seeking to get too close to the prize I plan to claim for my own.

Although I can't blame them. *She is beautiful.*

Within seconds, her hips have found their way to me and my manhood responds. I keep my hands firm at her waist letting her sway guide our movement in full. It takes everything within me not to kick everyone out of the club and take my delight in her right here on the dance floor. As my thoughts linger on the possibility of making love to her in this instant, she turns to face me, and I almost go numb.

I'm not sure if it's the way her caramel-coated skin glows all its own or how the Altrinion embers of red shine through her being, but I am lost in her lure. Her eyes deepen into mine with shimmering flames like fire and I immediately know her truth. She is Altrinion. Slowly, she trails her petite fingers up my shirt and the strong essence of desire leaks from her pores. She wants me! Laced with her sweet and calming scent, her pheromones tell the truth of her lust as her luscious pink lips drip open with wanting.

How I want to kiss her! I want to fill her lips with all of me. I want to taste her on my lips. All of her!

As we continue grinding on the dance floor, I swing her leg around my waist, and she lifts up and presses her femininity against me and the warmth from her body pulsates through me and my manhood responds. Harder. I know she can feel me, and she doesn't mind.

Nor do I. Crap! What is she doing to me?

I exhale along her neckline softly and her body shivers in my grip. I try to read her mind, but I cannot. Beyond the loud thumping of my own rekindled heart all else is silent. The music comes to a slower beat and I twirl her around and gently slide her down, releasing my hold. Once more, my manhood takes a stand, stroking her precious place as I lower her to the ground, and I hear her grunt in willful desire.

Oh the things I want to do for her and to her! Right here and right now. But I cannot. I feel the raging beast within yearning to be free, but I will not allow any harm to come to her—especially not by my hand. Although she does not yet know it; she owns me. Every part of me willfully submits to her entreat. I know nothing about her but this: she needed tonight. She wanted tonight. There was a deep longing in her to be caressed, to be touched, to be loved—and to be free. I want to make her every desire come true.

So, I say no to the beast within me. He no longer holds sway because she holds my all. My heart.

Leaning down, I rest my lips on her neck, kissing her softly while inhaling her wholly. "Mon cœur t'appartient," I whisper in her ear. Though she may not know it, my heart already belongs to her. The next time I see her, I plan to make her heart mine.

Chapter 14

Jackson

"Jackie," Sophie's voice seems distant although she's seated across from me. It's at least the third time I've heard her call my name. I've wanted to answer each time, but I cannot. All my mind does is replay my conversation with Kyra.

My aunt even gave me a big portion of her famous wedding soup but I'm sure it's cold now since I've done nothing but stir the spoon repeatedly for the last forty or so minutes. Perhaps my aunt is upset I'm not eating, or she's grown tired of the sounds of my spoon scraping the sides of the ceramic bowl, but her firm grasp is enough to revive my wandering thoughts. If she hadn't grabbed my hand this time, I doubt our eyes would connect.

"I'm here, Sophie. I'm sorry. I'm just—"

"Distracted. I know. You've been like a statue ever since you spoke with Kyra yesterday."

"I suppose," I quietly respond.

"Truly, I wish you never gave her the time of day. Ever. You know I was never a fan of her anyway."

"Ha! Sophie, you've never been a fan of any girl I've brought home."

"Impossible! That's not true and you know it. There was that one girl, Eva, or was it Everly? Oh whatever her name was, I recall liking her quite a bit!"

"Her name was Evelyn, and we only made mud pies together! I don't think I've seen her since the fourth grade!"

"Well, there must've been something special about her."

"I suppose she did make one hell of a mud pie. So, there's that!"

We both burst into laughter and it's the first time since *that night* that either of us have shared a laugh or even cared to do so.

Sophie squeezes my hand in hers and smiles, patting it firmly to regain my attention.

"You know, Jackie, there is still one woman, that I've liked—dare I say loved more than all the others," Sophie says in a warm tone with a sincere smile to match. "What are we going to do about getting her back?"

"I did speak with her briefly. Now at least I know she's safe. She's keeping in touch with Dacari. I think she just needs some space. Perhaps I owe her that much."

"That's rubbish and you know it, Jackie! You need her as much as she needs you. The last thing either of you need is any more space between you. Now is the time for her to learn the truth—from you."

"But what is that truth, Sophie? Just the other day I was ready to pour out my heart to her—tell her everything!"

"So what has changed?"

"The truth, that's what."

"Jackie, I don't understand."

"Last night when I spoke with Kyra, she told me that there are some who believe Damina is Fated. No one, not even Delia or Damina's father have mentioned that she might be Fated."

Sophie's gaze darkens, and she shifts in her seat, pulling her hand from my grip slowly.

"Jackie, the last thing you should be worried about is anything that comes from Kyra!"

"Unless there's truth to it. Tell me, Sophie, what do you know?" I demand. I know she's stalling.

"There's nothing, really."

"Sophie, tell me the truth! Is Damina Fated?"

"If you are asking whether she is Fated to be with another in such a way that it's a curse to not only her, but her very existence and all of mankind then, no. But if you're asking whether she bears the marking—perhaps."

"Perhaps? Is that really all you have to say? Perhaps?

You're telling me the one woman that I love is Fated, marked, cursed to be with another so much that it will bring ruin if the two are torn apart? How could you let me get this far knowing all of this? Even more, how could Delia or her family—"

"Do you recall your vows to her father?"

"Of course, I do! I'll never forget them!"

"Well then you remember that you vowed to protect her—even from herself!"

"What does that have to do with anything, Sophie?"

"It has everything to do with it! Maybe the Duacin Elders wanted to prevent her from accepting her Fated state. That's why your wedding was so important. Your ability to cloak her with your lupine nature would nullify the curse."

"So that's why they were apt to allow me to marry her? It was all a ruse?"

"Of course not, Jackie! They adored you. And you are a good man! They wanted you to marry Damina for all the right reasons—for all the reasons any family would be proud of. You being a Prime Alpha was just the icing on the cake!"

"I can't believe you knew all this time and you've said nothing? How could you do this to me? To Damina?"

"You love her, don't you?"

"Yes, Sophie. You know I love her with all that's in me!"

"Then nothing else matters."

"Except it does. Both Damina and I have the right

to know the truth of our lineage. These lies are exactly the fuel Keiron needed to execute his deception. I knew he had help. What I didn't know is that we were the ones helping him!"

"How do you mean?"

"Keiron knew I hadn't been upfront with Damina about her being an Altrinion, me being a wolf, or about my past with Kyra, and he used it against us. Somehow, he must've discovered she was also Fated. He convinced other den leaders that I couldn't be trusted to do what is necessary should Damina succumb to her curse. And he was right."

"How would Keiron know what you would or wouldn't do."

"Oh, come now, Sophie. We both know I'd die first before taking Damina's life. Fated curse or not, we know there's no situation possible where I would take Damina's life. No way."

"But that's why your wedding was so necessary. *It still is*. That is why you must do everything you can to reclaim her as your wife. Jackson, her father trusted that you would be the only one to protect her from herself and I'm sure this is what he meant. Only you can walk her through what is to come!"

"How can you be so sure, Sophie?"

"Because I know you love her! Not only that, but she loves you too! Sure, she's upset now, but she will soon realize you're only doing everything in your power to care for her and protect her."

"And what about the packs and den leaders? Kyra says

I've lost my standing with most of them. Many think I've given so much to Damina that I'm blind of their needs. Is there truth in what she speaks?"

"Jackson, every leader has to endure the disgruntled underbelly of those he leads. Sure there may be grumbling—but that comes with the territory. If you're doing good, they will say more can be done. If you're doing horrible, they'll say they want someone new until they get your replacement. People are fickle."

"Sophie, you don't have to say that because I'm your favorite nephew," I say trying to soften the mood.

"Yes you are my favorite, but even you know I'd never stroke your ego just to pass the time," Sophie adds in a mildly censuring tone.

"Thank you, Sophie. You know I love our talks," I say pushing away from the couch. I pick up my jacket from the arm of the chair and head toward the door.

"Jackie, you barely touched your food! Where are you going?"

"Well, I can tell you this. I'm done talking. Now it's time for some action. And since the den leaders and packs feel they haven't seen me in a while they'll get to see a great deal of me tonight—under a full moon!"

Dalcour

I DON'T know what's worse releasing her from my grip or the daggering pain piercing through my newly revived heart upon leaving her side. Sure, I've felt pain before, but nothing like this. At her side, a cascading stream of peace washed over me like dew resting on the leaves on a midsummer's morning. If it weren't for the beast raging inside me to be free, I have no doubt I would have never left her alone.

Still, even the beast within was somewhat subdued in her presence. Perhaps even he wanted nothing more than just to be near her. But I can't risk it.

As I take my flight away from the club, the throbbing beat of my heart fades to a quieter rhythm, but it does not die. For that I am thankful. If what I now feel even faintly resembles true love, then I anxiously await the joys of experiencing love in full bloom!

Thoughts of her body pressed against mine stir my loins with titillating desire. But this was unlike any fleeting guise of lust. I want to know her. What does she like? What does she want? Need? I also know I would gladly end any who seek to harm her, and I would do so without question. I only want to keep her safe, loved, and protected. Always.

Once more, Trieu's warning flickers through my mind and the lingering notion of threats against my newfound love, fuel a burning rage within me. Knowing she is with Braelyn and under the watchful eye of Jerrica gives me some peace that she is safe.

However, tonight is a full moon and that means there is still more to fear. Not only does the threat of the full moon terrorize my thoughts but so does my brother's scheming. Mania fills my mind at all the possible perils lurking in the distance and I know I must do what I can to ensure no harm comes to my beautiful lady or those I care for.

I hear a faint cry and tussling from the ground at the edge of the Quarter and I make my way to the area.

"My Lord Marchand! Always glad to have you lend a helping hand," Cedric's bright tune is welcoming despite his scuffle with a large Scourge as I land in the wooded lot. His wide smile meets his eyes, and he tosses two mangled Scourge arms at my feet, obviously proud at his triumph.

"Looks like I came too late for the party," I answer kicking the Scourge husks aside.

"Never too late, my lord," he answers pointing behind me. My instincts drive my elbow deep into the belly of a lanky vampire approaching my rear. Lifting it overhead, I body slam the creature into the ground, burying my feet into its chest wall and reaching down to pull its slimy head from its body before it combusts.

"Nice work!" Cedric laughs as he lunges his sword between two Scourges, impaling them to the ground.

"Good work, yourself!" Cedric's wife, Abigail exclaims as she leaps from atop a large tree branch, slicing through three small vampires with one sweeping thrust. She lands flawlessly at his side and the two share a quick kiss before simultaneously plunging their blades through the heads of the Scourge at their feet.

"Looks like I'm interrupting date night," I chuckle, walking toward them after a quick glance at our surroundings.

"I'm sorry, my lord. Abigail and I just like stealing moments when we can," Cedric says almost bashfully, lightly squeezing Abigail's hand, and they share knowing glances.

"No apologies needed," I respond and continue staring at their small bouts of affection while they discard the Scourge husks as they burn.

"Well, I'm glad you asked us to patrol the perimeter. For it to be a full moon there's an uptick in Scourge activity tonight," Cedric replies while wiping his blades and putting them back in their sheath as he makes his way toward me.

"He's right, my lord. Usually, the vermin know to stay clear of the woods during a full moon. But tonight it's like they're after something," Abigail adds coming to her husband's side. She keeps her eyes tight as she gazes around the lot, searching for any signs of danger.

Or someone. The thought of Scourge tracking Damina's scent or even looking for her enrages me.

"Do you think it could be Decaux, my lord? Perhaps he's pulling another coo," Cedric offers, watchful of my response.

"I wouldn't put it past him," I answer dryly as I put a final end to one remaining Scourge trying to slither away under a bushel of leaves and pinecones. "Any word from Titan? Are other areas just as populated?" I question.

"Yes, both Titan and Lux have reported an influx of activity tonight," Cedric replies.

"And what of the Skull wolves?"

"Not many, my lord. I'm sure most are staying away from pack soil tonight. Most of the trouble have been Scourge. What's more surprising is that the Guardians have done well to keep a census if you will on how many are in the City and neighboring parishes."

"Cedric, what are you implying?"

"I think it's highly possible that someone is making more Scourge," Abigail answers softly, looking at me under her eyes, almost hesitant.

Or creating an army. Crap! What is my brother up to now? I've seen him do this before—back during the Great Fire of New Orleans. He created his first Scourge army; bred for one purpose to destroy mankind and any who oppose him.

"She's right, my lord. And these vermin are different. You can tell they are new, smaller—more fragile. Some haven't even gotten full fang, still wet behind the ears!"

"I'm glad you've shared this with me. Have you told Titan?" I ask.

"Yes, him and Lux ran into large herds with both of their company just an hour ago," Cedric quickly answers.

"Good, well tell no one else. Let's keep the perimeter strong tonight. But let's not start a panic. I don't want people afraid for no reason. We've got a lot we're working towards and the last thing we need to do is make the nobles or the human faction nervous."

I've done well over the last hundred or so years rebuilding much of what my brother destroyed in New Orleans. Now, with things so close to perfect I dare not risk an intrusion of his brutal attacks. I've worked for years resetting the beams of balance in the supernatural world all while repairing the breach he created between us and humans. I will not allow him or anyone else to undo all the good that has been done.

"We understand," the duo nod in affirmation. Even now I stand in amazed at their synchronicity. They are the epitome of unison.

Abigail gets a call on her receiver, and she turns away and responds.

"My lord," Cedric begins, pulling my elbow and leading us away under a small tree. He quickly glances over his shoulder at his wife who pays us no attention as she lashes at her caller, apparently annoyed. I gesture for him to continue. "Is there something more that you're not saying? I mean, I hadn't expected to see you tonight, especially after your recent rip through the City a few days ago. I hope you know you can trust me when I say, I'm here for you however you need me."

"Thank you, Cedric. Out of everyone you still remain one of the most observant. Yes, the last few days have been a firestorm—especially with everything my brother is pulling. I just needed to get away from the noise. The mansion is swarming with Jerrica's new pet project and though I haven't seen him in a while, Brian and I need to keep our distance."

"Ah, I see," Cedric replies with an undercurrent of suspicion burrowed in his brow line. "Are you certain there isn't anything—anything more, my lord?"

"Nothing to worry about I assure you," I lie, working

hard to scatter my thoughts. Thankfully, after five hundred years I'm rather adept at burying my truth from others, making it painfully difficult to read me.

Cedric relaxes the growing frown on his face and smiles. I know he's not buying the bull I'm selling, but he opts not to push the issue.

"Dearest," Abigail calls from behind us to Cedric, "my apologies for disrupting you two, but we must head over to the westside. Sonja tells me there have been more Scourge sightings and Raja and Demeter's company never made it to post."

Cedric blows a sharp curse under his breath, before staring back at me with a half-irritated grin. I can tell this is not how he planned to spend the night with his wife. For the first time, I feel a tug on my newly beating heart and a small part of me almost understands his apparent angst.

"Well, I suppose the night is far from spent. Duty calls." Cedric's faux chipper tone betrays him.

"No, you two stay here. I'll go. I could use another round with some Scourge anyway. Besides, maybe you might be able to salvage whatever is left of your—um, date night," I swiftly reply.

Both instantly protest and shake their heads and try to convince me otherwise, but faintly, I hear their harmonic sighs of relief. Tonight, I'm more than empathetic to their plight. Soon, I shall have such a quandary of my own. And in that, I take great delight.

Chapter 15

Jackson

I've finally seen the new me and it's nothing I've ever thought possible!

While this by far has been the most painful lunar phase to date, I have never felt so powerful. So strong. My normal phasing typically consists of a few broken bones, setting and resetting, as I transform from the appearance of a man into my wolfen form. But everything about last night's turn has my muscles still pulling and contracting even as my splintered bones swell beneath my newfound musculature.

As I stand taller than my usual height, I gaze at the chorale of den leaders hovering over in submission and awe at my new form. And if it weren't for the glass doors of my aunt's terrace reflecting my image,

I would hardly believe it myself. Now I understand what Gregory meant when he said he witnessed my new transformation.

In fairness, I thought he was only trying to stroke my ego in my sullen state. Truly, I thought creatures like the one I saw reflected in the glass doors staring back at me were myths—or only existed as legend. Now, as the sun rises upon me and the den leaders, I now know there is more to me than even I understood.

One resounding growl rumbles through me as my spinal column snaps back in place and my protruding canines and lengthened nails retract to their normal state. The surrounding den leaders howl in response, baying at the retreating apex as the sun looms on the horizon. And with it, each one drops to one knee to the earth while resting their elbow to their opposite knee, showcasing their submission.

My chest swells and constricts as air ripples through my lungs and I pace back and forth in front of the packs, working hard to catch my breath in hopes to douse the lingering jitteriness raging within me.

"To our Prime Alpha!" Gregory shouts first, leading the chorus of den leaders. Each echo in response, pouncing their fists to their chests as they bellow a militant roar.

It's been years since I've called for den leaders to shift on prime pack soil.

Most came likely to pry about my nuptials—or the lack thereof. A few came out of simple curiosity while others came with hopes to challenge me in some fashion.

Some didn't come at all. I've asked Shawn to follow up on those who didn't present themselves. Perhaps they're with my treacherous brother.

I'm not sure what any of them expected when Gregory summoned them at my behest to our pack soil at my family's ranch. What they got was not something I think any of us could prepare for.

From the first crowning of last night's moon, my wolf insisted he would be stifled no longer. Normally, it's the apex of the moon that ignites our transformation. While Prime wolves can always change into form at any given time, like most wolves, none of us can truly resist the summoning of the full moon. It calls to our very primal nature like no other.

But something happened last night that I neither intended nor expected.

There was at least another hour or so left until the full moon was set to reach its apex when a loud, grizzly-like roar ruptured through my being as my wolf took form. I hadn't said much through the evening and my mind fluctuated its course over and again. I knew I needed to say something, but I wasn't quite sure of what to say. Or how.

Thankfully, my wolf knew exactly what needed to be done.

With my first yelp, leaves rattled as the tree trunks shook and the dens immediately grew quiet. Then another roar issued from me and the moon's brightness showed its fullness.

At my wail, the clouds lift their cover, giving

way to the full moon in our view and the wolves transformation is instantaneous. No one under the sound of my howl or standing in the light of the moon withstands our entreat.

While everything about this moment feels both mystical and perhaps a bit more than supernatural, it is no dream nor nightmare. This is real. Den leaders from all around the mid-Atlantic gaze at me with a reverential glare that both strengthens me and stirs me with awe.

But as life changing as our phasing was, it was our shared hunt that solidified the unity amongst the packs more than I thought possible. We shared no words that human minds can interpret, but we were able to communicate with one another on a level those of original lineage can understand.

"We are with you and await your word," shouts Isaac, leader of the lower York County den. The remaining leaders once more chorale in unison, still on their knees.

"And I am with you," I shout back followed by a loud roar. Slowing my pace, I take note of each den leader, making eye contact with each of them as I pass by. I need them to know I see them. Even more, I need them to know I'm here with and for them. When they leave this place, they must know we are in this together.

We are family.

"I know some of you think I have failed you. You feel that I have abandoned you. And maybe I could have done some things differently. Maybe we all could have done some things different. But the time for apologies is passed. As leaders of the Prime wolves, we have a responsibility to end dissension in our ranks. There are growing threats that seek to end our way of life— and life as we know it! Unlike my ancestors, I will not skulk to the shadows and hide! You have my vow that I will stand and fight! All I ask is that you fight by my side!"

A loud chorus endorses my sentiment with another militant roar as they pound their fists to the ground, and it shakes in response. Both Gregory and Shawn's proud smiles of admiration shine brightly as the sun rises, showcasing the shimmery dew of the tree leaves around us.

As I walk toward the steps of the back patio, I spy Aunt Sophie watching me through the glass. Her eyes dance with delight and while it's hard to fathom, the look in her eyes tell me she's prouder of me now, more than ever. She nods in approval and smiles and I respond in kind and turn back to face the wolves.

"That is why I need you here today. Together we can uphold our vow to protect the keepers of the balance, those of Altrinion lineage. And yes, my fiancé, Damina happens to be one of them. I know many of you have heard disparaging remarks from my brother about my betrothed. I say this to you now because I want to bare my truth to you. For too long secrets and lies have been both our demise and downfall. Now is our time to take back all that we lost—and for me that also includes Damina! Long before I knew she was supernatural, I loved her. I love her still. And I still believe it is that love which is capable of overcoming any curse or anything that comes our way!"

"My lord, how then can we overcome such a curse as the Fated Ones? Especially when you have yet to mark your lordship and take your rightful place as Alpha Lord?" Jesse, den leader of the Glasgow pack mutters. His tone reeks of fear and his shifty stance tell me he was afraid to ask.

I smile in return and gesture toward him to approach me.

"You have every right to question me, my friend," I respond with my hands on his shoulder. I feel his tense muscles relax in my grip and a small smile creeps on his face. "As a matter of fact, you all do! For too long, I've kept myself guarded. But how can I expect you to follow and serve by my side unless we have transparency between us? Last night proved one thing, I am more than your Prime Alpha! And I suspect that if and when the time comes for me to enact my lordship if you will, then I shall. What I want to focus on now is not letting it get to that point. We cannot repeat the mistakes of our ancestors by taking the rank of Prime Lordship for granted. It is a great responsibility not to be taken lightly and used as only necessary. Having control of all animal life is no small undertaking. Our ancestors abused their powers, and we've been trying to play catch up ever since—but not today. No. Today, we will become proactive. Not reactive. That is why I need your help to reclaim my bride!"

"We are with you!" Isaac and Jesse shout with the remaining leaders resounding their sentiment.

A strong wind blows through the woods behind us, and we howl in unison with nature's melody breezing at our backs. I lift my hands, encouraging all the leaders to stand to their feet. I greet each of them as they pass by me on the steps. As each leader takes my hand in their grip, I feel like a connection once lost has been restored.

Although I hate to admit it, perhaps there was some truth in Kyra's words. For too long the packs and den leaders have been disjointed. Keiron leveraged that instability to my own demise but I believe today we laid building blocks to a better future.

What they needed wasn't just someone to talk to them and trifle with their own inherent fears. Instead, they needed to *see me*. I can't believe I didn't see that all along. It's the one thing I've longed for between me and Damina—*for her to see me*. The real me.

The wolf I've long kept hidden is the real me. For wolves, especially alphas, nothing is more sacred than the moments between our humanity and our supernaturality. I think my wolf knew that. He gained the confidence of the koi-wolves when I shifted from wolf to man. And he knew it was time for those who truly follow me to see the same. My transformation before the den leaders proved that I was willing to be at my most strongest and most vulnerable before them.

"What do you require from us?" Shawn says as he

and Gregory join me on the patio.

As much as I wish to linger in the swelling joy of regaining the confidence of the den leaders, I know I must plan to reclaim Damina as my own. And to do so there's only one name that comes to mind.

My brother, Keiron.

"Find my brother and his band of traitors!"

Dalcour

I FEEL like my favorite cartoon, Charlie Brown. For the last few hours, everything Jerrica has said to me is as muted as the words of the teacher of the Peanuts gang. Nothing she says seems of any importance; at least compared to my longing to finally see Damina.

All I do is listen intermittently for her name.

Damina.

Frankly, it's all I care about at this moment.

Ever since I came back from taking Cedric and Abigail's post at the westside, putting an end to the large crowding of Scourge seeking to descend on the City, I've been jumpy at the thought of seeing her again. Once more, I feel like a kid at Christmas and boy I can't wait to unwrap and open my gift. This day couldn't come fast enough.

As Jerrica continues talking, something about her ongoing dislike of Chartreuse Grenoble, I hear a growing number of footsteps leading toward Jerrica's back office in the adjacent parlor. Without a moment to pass, my face is pressed against the doorway as the sweet and calming fragrance of Damina drifts through the air, letting me know she is near.

I hear several voices, but it's the dulcet and harmonic cadence of her words that sing like a melody to my ears. My heart throbs in my chest and my pulse quickens as my anticipation grows with each passing moment. I want to see her. *I need to see her!*

"Well someone seems eager to get out there and meet the team!" Jerrica says joyfully, breaking my panic before it sets in.

"That is why you wanted me here today, right?" I respond, playing it cool.

"Then I suppose there's no need to hold you hostage much longer," Jerrica answers while briefly searching my face. I know she can tell something is off with me, but I'm glad she doesn't press it.

Rounding the corner to the hallway my heart races with delight and anticipation! I do everything possible to douse the growing fervor in my loins; lest Jerrica gets the wrong idea. Besides, I'd hate to formally meet everyone with my manhood leading the way. *We can save that for another time.*

Annoyance creeps over me as I realize this hallway seems longer than usual and instead of using our abilities, we're sauntering like mere humans trudging through a garden. I can't get there fast enough. Unfortunately, Zamora is leading us down the hall, and she and Jerrica are taking their sweet time. It's taking everything in me not to push past them both.

And while they are certainly trying my patience, I know that when I finally see her face it will be worth it!

"Listen, everyone," my heart skips as I hear Damina address the team. "Remember to remain steadfast and know you're not in this alone. We are a team and together we will make something greater than even we can imagine. Something quite beautiful."

Oh, we're going to make something beautiful all right. Try as I might to force my intrusively dark thoughts aside, my mind can't help to imagine her laying next to me on my bed.

Even without yet seeing her face, her words drip like honey in my hearing. *Just a few more steps to go.*

"Now you see why we needed the likes of Ms. Nicaud to lead this team," Jerrica announces over her shoulder breaking me away from my fleeting thoughts.

"Haben Sie Angst, dass ich sie zum Schlachten führe? " I jokingly ask in German whether she's afraid I'll lead them to slaughter. It's something her mother would playfully say of her father's inability to care for his children. Jerrica laughs loud and her eyes dance when she looks over her shoulder at me. A part of me feels like I needed to share one final moment with her now because soon all my attention and affection belongs to Damina.

Seeing Colin's daughter Claudia as I enter almost sullies my mood entirely. Her big wide eyes and fire-like hair makes her stand out more than I care to see. I even thought I caught her pushing up her cleavage just as I came into the room. Little does she know there's absolutely nothing she can do for me.

My eyes scan the room, looking hard for my beautiful Damina. But with Jerrica's finalists crowding us as soon as we crossed the threshold it's almost difficult to see through the lot of them. Some of the team I know, like Mark, Dilano, Dorine, Padma and Vonnie. There's a girl with Dilano that I've never seen, but she is not who I'm looking for. Still, I know she is here. I can smell her.

I spot Braelyn on the parlor steps pulling a woman's arm from behind and my heart races with joy and a tinge of trepidation knowing my beautiful lady is only a few steps away. Pushing through the crowd I'm behind Braelyn in an instant.

"Oh, but first you've got to meet Dalcour," Braelyn gripes to Damina.

"Well, I suppose it's a good thing I'm standing right here," I say, lifting myself to one step so that I'm in direct eye contact with Damina. I want to see if I can catch the same sparkle in her eyes, I saw at Razors last night. Only a spark too faint for human eyes to detect remains, and my heart warms knowing she is Altrinion. Like me.

Damina gasps slightly for air and her parted lips are indeed the sexiest thing I've ever seen! Everything in me wants to press her mouth with mine until our tongues are entangled as one. The way her bouncy, copper coils drift at her shoulders makes the silhouette of her frame and loveliness of her face stand out even more. Her maxi jumper hugs her in all the right places without revealing too much. Still, my eyes can't help but to wander to the thick line of her cleavage and thoughts of seeing her in all her glory awaken the primal beast inside.

With everything within me, I stifle my urge just enough to keep the beast at bay. Yet and still, I know I need to feel her, so I take her hand in mine, allowing only the warmth between us to fill the space between our fingers. I can't let the beast out. Not now. Not here.

"I'm glad to formally make your acquaintance, Ms. Nicaud," I quickly state, breaking the silence.

"Oh, you can just call her Damina. She's laid back," Brae says coolly and blows through her pink bubblegum. I give her an irritated glance, but she ignores me. I wish she would leave us here alone.

"Well then, Damina, it's good to finally meet you," I say, squeezing her hand just enough to keep her attention on me. Her eyes glaze over my chest and down through the length of me. It's evident I am affecting her as much as she affects me.

Damina's silence grows deafening and Braelyn uses it to poke fun, but Damina doesn't seem to mind. And while I smile at Damina, I give Braelyn a rebuking glare, and she bows away from us and rejoins the team.

"I'm sorry about that; Brae can be so—"

"BAD?" Damina interjects with a small chuckle that matches her smile. I'm glad she's not as annoyed with Braelyn as I am.

"Yes, I guess you've learned that about Braelyn rather quickly. Why don't we go outside on the patio and talk? I've heard so much about you from Jerrica already, but I'd rather learn more about you firsthand."

"I've heard a lot about you too, Mr. Marchand—"

"Please, just call me Dalcour," I don't need any formalities between us. I don't want anything between us. Instinct firms my grip in her soft, delicate hands and I squeeze just enough to keep her not more than an inch away from me.

"Okay, Dalcour. But I'm sure Jerrica wants you to talk with everyone here first. They're all eager to get to know you. Really," Damina's breath hitches, as she snatches her last word back tight, darting an icy glare aimed at Claudia and her tag-along, Dauphine. Damina gazes back at me and smiles weakly, likely still annoyed with the onlookers at our back. Perhaps it's the little wrinkle at the bridge of her nose or the way she crinkles her upper lip when she's irritated, but I have a feeling Ms. Nicaud is a force to be reckoned with if the opportunity presents itself.

Now, I'm even more intrigued.

Before I can protest, Jerrica's pitchy voice breaks through our forming silence. "And as usual, Damina is perfectly correct. I really want you to greet the team, Dalcour. You and Damina will have loads of time to get to know one another!"

With reluctance, I loosen my grip from Damina and try hard to smile between the two women. This is awkward. The one woman I want to my left and the one who wants me to my right. But I'm not ready to let on that I already know who Damina is to Jerrica, so I must keep up the pretense.

"Sure, Jerrica, you lead the way. But Damina, I look forward to talking with you soon," I say before turning quickly on my heels toward where the team stands. I need to get this over as quickly as possible.

Once again, a stinging ache rips through my newly beating heart as we part. As we reach the team, I look around for Damina and I realize she's escaped again. My eyes scan the room and I find nothing but her lingering scent. It's the only proof I have that she was actually here and all that's keeping me lucid.

After a little over fifteen minutes of rambling with Jerrica and the team, my patience wanes when I realize Damina never came back to the parlor. I also notice her scent is fading—that can't be a good thing. Thankfully, Jerrica's phone rings, and she rushes back to her office and I know this is my chance to find where my beautiful lady went.

It doesn't take long for me to catch the drift of her effervescence which leads me onto the front porch. I'm not sure if it's the way the light from the setting sun shines against her honey-kissed skin or how the early evening breeze captures her sweet scent, but for the first time my knees buckle, and I am lost in the trance of her.

As I await the lingering sun to set, I can't help but admire her from behind. I wonder if she knows just how beautiful she is? In my five hundred years I've never seen anything or anyone so beautiful! I'm awestruck at just the sight of her!

I want her. Always.

Leaning on the doorpost, I allow my voyeurism to hold me captive to the beautifulness before me. I can't help wondering what she's thinking. If I didn't know better, I'd swear that last exhale released something toxic from her. Stress, perhaps. Or could it be she's freeing herself from the one who hurt her heart? The thought of anyone hurting her sickens me with rage. I'll gladly kill anyone who does her harm—and I'd do so without hesitation. Still, her mind is closed to me. I can't read her at all and it's frustrating!

The last shadow of the sun subsides, and we're left with only the glowing red and purple hue of an early summer's eve. As soon as I cross the threshold of the doorpost, her fragrance smacks me in the face and I sense the molecules of our pheromones collecting and binding as one and my thoughts run wild with desire.

I swallow the thick air in my throat and suppress my urges once more. Damina deserves better than a lust-filled beast. She deserves the very best of me and I intend to give it to her.

"So this is where you ran off to?" I question as she turns around, somewhat startled. Warm red fills her cheeks and immediately I know I'm affecting her even more. Her eyes dance and a small smile nestles perfectly between her cheeks and it's evident: she's happy to see me. Very good.

"Oh, I just needed some air. It was stuffy in there. Besides, my ride should be here soon," she says, her voice slightly trembling. I wish I knew what is causing her consternation. I hope I'm not coming on too strong. But then it hits me; she's waiting for someone else to come get her. Not good at all.

"You're not staying at the mansion," I respond leaning on to the porch railing.

"No, I already had arrangements elsewhere before I decided to, um, take this project on."

"I see." Crap! I thought everyone was staying here. Now I really want to know who's coming for her.

"Don't you live here?" Damina asks and I see her eyes dance again. *Good,* she's still interested.

"Well, it is my family estate if that's what you're asking, and I do have a room."

"Oh, so it's not your home then?" She almost sounds disappointed. *Even better*.

I can't help chuckling as I work to push aside the blushing feeling that warms over me. "No Damina, it's not my home. But then again, home is where the heart is, right?" I answer, my tone dark and lush. I deepen my gaze into her own and a sharp pulse of kinetic energy stirs through my core. *I really want her.*

I want to tell her that she is already my home *because she has my heart,* but I know my time has not yet come.

Chapter 16

Jackson

The last twenty-four hours have been amazing. While it's hard to fathom the word amazing apart from all things Damina, I have to admit I feel quite exceptional. The only thing that would make how I feel more tenable is to have Damina back with me where she belongs. And as I stare around the long table of den leaders, I now know I have people by my side who are committed to that goal.

This is probably the first meal we've had together in ages! Together we've phased, hunted, laughed, cried, asked for and been forgiven. We've dispelled rumors and laid all our cards on the table. All of us know the only way we can take hold of the bright future is to do so together. I've had grown men confess they've held undue grudges against one another, and I've experienced the joy of reconciliation when they agreed to let bygones just be. Even the female alphas have laid their trifles aside to ensure the betterment of our people and it's been glorious to behold.

A newfound joy springs within me I never thought I'd see again apart from Damina. Yet and still there's a sweeping peace in seeing harmony restored among the den leaders. Not that I'm glad to have Damina and I at odds, I am thankful that through this pain something good has come from it.

For that, I'll forever be thankful.

Sure, sharing our moonlit phase aided our angst since all truth and secrets are revealed during our transformation. I guess that's why wolves are so selective with who they share such a ritual with. But I know that as I became barren in front of them, they saw the truth—when they saw me. There was no folly or ill-will. No, I'm not perfect-they saw that too. My shortcomings, lack of patience, bad temper and all. But they also saw a man who was heartbroken and longed for his one true love. They saw just how lost I am without her. They saw that she means the world to me and that is a truth I'd gladly share with the world.

Now with all our pretense and posturing aside, we can finally walk in agreement. Together.

As we wrap up our evening, I give instructions for each of them to give no quarter to any leader who refused to come tonight or any pack resident who refuses their leading. We all agree on one thing: there is no place among our ranks for traitors. That includes my brother.

Merle, den leader of the Bay Area pack hangs behind as everyone heads out and I know why. He's the newly installed leader since Kyra was eschewed. During our transformation, I could sense he felt remorse for taking part in removing her from leadership, but I can see he did it for the pack and not out of any mere grievance.

"Sophie didn't call you in for kitchen duty, did she?" I question jokingly. I know the truth, but I'd rather not call him out on it.

Merle gazes at me, his shoulders sunken and sweat forming at his brow. I work hard to brighten my smile as he saunters forward, the last thing I need is him doubting himself. Kyra has that effect on men.

"No, my lord, she didn't. But I can certainly lend a hand if need be," Merle responds, with his head low and shoulders hunched.

"Well, then what can I do for you?"

"I—I um...just wanted to tell you that I had no intention of having Kyra eschewed. She just—um—"

"She screwed up. No need to sugarcoat it, Merle. There's also no need for you to feel remorseful."

"But that's just it. I do. I know she messed up and I know the harm she caused—most of all to you—but—"

"You love her."

Merle gulps loud, swallowing the thick air in his throat and gazes around the room. "I mean, I do—but she doesn't see a guy like me. How could she?"

"I don't know Merle. Maybe one day Kyra will

finally see beyond Kyra. There's no room for anyone as long as she's in the way," I respond. Merle's eyes rise and fall. A part of him feels slightly insecure and the other defensive of her. It's almost impressive. But I know what he really wants, and he's too fearful to ask. "Look, Merle, you're the alpha of the Bay Area and den leader. You don't need my permission if you want to pardon her. But you should speak with the den council and ensure you're all in agreement. Just be sure you can trust her. You not only carry your secrets but now mine. If she proves worthy, then so be it."

"Thank you—thank you, sir!" Merle's eyes beam with hopefulness and his tense frown relaxes to a smile.

"You are more than welcome. That's what I'm here for. Once we find Keiron, Tye, and whoever else is helping them I will release her to your care. Is that, okay?"

"Yes, my lord. Yes. And I will do whatever I can to not only help you locate your brother and Tye but your beloved as well," Merle says in a more confident tone, with his shoulders squared. After a brief hug, he gives me a sturdy handshake and heads out the door.

Only Gregory, Shawn and Brandon remain, and Sophie has them on full clean-up duty. We caused a bit of damage to the barns, surrounding fences and woods during our transformation and hunt. Mostly, I know she has them collecting any animal debris left from our hunt. A part of me feels like that's why Sophie hasn't opened the land for phasing in decades.

Even though it's pack soil, and they have a right to come here, she hasn't made it welcoming to do so. Being the Prime Alpha I could always invoke rank like I did tonight and insist on bringing everyone here, since it is my family's estate after all. But I see no pleasure in causing Sophie any unease. Especially after everything she's done for me.

"Need any help with the dishes?" I ask as I enter the kitchen.

"Indeed not!" Sophie exclaims as if me asking were almost an expletive.

"No need to get huffy, auntie. I'm just messing with you. I already knew your response."

"Ha! You know me well," Sophie adds as she dries off a large casserole dish. She tries to put it in the cabinet, but her height halts her efforts. Turning her head, almost annoyed, she hands me the glass dish.

"Ah! So you only need my height and not my help! I see—" I tease, placing the dish in the cabinet.

And you knew that without me phasing with you. Sophie mutters under her breath. I'm sure she didn't expect me to hear her.

"What's that supposed to mean, Sophie? As a matter of fact that brings up a good point. Where did you phase last night? Don't tell me you stayed in the cellar?" I ask.

"Jackie, please! I've been phasing in the cellar for well over forty years. And I have no desire to bare my sixty-ish behind in front of you younglings!"

"Now, Sophie you know we don't see things that way.

Besides, you always told us it was the most natural thing in the world."

"Yes, it is, but not for me. Besides, it was for the den leaders. I'm just on the council."

"You're more than that and you know it!"

"Perhaps. But let's just drop it okay?" Sophie's tone is indifferent, but she feigns a faux smile and swats my shoulder with the kitchen towel as she ambles into the den. Ever since my transformation, my senses are heightened, and I can almost smell the stench of fear a mile away.

What could she possibly have to fear?

"Sophie, what's wrong?" With my arms folded, I lean against the oak pillar separating the den from the dining area and keep my eyes locked on her shifty posture.

"Jackie, please! I'm just tired! It's been a long couple of days and I just cooked and cleaned up after fourteen ravenous wolves. I'm spent!" She says patting her knees as if they were dirty. She's nervous.

"There's something you're not telling me. Some reason or something to do with phasing with the wolves."

"Look, Jackson I—"

"And now you're calling me Jackson. You never call me Jackson. What's wrong?"

"It's nothing is what it is!"

"Sophie!" I bark and the rumble through my chest makes her jumpy.

"I was just going to say while it's nice you phased

with the dens today, I don't think you should make a habit of it."

"Who's saying we're making a habit of it? I'm sure it won't be feasible to get everyone together every full moon anyway."

"Good. That's all I'm saying."

"No, it's not. There's more and you know it. What's the big deal if I wolf out with everyone? I mean didn't you see the morale today? Everyone was boosted. So free!"

"Jackie, you aren't some random alpha. You're a Prime. And as such a leader like you can't just reveal himself to whosoever will!"

"Well, Sophie I don't plan on doing that, but what's the big deal of who I choose to reveal myself to?"

"Somethings just aren't meant to share—not even by you."

"What things? I laid everything out on the table. I have nothing to hide."

"Perhaps you do, and you don't know it. Just trust me on this, Jackie. You know I'd never lead you astray."

"Well, Sophie, I made a promise to those den leaders today and I'm not gonna back out of a promise. I never have and I'm not going to start today."

"What if that promise is too much for even you to bear, Jackie? Just promise me you won't phase with them ever again!" Sophie's tone is covered and her expression grim.

"*Ever*?" I mumble, unsure why Sophie's gaze has darkened.

"It's for your own good," she pleads in a bleak tone as her eyes search my face for understanding.

"Tell me the truth, Sophie! What could we possibly have to hide?" I snap back, refusing to conform.

"The truth is what. The truth about the Primes. The truth about what our ancestors did."

"Tell me now!" My patience is all but spent and I refuse for any further secrets to linger.

"It was us! We are the reason the Dunes are cursed!" Sophie belts as tears flood her face.

"What do you mean, Sophie? How can that be? The Dunes are the ones who turned on the Altrinions, not us."

"I'm not sure if your father ever intended to tell you, but if you accept lordship one day you will be burdened with the truth of every Prime Alpha before you. That's why your father never wanted you to bear such a yoke. The truth is that long ago there were two sets of primes: Alphas and Betas. The Alphas were responsible for the overall watch and care of the supernatural balance and the Betas were directly responsible for guarding the Altrinions. It was known that should a Prime ever get out of step, the Betas could rightly challenge for alpha status. And so, to keep the Betas at bay, the Alphas arranged a plot with a changeling to trick the Betas."

"But I know the Betas claim a changeling tricked them, but I had no idea Alphas were responsible."

"Yes, and what do you think will happen if others find out what our ancestors did? You could be challenged or worse!"

"Well, why did the Elders or the Order curse the Betas if they knew?"

"The power of the Great Oak prevents them from seeing through the dark shadow cast by the changelings. Changelings are evil, malevolent beings. So it's no more than hearsay to the Elders. That's why Jackie you must keep these things secret. No one can ever know the truth!"

Just like that, the would-be veil of my joy is snatched from me. And I know what follows and it isn't the truth.

Dalcour

ONCE AGAIN, I'm giddy like a kid on Christmas morning and I owe it all to *her*. I can't wait to see Damina again! I could've stayed on the porch talking with her forever, that is until *he* came. Brian. Ugh! I wish Jerrica had assigned anyone other than Brian to look after Damina. But even that didn't stop me. In fact, not even the bloodletting of her puncture wound from the wood railing could keep me at bay. As much as the beast within clawed to sample just a drop of her, I used everything within me to keep him at bay. Sure, Braelyn tried to convince me to stay put, but I couldn't. My heart ached to see her again.

To be near her.

Going back to Bessie's place wasn't exactly on my bucket list either, especially with Melvina's border blocking my entrance, but I would have walked through the flames of hell just to see her again. Not that I enjoyed running into Bessie or her treacherous brother, Javier, but I was quite impressed to watch Damina throw her weight around. The way she stood up to Bessie's spite-filled rebuke for keeping company with me, made my heart leap. Even more, I've never known a time when a woman was so overcome with keeping me to herself that she pulled me into the streets by her own might. If I learned nothing else from last night, I know Damina Nicaud is not to be trifled with.

Although I found it frustrating not to be able to read her mind, I was happy to know her walls were relaxed enough for me to compel her to truth. And she didn't hold back. Damina now knows I've been enraptured by her since the first night I saw her at the Tavern and even how much I enjoyed our sensuous grind on the dance floor. Not that she seemed to mind. I suspect she liked it as well.

We shall see.

Puzzling enough, what I most enjoyed was our *non-kiss*. I wanted to kiss her lips. Really, I did! Her scent is intoxicating and her curvaceous frame calls to me with a forbidden lure. It's definitely a challenge restraining myself around her.

She is worth it.

Resting my lips upon her forehead sent my loins into a frenzy and it took every ounce of decency in me not to rip her clothes to shreds and take her in the middle of the promenade. While it sounds indecent, worse things have happened in the Quarter; especially during Mardi gras. What's more is that I am sure she wanted me to kiss her. The way she gripped my hand, allowing me to pull her close enough for our bodies to touch lets me know she's beginning to drop all barriers with me.

Today, however, I have every intention on testing those barriers. There's no Bulwark in heaven or hell capable of keeping me from experiencing everything that is Damina Nicaud.

Jerrica's headed to London to acquire a few antiques, and she asked Damina to accompany me to the Hall of Isis to pick up statues for the maze garden and some other things for the mansion. I'm looking forward to spending the day with Damina and I hope she's ready for what I have in store. While I suspect Jerrica is delighted that I'm so taken with Damina, I can tell it's still uncomfortable for her. I have no doubt her venture to London is to get a little separation from us.

Still, I'll allow nothing to sully my good mood. In fact, I'm thankful for this dreary morning. The forecast of rain and cloudy skies ensures I can spend daylight hours with Damina without the sun's interruption. And should the sun sneak its way out, I'll summon every bit of the Altrinion Force within me to bend nature to my will. Nothing is going to keep me from her. Not today— or ever again.

Whipping my Audi in the middle of the courtyard in front of the Tavern with Imagine Dragons blaring through my system scares most of the locals as they set up their curbside stations. While I hate causing such a stir, I can't get to her fast enough. I only hope she's outside so that I don't have to make a scene. Although when I see Melvina, with her hands on her hips giving me a disapproving maternal glare upon my arrival, I know I've already made a scene. At least a little.

I'm just glad that Melvina likes me; even if she has to barter the peace between Bessie and me. And from the looks of the admirable smile, she dotes on Damina as she exits the Tavern, I can tell she's quite fond of her too.

Unfortunately, she's not the only one.

Calvin's cagey eyeballing of Damina's rear as he holds the door open for her doesn't go unnoticed by me. For a couple who claim ardent devotion to their marriage covenant, both he and his wife Bessie could use a lesson or two in restraint. *I'm certainly not opposed to giving Calvin a refresher course.*

He glowers quickly in my direction when I get out of the car, but I refuse to let him sour my mood. Watching Damina's graceful stroll toward me is enough to ward off any mal intent from Calvin or even the beast within me.

She looks lovely in her creamsicle peplum top and white capris. The way her blouse accents her curves and perfected waistline coupled with how her pants caress her curves in all the right places, almost makes me jealous. What I wouldn't give to trade places with her clothes!

"Now don't you look tasty this morning," I say, twirling Damina around and pulling her into my arms. She nestles her head at the nape of my neck and it's the best feeling—ever. It feels like home. It's where she belongs. "I could just eat you up," I add with a peck on her forehead.

Damina tucks her hair behind her ear and smiles wide. Her big, bright eyes gaze at me with an innocence that almost makes me want to repent of any evil I've done past or present and vow in this moment to be a better man. Staring into her eyes and trusting smile, I take in her delectable smell and savor it, knowing I will do whatever I can to be the best I can be. She deserves that and so much more.

"All right you two, there won't be any eating anybody up this morning," Melvina says as she walks up behind the two of us with her hands of her hips.

"Miss Melvina!" I laugh while taking her in my arms for a hearty embrace.

"Oh, now don't hurt this old bag of bones!" Melvina says, pulling from my grip. "How have you been, sugar? Have you been misbehaving?" She gives me a knowing glance and I hear her thoughts drift between my recent misadventures at the Tavern and my beastly onslaught a few days past.

"Well, I have been on good behavior as of late, Miss Melvina," I reply almost bashfully. Although I'm more than twice her age, I respect Melvina wholly. She's the only one who has shared any maternal-like affection toward me since my mother's passing. Even when she rebukes me, I have no doubt she not only cares for me but sees the good I'm trying to do.

After Melvina gives Damina a bag of breakfast pastry and coffee, I help Damina in the car because I know what's coming next.

"Are you sure you can do this, dear?" Melvina asks in a mild but censuring tone.

"Do what?" I reply coolly, looking over my shades into the car and see Damina stuff pastry into her cheeks. She must be hungry. I send a quick text to Khalil and tell him to set up the courtyard at the Hall for lunch for me and Damina.

"Now don't you go ignoring me, fooling with your texting and such!" Melvina reprimands, pushing my hand down, with her hand tight around my wrist. "I know you hear me talking to you!"

"Yes, Miss. Mel. I hear you. And no worries, I can do this!" Loosening my hand from her grip, I hold her shoulder tight and smile, tipping my eyes over my shades once more. "Besides, I've never felt like this before—ever!"

"Like what?"

"Like this!" I quickly reply, bringing her hand to my chest, allowing her to feel the thumping of my heart.

Melvina steps back, with her mouth gaped open at my revelation. "Is she?" Melvina sputters, looking back and forth at me and Damina.

"Yes, I think she is. No, I know she is. She's the one!"

"You know what this means, don't you?"

"Yes, ma'am! It means I must stay on my best behavior!" I give Melvina another quick hug, and she smiles wide as I jump in the car

She is happy for me.

"Are we ready to go?" I ask, squeezing Damina's shoulder. Damina nods briefly as she continues chewing her food and I marvel at how adorable she looks with her stuffed cheeks. I sincerely doubt this woman can ever look bad; not even when she's eating.

I truly wish I were a better driver, but I'm not. Perhaps it's because I abhor the restraint of using an automobile instead of taking flight. Cars are so slow, and the drivers move with no sense of urgency which is one of my main gripes with driving. Altrinions are made to move with lightning speed, not limited to the confines of some tethered piece of scrap metal. But alas, for today it is my lot.

"Really trying to beat the morning rush, eh?" Damina questions with a half-worried grin. I can tell she's not a fan of my driving skills, but that's only because she doesn't understand I could never let any harm come to her.

I do my best to distract her from my rickety navigation by naming points of interest along our route. Thankfully, she obliges my rant and is genuinely attentive to my leading. That's a good sign.

Before I can ask if there were any things she wanted to see while New Orleans, the phone rings and Titan's name appears on the screen. Crap! This can't be good.

"You don't mind if I take this call, do you?"

"Sure no problem, take your call," Damina answers sweetly.

"I'm busy. What is it?" I snap at Titan, although he has no idea what he interrupted.

"We had another breach," Titan responds immediately while also ignoring my harsh tone.

"Where?" I mutter under my breath as I glance over at Damina. She's texting someone. Who is she talking to? I wonder.

"At the Crescent Star hotel in Baton Rouge."

"What's the damage?"

"About twenty-three dead; mostly human and Altrinion."

"Well, fu—" I catch myself as I peek over my shoulder at Damina once more. Her eyes catch mine and I see in her that my disposition is a bit unnerving. I have to be better for her. *Try harder!* "Look, Titan, this is what I hired you all to do. Clean this up!"

"And what of Decaux?" Titan questions, still snubbing my brooding.

"Just worry about cleaning up this mess! You can worry about him another day," I shout back, ending the call.

Taking a deep breath, I try to shrug off my growing irritation with my brother. He's insistent on starting a war for no reason other than his feeble claims of retribution from wrongs committed long before now. His incessant thirst for bloodshed has almost become unquenchable. But now with Damina in my life, I almost hate bringing her into this world.

Yet, my annoyance with Decaux seems almost insignificant at the sight of Damina's now pale face as her phone buzzes against the windowpane. Her expression is frozen and lips quiver slightly at the sight of a name that seems to torment her entire being.

A raging fire kindles inside of me and I press hard to force feelings or inerrant jealousy to the far corners of my mind. My thumping heart seems to fall to the pit of my gut and only one concern raises my brow.

Who in the hell is Jackson?

Chapter 17

Jackson

"There he is! Turn left now!" I shout to Gregory, pointing to Tye as he sprints through a narrow alleyway. Shawn finally got a beat on Tye's hideout in Georgetown. We've waited outside the loft where he's staying waiting for him to come out. While a part of me is surprised he's stuck around as long as he has, I'm also curious as to what he's been doing since his betrayal.

"No worries, Jack-O! He's got nowhere to run," Gregory quickly replies, whipping his car in the tight space of the alley.

Jumping out of the car, I wince as Gregory's car doors crash against the metal trash cans along the corridor. Shawn pops out from the backseat in a flash and he and Gregory race toward Tye and begin pulling him down from the tall iron fence. Gregory flings Tye across the alley, slamming him into the windshield. Tye gazes up at me through a thick bloody film dripping past his eyes and he smiles, showing equally bloodied teeth and laughs.

He coughs up blood, tugging at his ribcage and it's evident he's more hurt than he's letting on. Nothing but insolence is what I see as he stares back at me.

"Is there something funny?" I roar, pulling his collar and throwing him to the ground.

Tye squirms on the pavement, writhing in pain. Shawn lifts Tye's chin up to meet our glaring eyes, "Answer him!" Shawn demands.

"I. Will. Not," Tye answers dismissively, turning his head toward the trash can, anything to set his sights apart from us.

"Speak, dog!" Gregory barks, kicking him in the chest, almost folding him into the large trash container.

"Why should I? I'll only speak to the real leader of the Primes, not some impotent, lovesick, puppy!" Tye sneers.

"Watch your words, mutt!" Shawn orders.

"You know that I'm right, Gregory! He's been so enraptured by that Altrinion he's forsaken his duty to his own pack and kin. He is not fit to be an alpha, a prime and much less, an Alpha Lord!"

"Shut your face, traitor!" Gregory lashes back at Tye, forcing the weight of his foot deeper into his chest.

"You know I'm right," Tye scoffs with another leer,

before spitting out a glob of blood on Gregory's pant leg.

"Gregory, my friend," I say pulling him back from Tye. "This is not our way," I add with a firm hold at Gregory's shoulder. In my grip I feel Gregory's muscles relax, but he keeps a watchful stance over Tye with Shawn aptly at his side.

"And now you see," Tye begins with his head leaned against the receptacle and his breathing sketchy. "Can't you see why we couldn't let his lack of leadership endure? We'd all surely perish. Look at him! Never ready to do what is necessary. I suppose his little curvaceous wench has taken whatever remains of his manhood!"

At his words, a deep, blaring growl resounds through me and my head whips to his direction. Cream-coated fur instantly rises beneath my skin along my forearm and jawline. My canines protrude and my nails lengthen. With the exception of a reflection of my sun-spun eyes, all I see is the purest level of fear staring back at me. New sweat forms at Tye's brow and more drips from his face. Even Shawn and Gregory jump back at my roar.

Stooping to meet his frightened eyes and gaping mouth, a noxious growl spits through me and Tye curves himself between the brick building and trash can, likely fearful of his demise.

"Look at me!" I demand.

Turning slowly, he circles his head toward me, but his gaze is set on Shawn and Gregory still flanked at my sides.

My wolf form recedes, and I watch as he marvels at my transformation. Though not a complete phasing, it's now evident to him that I am no longer the alpha he once knew. I am becoming something *more*.

"Think whatever you will of me. But you will not disrespect Damina! Not in my presence! Not ever!"

Tye's scowl lessens, and he pulls away from the wall and continues searching my face. I hear the racing of his heart subside and I witness a small smile form at the corners of his bloodied mouth. For a moment, I see a trace of the man I once called my friend peering up at me. I even detect the hint of a kindness behind his eyes that once established our bond long ago.

A loud, menacing yelp breaks through the dissonance of our forming reconciliation from behind and dark, threatening eyes stare back at me. Once more, Tye's face is marred with a malign grin which dimly resembles the friend I once knew.

"Jack-O, we've got two rogues in the building!" Gregory shouts.

"We've still got some sunlight! They won't come out yet," I yell over my shoulder as Tye cackles behind me.

"We're not all rogues!" Keiron calls from the edge of the alleyway.

"Brother, what are you doing here?" Even the shadowy outline of my brother's form enrages me from afar.

"Well, not everyone was invited to your little lunar-light shindig at Sophie's place. So, I thought I could introduce you to a few friends of mine. I hope you don't mind, I brought a few guests," Keiron's spite laced words jar my rage and I no longer see my brother.

I only see my enemy.

Two hulking figures drop from the top of the buildings down onto the rooftop of Gregory's car. Shawn and Gregory snarl in their direction as another four men crowd the entrance of the alley behind Keiron. Tye heckles both Shawn and Gregory, taunting them through his painful bouts of laughter and groans.

"Well, brother, I do hope you'll treat my friends with better care than you did Damina. Speaking of her, I best run off and go check on our little fated damsel. Have fun!" Keiron's threats hardly go unnoticed by Shawn and Gregory and both men shoot worried glances at one another before staring back at me.

The two scoundrels on Gregory's car lunge at Shawn and Gregory but both are snatched in midair as my men slam them into the brick cavity walls of the alleyway. I'm not sure what the fools hoped to gain in their attempt, but neither Gregory nor Shawn lack brawn or might. For most, the sheer size of them alone is intimidating enough. My brother's thugs have obviously been drinking from the same foolhardy spicket as Keiron.

Still, I don't have time to marvel their feat when Tye yanks my leg from below causing me to press against the wall, using it as momentum to lay a sidekick into his chest, knocking him out cold.

Turning to face the alley's edge, I spy Keiron one

last time before he runs off, leaving those in his employ to fight his self-imposed battle.

Coward.

As he makes his escape, his urchins' race in toward us. Meeting them head on, our brawl is effortless! They are no match for us as we wrangle them like silly putty.

"This would go a lot faster if you'd just turn into the Big Bad," Gregory taunts over his shoulder as he plunges his knee through the abdomen of one of Keiron's goons and kicks him into the car.

"What is the Big Bad?" Shawn shouts back while ramming together two heads of a smaller pair.

"Stay focused! More are coming!" I yell at both Shawn and Gregory when I see another three men race into the alley. Hissing, snarling sounds grow louder as the sun's light is overcast by darkening clouds, and the rogue Skull wolves make their way closer to the threshold. Gazing up at the crescent-like slither of the sun that remains, I pray for the sun to reclaim its position and pierce its way through the thick, cloud-covered sky if only to keep the Skull at bay.

"The Big Bad Wolf," Gregory yells back to Shawn, and they both set their gaze on me. I knew what Gregory wanted when he first opened his mouth. But he understands not what he asks.

I can't phase here. Not now. Not like this.

Ever since my last talk with Sophie it's become clear that I must be careful who I reveal my truth to. As an alpha, transparency is a must and I cannot lay myself bare just in front of anyone. There's too much at stake. Too many secrets and far too many lies.

So for now, the wolf must remain silent. Dormant.

As much as I would like to, I can't call on my wolf for help.

I must do this on my own.

Dalcour

I'LL MAKE *her forget the name Jackson soon enough.*

At least that's what I tell myself as I walk her through the Hall of Isis. Seeing her exuberance as she marvels at the art I've collected throughout the centuries makes my newly beating heart flutter. Not once when I gathered these things, did I think how it might impress the one who would capture my heart. But now I find myself blushing at her admiration of my accomplishments.

Even as I introduced Damina to Mikkel, our resident director of the Hall, my chest swelled with pride. While her beauty and intelligence alone are enough to make any man proud to have her at his side, I think it's knowing that even though she could be somewhere else; she is here with me; *wretched soul that I am.*

So, it's no wonder why no sooner than she confessed, "... I'd rather you'd just kiss me and get it over with already," I plunged my mouth to hers. Sure, I might have compelled her to tell me how she really felt about me, but I needed her confession to be her own.

I can't afford to be wrong about *us.*

Now with her body pressed between me and the marble columned wall, there's no doubt our attraction is mutual. The passion I feel for her is all consuming—like a fire. From the way she walks to the sweet manner in which she talks, I am wholly enraptured by her. But it's the current sweet entanglement of our tongues, locked together like magnets, sending shivers up my spine and strength to my manhood. Her tight hold on my shoulder blade and the nape of my neck is strong, forcing our bodies so close making me ravenous with shameless abandon.

I could make love to her right here. Right now.

Even more, I can tell she wants me to. She surrendered to my embrace as if I erased all her cares and supplied all her needs. Her body is screaming for a release and I know I am more than capable of assuaging all her desires both sensuous and otherwise.

Glittering colors of electric blue and shimmering gold hover around us as we slowly drift above the marble tiles as I invade her mouth deeper and deeper. Holding her face close, I pull away just enough to make sure I'm not dreaming, and I can't help admiring the beautifulness that is Damina Nicaud. Her eyes dance with a fiery hue while her lips gape open with desire, longing for me to delight once more in the pleasure of her mouth.

Every inch of Damina clings to me, screaming to be touched while equally touching me in all the places I long for. The shape of her slender yet curvy silhouette fits my muscular frame like she was made just for me.

And I believe she was.

Tugging her legs around my waist, the warmth of her preciousness at my abdomen is almost my reckoning and I feel the beast within begging for his release.

Still, I refuse to allow my shortcomings to bring her any undue harm.

I've never been impulsive. But being with Damina makes me do things I never thought I'd do. And right now is the best of them all.

Slowly, I pull away from her once again, gazing at her lovely smile as I release us back to the floor. Damina presses her body back against the wall, allowing the coolness of the tile to relieve the warmth exuding from her body. Although I'm certainly not embarrassed, we both chuckle when she slides down my body past my protruding manhood, making her way to the floor.

From the looks of it, she's rather pleased with herself; she knows she's getting to me. I admit, knowing it pleases her to see me this way, churns my desire for her more than I thought capable. But for her sake, I can't let even our desire for one another cause us harm.

Pulling my shirt from behind my belt to cover myself, I squeeze her shoulder and try to divert her eyes. "Wow! That wasn't quite what I expected you to say, Ms. Nicaud, but I hope I obliged your request. I only want you to have sweet dreams of me, Damina. Now, if you're done seducing me, can we please get back to our business for the day?"

Damina chuckles, covering her mouth and tucking her hair behind her ear in the cutest way possible. As her eyes wander around the Hall, her expression changes, and I instantly know the conversation is going back to a place I'd rather not share—at least not right now.

My wealth.

"Dalcour," Damina begins as she tugs at her shirt when she notices more guests have entered the Hall.

Trailing my fingers down her arm, I try my best to bring her back to me. "Yes, Damina," I answer.

"There's still the issue of all this!" Damina says pointing around at the array of art surrounding us.

As much as I do not want to discuss this topic, I do my best to appease her intrigue. Despite it being the 21st century, she seems more surprised that a man of color has amassed such treasure than of the treasures themselves. It's somewhat disappointing to know such stereotypes remain—even among our own. I work hard to move past it, making a mental note to revisit the topic at another time.

"So yes, Damina—I'm rich. But I'm more than that—" I say after giving her a quick run-down of my global holdings.

Her mouth gapes open once more, but this time not in a manner of passion, though I'd be happy to oblige, but one of pure awe. "Whoa! See Dalcour, that's what I mean. What could I possibly bring to your life that you don't already have?"

"You." There is no pretense in my speech and my

tone is clear. I want and need her to understand the gravity of my feelings for her. This isn't puppy love, and I didn't just steal a kiss under the high school bleachers. No. I know she doesn't quite understand, but she is mine and I have every intention of making sure she and the rest of the world understand this truth.

For the first time, the veiling of her mind is lifted. A fluttering of emotion and random thoughts invade my space, screaming at me all at once. I work hard to decipher each erratic stream that blares through her mind, but it's too much to take in. She's an Altrinion. I'll have to be more specific to get in her mind, but I do grasp just enough intel to make my intent clear.

"Damina, you know Newton was on to something, but I don't think the laws of universal gravitation were only referring to particles proportional to their own masses—I think he was referring to us," I respond, pushing through her thoughts. She ogles me for a moment, slightly stunned I picked up on her internal Newton reference, but I smile quick, trying to evade her budding curiosity. Pulling her back into my embrace, I hope my lure is enough to keep her mind off my wealth, if only for a little. "There's no escaping me now, Damina Nicaud—it's Newton's Law after all."

"Right, Newtons Law," she laughs, allowing herself to give way to my hold.

After a little coaxing, we finally near our exit to the patio when Damina tugs on me and I see the same incessant glare in her eyes. It's obvious she's not going to let this go. I sense my patience waning, but I'm surprised that it's not like my typical brooding that both Jerrica and Braelyn have to endure. Interesting.

"Dalcour, you sell these things?" Damina asks, her curiosity peaking.

"Yes, some of them are for sale but not all. Like I said, they're just things, Damina."

"And you own all of them?" Her eyes are locked on me and she's pulling me in.

Crap! *Does she know what she's doing?* The way her pitch dropped an octave coupled with her narrowed gaze are classic distinctives of Altrinion compulsion. As much as I'd hate to answer her and bring my vile brother into the conversation, even I can't refuse her.

"Well, not exactly," I begin, trying hard to resist but her pull is strong. *Woman, what are you doing to me?* Damina's gaze digs deeper into mine and she owns my truth. There's no resisting. "At least eighty percent of the things you see here are mine and the rest belong to my—um, my brother," I add reluctantly.

"Your brother?" She quietly mutters, obviously surprised. Good. Although I despise mentioning his name, it seems just the mere thought of him douses her compelling reach within me.

"Yes, my brother, Decaux—but listen, I really don't want to talk about him right now, okay?" I reply with just enough strength left to fully escape her inducing inquiry. She pauses once more before asking whether I'm the owner of the Hall of Isis to which I affirm her inquisitiveness and gesture for her to step out onto the patio.

Seeing the sheer awe laced across her beautiful face when she finally sees the surprise I've arranged for her almost makes her incessant inquiry worth it. She drops her mouth open again, and it's still indeed the sexiest thing I've ever seen. Every time she does it, I think I might lose my wits. It's such an invitation! I doubt I'll have enough strength to muster restraint much longer.

"Thank you, Dalcour, but you didn't have to do all of this," Damina says softly, her posture bashful.

"Actually, I did. But I do need you to do something for me," I begin taking her hand in mine, hopeful to ease the nervousness I sense budding within her.

"What?" She questions as her gaze deepens into mine and her voice pitchy, once more compelling my truth. But this time I don't mind.

"Let me love you. Please." The world around us goes quiet as our eyes lock onto one another and I know one thing, I'll do whatever I must to show her the enormity of my affection for her. And I'll do so until the only name captured by her love is mine.

Chapter 18

Jackson

*E*mptiness floods my soul as I witness my beloved snatched from my presence. Only a faint hint of her sweet and peaceful fragrance of vanilla and eucalyptus remains in the meadow. While a loud, yelping chorus of howling wolves echo in the distance, it's the jolting pain of my aching heart ringing loudest in my ears.

How could I let my guard down? It's my duty to protect her.

How could I let her slip away?

Just like that, she's gone.

But I cannot allow this to be our end. I refuse.

Fury rises inside of me and a low churning growl rumbles in my chest and sweltering heat blazes through the coat of my fur as my roar extends far *beyond the meadow. The gray wolves behind me echo my howl causing the Great Oak to sway as golden leaves swirl through the air. A bright iridescent fog fills the area and sparkling lights pop and fizzle all around us as the wind resumes its force pushing us away from the cliff's edge.*

Instinct drives a forceful growl through me as rage consumes my being, causing a gaping tear in the illuminating fabric of the misty fog. A dark gray wolf, sizeable and larger than the rest, flanks my side and roars in unison and the thickness of the mist weakens. One by one, an echoing howling chorus of wolves bay along with us at my rear and the popping firecracker-like lights resound like an explosion and the forming haze evaporates.

I rush to the edge of the cliff, hopeful to see her, but four mountainous waterfalls are in my view. Piercing my gaze tight, I try to peer behind each of the flowing fountains, but the thick streams block my attempts. I know she's probably in one of the caves behind the falls, but I have no idea how to get to her from here.

The large dark gray wolf bays in my direction and the wind shifts once more, allowing the remaining golden leaves to fly overhead. Each leaf crackles and fizzles as it connects with the spray from the waterfalls; allowing a slither of sight through the caves. The wolf howls at me once more, lowering his body and pawing at the earth beneath me. More leaves hover around us and I issue a loud growling howl, sending the leaves crashing like fireballs into the falling streams.

Peering again, I see a bright blue ember shimmer through the third cave and I now know where my beloved has gone. Turning behind, I see my company of wolves has doubled and I growl a low rumbling roar, and they all howl in unison as the leaves hurl like comets toward the cave.

My tail straightens high and stiff and I howl again, feeling my muscles contort beneath my fur and I know the alpha in me is pining for his eventual release.

The loud buzzing of my phone in my shirt pocket jolts me awake in a panic.

Crap! It's not her.

"What is it?" I snap, annoyed the caller isn't Damina. Neither my nightmare nor our estranged state assuages my growing concern for her.

"I'm sorry to bother you, Mr. Nash. It's me, Nicolaus," he responds quickly. To this day I'll never understand why he announces himself. It's like he forgets the 21st century came equipped with caller ID.

"Yes, Nicolas I know. How can I help you?" I ask softly, trying to temper my mood. He's just a young guy doing his job, I need to back off.

"Yes, sir, well I have some news on the information you requested."

"What information? I'm sorry, everything has been a blur as of late," I add rubbing my eyes, gazing around Damina's condo. I look up at the wall clock and see it's well past seven in the evening. I got here late this afternoon.

Gregory, Shawn and I spent most of the day trying to get a confession out of Tye and a few of Keiron's goons we were able to bring back to one of our holding dens.

I've barked so many orders to almost every Den Alpha and council member over the last few days that I'm starting to lose count. Even Brandon has sobered himself enough to keep watch on Damina and Allyson's place while I'm away. Isaac and Jesse have ensured Damina's family is safe, keeping a close detail on both Delia and Dacari at all times. I've also given instructions to Merle to use Kyra's former brute trackers to search for Allyson and her Dunes Paw boyfriend.

With everything going on I can hardly recall what I've asked from Nicolaus.

"That would be regarding JJ Properties, sir."

"Ah, I see," I mutter, thumbing through my phone. I had hoped to hear from Damina by now. "Anything interesting?" I ask while noting an urgent text from Gregory to call him.

"Actually there is," he answers quickly before I have a chance to brush him off.

"Can it wait? Or better yet, send me an email."

"Well, I can send you the particulars, but I think you'd be interested in what I have to say now," he begins.

I really wish he would get on with it.

Just as I rise from the couch, to wake myself enough to pay attention and stop the replay of the dream in my mind, Gregory and Shawn burst through the door. I cringe when I see the bent wooden frame near the deadbolt. *We're going to need to fix that.*

"Jack-O!" Gregory shouts, rushing in and sliding along the wooden floors into the living room. I raise my hand, cautioning for him to give me a few minutes. He and Shawn stare back at one another, almost exasperated and I can't help wondering what's giving them worry.

"The company, JJ Properties is owned in part by a Jerrica Jeffers and a name, please excuse me if I mispronounce it, a Dalcour Marchand. But the strangest part is the records for these holdings date back more than one-hundred and thirty years."

Despite his rambling, there's one name that stands out, filling me with dread. *Dalcour Marchand.*

"*It can't be*—" My words are almost breathless. I look up, my eyes laden in alarm, unsure how to respond. Gregory and Shawn's reactions mirror my own and they are just as pensive, curious of the new alarm wreaking havoc within me.

"Of course I thought it was odd too, but when I checked and rechecked the records, I got the same results," he adds.

"Are you certain?" I hurriedly question.

"Yes, sir. I can email you a brief now if you'd like," Nicolaus adds.

Gregory bites his lip as the distress in his posture builds and a growing, urgent fear gnaws within me.

"Send it now," I finish with a dry tone as I hang up the phone before Nicolaus affirms my request. Both Shawn and Gregory call my name, pulling for my attention, but I have none to give.

Not once had I ever considered I'd run into a Marchand in my lifetime. Throughout the centuries my family has done well to keep far from the less admirable of the Altrinion Order—such as Dalcour Marchand. The atrocities he and his brother Decaux have committed through the ages are countless and we've made it our business to steer clear of their path. Sure, rumors of their heinous deeds reach our ears often, but never would I think it would come this close.

Had I known Harold Emmerson had any dealings with the likes of the Marchand brothers, I would have kept him away from Damina. While I can't fathom what type of connection Emmerson and Marchand share, the mere fact he wanted to put Damina in an inch of Marchand is more than infuriating!

"Jackson!" Shawn yells while tugging my arm, breaking me from my rageful trance.

"What is it?" I snap back, breaking free of his tight grip. All I can think of is Damina. The only solace I find is knowing she tossed this invitation into the trash. Now, I'll do her one better and burn this wretched information before she returns. There's no way I'll allow her to involve herself with the likes of Marchand! Thankfully, since her parent's death, I know New Orleans is the last place Damina wants to be.

"Look, you know how you've asked us to keep a beat on any unusual supernatural hotspots or activity since Damina left?" Gregory begins.

"Yes," I answer gruffly, shrugging my shoulders,

unsure of where this is going.

"Well, a few nights ago we heard rumors of a rash of murders. Since it neared the full moon and there'd been a rise in Skull activity, we didn't think much of it. That is until we got word of transcendent occurrences happening in the same area. Then we got the call tonight about another transcendency in almost the exact spot. There are even rumors of an uptick in Altrinion sightings."

"Where?" The beating of my heart slows its pace as the same foreboding dread fills my soul once more and I almost hate to hear the response. Please let my premonition be wrong.

"New Orleans." And with Gregory's words, my heart stops.

Dalcour

LOVING HER is all I wanted. All I needed.

From the moment I saw her in Bessie's, I knew nothing more than my heart longed to make her part of my world. I wanted her by my side, in my bed, and in my heart always and forever. Even as I professed my love to her during our lunch at the Hall and the many times I proclaimed my affection toward her as she traipsed through the halls of this old mansion today, I am in awe how quickly she has enraptured my heart and become my world.

One would think I would stray far from the foolery

that lead her to New Orleans. Sadness and fury rang within me and my heart grieved with her as she recounted Jackson's betrayal of their pending nuptials. For the first time, her cloaking was fully unveiled to me. Whatever power responsible for hiding her truth from me had now rescinded its reach as she exposed her vulnerability. In that moment, her thoughts intertwined with my own sending me into both peril and passion and I witnessed her pain as if it were my own.

So why am I now watching her through fear-wrought eyes?

Because I am just as treacherous as Jackson.

At least in her mind.

Watching streams of fury and regret pour past her cheeks strikes like daggers in both my heart and soul. The truth is, Claudia means nothing to me but that's not what Damina sees. How could she not? Her recent experiences have taught her to expect this from men. And now, even from me.

I only needed to settle the forming blood rage within me after witnessing Damina's injuries, but I should not have listened to Braelyn's suggestion of feeding on Claudia. Not only has it given Claudia the wrong impression but doing so hurt the one who alone holds the lock and key to my damned heart.

"Damina, wait! I can explain!" I shout from the top of the stairs. Slowly, I pace down, keeping my gaze on her. With one hand on the doorknob and the other dangling at her side, wrapped in bandages from her injury in the garden, I know if my actions are too sudden, I'll drive her away.

Crap! I can't hear her thoughts anymore either! She's closed herself to me—and rightfully so. For a moment, her expression softens as she searches my face and I'm hopeful she can interpret the truth behind my eyes. But that hope is short lived as Claudia ambles behind me and I can sense spitefulness exuding from her pores. Unfortunately, so does Damina. I watch in both remorse and fear as Damina's flame-filled eyes rest on me and I can almost feel her heat burn at my temples.

Braelyn pushes her way between Claudia and me and knocks her into the other side of the hallway. Claudia's cries are loud but there's another sound growing louder from outside the mansion.

The loud sound of a car's horn sends Damina rushing through the doors in a motion so swift it's almost too fast for my eyes to comprehend. As much as it burns me that she's gone—especially due to a misunderstanding—I'm now more angered as to who has come to her aid.

"Braelyn! See if you can find out where she went! Cedric and Lux go and put a call in to one of your contacts at Bessie's place and see if Javier or Calvin have come for her. She doesn't know that many folks in New Orleans, so the list of potentials is short," I bark my orders in such a thunderous flurry almost everyone scatters from my sight.

"Hey Big D!" I hear Mark call up to me from the

middle of the foyer. He offers a brief smile as I make my way down the stairs, but as I notice Brian come to his aid to steady him against the wall, my inner-fury returns.

"What is it, Mark?" I work hard so that my words aren't too curt. The last thing I need is for anything to breakout between me and Brian again. We haven't spoken more than two words since our last encounter. While he is ever dutiful and helpful to both Jerrica and Damina, I don't have patience for him tonight. Mark, on the other hand, is another story. I promised his father Abraham I would look after him and this revitalization project is a part of me fulfilling that oath. Besides, knowing he was hurt along with Damina today gives me a measure of empathy.

"Look, I know you are in a hurry to find Damina, but I'm sure we could just track her," Mark states.

"Are you suggesting we track her scent? Not a bad idea since she's injured, but you're in no position to do it unless you wolf-up and I didn't think you peaked yet for such a transformation."

"Mark is an alpha, Lord Marchand and thus certainly capable of phasing at will," Brian adds with a puffed chest to match his usual stoic posture.

"Capable perhaps, but I don't have the time to try out any of his new tricks tonight."

"Um—guys—actually I'm not talking about wolf tracking. I'm talking about tracking the Hitch driver who picked her up. I'm pretty sure I saw a Hitch logo on the side of the car she jumped in. If she used the mansion WIFI I'm sure we can find out her destination," Mark says in his normal breezy cool tone.

"That's actually a pretty decent idea for a mongrel such as yourself," Braelyn snips from overhead. "Too bad I'm already light years ahead of you," she teases while perched on the railing with her laptop.

Mark looks up at Braelyn and the two exchange knowing glances. *Great, she is really into him!* As much as I would love nothing more than to badger both Mark and Braelyn about their budding affections, I must ignore it. At least for now.

"My lord," Lux begins as he and Cedric rush from the parlor. "We phoned our contacts at Bessie's, but no one has seen her and both Calvin and Javier are accounted for."

"But there is another problem," Cedric adds.

"What is it?"

"We aren't entirely certain if it's related to what took place in the Tremé or not, but a group of Scourge have been sighted not far from here."

"Where?" Brian says, coming between me and Cedric. While I know he's itching for revenge, the last thing I need is him putting himself in danger while Jerrica is away in London. Though I'd never admit it, I could use his skills to help me look for Damina.

"Well, I hope it's nowhere near Saint Roch's Cemetery because that's exactly where Damina requested a Hitch."

Once more, dread and fear flood my soul as I turn back to Cedric and Lux, awaiting their response. But they don't need to reply—the despondency marred across their faces tell me my fear is well placed.

I'm fully dressed in minutes and in flight to the cemetery with Cedric and Braelyn. Lux follows just behind us along with Mark and Brian. Although I told Mark to stay back at the mansion to nurse his injury, he insisted Damina's injury was his fault and that since she is Altrinion, it was his duty to protect her. Even though he didn't take time to phase, he seems to be healing slowly and is rather confident of his ability to help.

Hovering near Saint Roch's conversations with Jerrica regarding Damina being unaware of her lineage plague my mind and I instruct both Cedric and Braelyn to resist exposing their otherworldly charms. I'll even have to work hard to keep my own beast at bay. The last thing I need is scaring Damina away or worse. Especially since I'm not sure just how much she saw tonight or how much she knows about who she really is.

"Okay, I'll do my best D, but perhaps you should've given your lady the same instruction! Looks like she's lighting a fire under the vermin from the looks of it!" Braelyn shouts over her shoulder while pointing below.

She's right. Damina's got one Scourge by the throat and the essence of her golden and blue embers shine through her like the Northern Lights. The strength and beauty exuding from her have me awestruck. With her hair glistening in a tidal wave motion and warmth like the sun emanating from her skin, her Altrinion nature is on display for all to see. Despite the sunset long past, the brightness that is Damina is all consuming and magnificent.

My how this woman gives me new reasons to love her more and more each day!

"Braelyn," I yell to unyielding ears and she passes me and Cedric, making her way into the courtyard first. She quickly puts an end to two small Scourge just as she lands and Cedric follows close behind, slaughtering each vampire without mercy.

Brian, Mark and Lux arrive just as I land atop a large sepulcher and snag the first offending leech I see making his way toward Damina. Holding the creature in my hand, Damina looks up at me and despite chaos raging all around us, she grants me a sweet, albeit brief smile. Her trusting eyes are still fueled by the Altrinion flame, but not laden with the same fury as before.

My heart races at the mere sight of her and she opens a slither of herself to me again and I know her truth. She is happy to see me... still.

If it means I have to bring an end to any and everything that seeks to cause her harm, I will do so. I'd gladly do so a thousand times if it meant she'd look at me like this—forever.

Then it hits me.

That's what I'm fighting for. I'm fighting for our chance at forever.

Chapter 19

Jackson

Staring at my phone waiting for Damina to call is driving me insane! Moments like these make me long for telepathy! Not just any kind of telepathy— but long range. The kind super intelligent bald men in wheelchairs use to find any mutant in the world. At least then I would know whether Damina is safe or not. From the moment Gregory and Shawn told me of the transcendent occurrence in New Orleans there have been similar hot spots popping up everywhere, making it difficult to narrow her location.

I've called Damina more times than I can count and still she hasn't answered. While my heart tells me she's okay, I have little trust in my heart as of late. Why should I? It's led me astray too many times.

That's why I'm in this mess now.

Now, I'm stuck trying to get the local den council to understand just how grave our situation has become. Though everything inside me tells me to abandon this *meeting of the minds* and tear through every city until I've found Damina, there's no denying the fact my passive leadership is likely linked to this rise in Skull activity and the uprising of supernatural hotspots.

Unfortunately, Isaac's gritty faux cough breaks my stargazing. "My lord, what exactly do you think we can do? If indeed your betrothed has involved herself with the Marchand family there is very little assistance we can provide," Isaac says in a tone more challenging than I believe he intends. Thankfully, the stench of fear emitting from him lets me know it's not outright defiance but cowardice now holding his state.

"I think we must do everything we can to help!" Gregory charges, standing up from the council table, thrusting his chair to the back wall. His patience is certainly waning. Though I'm sure he's more frustrated, I brought my concerns to the council instead of going straight to Louisiana without their permission.

Alas, for far too long my leadership has been seen as rogue, so I at least wanted to give the council the chance to express their concern. Besides, we are not yet certain that Damina is in New Orleans. We also heard from another source she took a train to Philadelphia from Union Station. There may be some truth to it since there have been a few Altrinion hotspots rising in the East Falls community. I know she has some family in that area so it wouldn't surprise me. Still, it's too early to tell.

Shawn jumps up to Gregory's side and echoes his sentiment and all the members of the council talk at once, arguing their pros and cons.

"Silence!" I shout rising from the table while beckoning my two right hands to keep their cool. "First, let me make it clear that I am *not* asking for permission. Make no mistake, I will travel through the underbelly of hell itself to reclaim Damina—at all costs! What this is—is a wake-up call. Many of you thought my leadership as docile over the last few years. I'm not saying you were right; but you weren't completely wrong either. The truth is, *we've all been too passive*. Resting on our laurels. I know my ancestors have long thought the best way to keep peace is to keep silent—but I now understand it is the farthest from the truth. Because whether we like it or not, there is a growing threat which no longer wishes to remain in the shadows. Sure, today it appears to be my brother Keiron and tomorrow the Marchand brothers; but I am convinced, now, more than ever, there are others who seek to break apart even the semblance of peace that remains! It is for this reason I've called you here tonight. We cannot—should not grow complacent in this hour!"

"I—um—I agree with Jackson, our Prime Alpha," Merle says sheepishly as he rises from the table. All goes quiet as he looks around the room. Most are more surprised he's said anything at all than the fact he now

L.C. SON

stands in agreement with me.

"Thank you, Merle," I answer quietly. He's impressed me more than I thought him capable.

He nods with his eyes and continues, "I've also heard of an increase in Scourge sightings and large Skull herds have made their way through almost every major territory on the east coast. It's apparent, something is coming."

"If this is true, then I ask you, Jackson, the same question as Isaac. What would you have us do? We've long pulled from fighting alongside Beta Primes in protection of Altrinions like your betrothed or otherwise," adds Sonja of the Havre de Grace den council.

"We must do whatever we must. Ensure our dens are trained in the old way—"

"The old way? Jackie—I mean Jackson, we haven't employed such archaic measures in centuries," Sophie begins.

"Then we must return. We must strengthen the borders and staking claim in our territories, forbidding rogue reformations from activity. How long has it been since we demanded a census? A full check in of every den—so that all wolves are accounted for and accountable to a den? It's our job to be the keepers of checks and balances."

Loud gasps echo throughout the council and I use the opportunity to take a deep breath. I know I'm pushing it. But I can't stop now.

"That's not all. We must seek to barter a truce with

the Betas and help them reclaim their status."

"Now, that's going too far, Jackson!" Jesse shouts, pushing back from the table. "There's a reason things are the way they are! Who are we to change the order of things?"

"Is it not our job to keep the order?" I shout back, challenging his haughty posture. The room goes quiet again and I exhale, working hard to regain my composure. I can't phase here. Sophie keeps her watchful gaze set on me, but I inhale again and work to stifle my growing ire. "Why do you think the Skull have increased in number? Because we are weak. They no longer see us as one unified pack. For too long we have merely survived, only living in a shell of what we call peace. Now is the time to thrive! And the only way we can do this is together! Even if it means reclaiming the manner of the old way, I charge each of us to do what we must and take up our rightful place as the primes we are supposed to be!"

This time, Merle is the first to stand, thrusting his hand together in a series of claps and shouts. It doesn't take long for Gregory and Shawn to echo his sentiment and the others slowly join them.

As much as I want to relish in this moment of merriment, I cannot. Something has changed. *Something is wrong.* Dialing her number once more, my heart races as a new warning fills my being and I know I need to talk to her. *Now.*

Dalcour

HOW CAN the one thing you never knew you needed feel so right? Not once since my wretched father forced my innocence from me when I took my first human life did I ever contemplate the revival of my desolately wicked heart. Yet, in this moment it's the only thing I can think about.

Holding Damina in my arms as she lays asleep on my chest awakens a joy in me, I never thought I'd find again. And it is that joy—the complete joy of having her in my life—that I will never let go. Whether she knows it or not, she is mine. Now that I have her in my arms, I have no intention of ever letting her go.

That's why seeing the name of her once betrothed on her phone, calling continuously as she curls into my arms kindles a raging fury in me that would burn a hole in my chest if it were not for the calming restraint just the sweetness of her presence brings to my life.

Not only am I in awe that I've not answered the phone, threatening him to never call again but I'm surprised at the self-control I've demonstrated as her beautifully sculpted body lays pressed against mine. With all her soft places nestled against the strength of me, I marvel that I've curbed my lustful appetite if for no other reason than knowing she is worth it.

I've waited centuries for a love like this. I can certainly wait until the time is right. Still, I can only hope that time comes sooner rather than later.

Once more, her phone buzzes against the nightstand

and my muscles instantly tighten as I peer through her purse and see Jackson's name pop up on the screen. While I've already assigned the keeper of our annals, Nara, to see if there is any supernatural link to this fool, Jackson, knowing he broke Damina's heart is reason enough for me to loathe him.

She needs to wake up and deal with him before I do.

As my body stiffens beneath her, I hear her take in a deep breath and I watch her smile at the pleasure my fragrance brings to her being. It makes me happy to see just how at home she is in my embrace and it almost douses my fiery and growing irritation with— Jackson.

Slowly, her fingers trace the outline of my abdominals and pectorals and her mouth parts open with desire, sighing with a low churning hum that vibrates through my. It takes everything within me not to succumb to her entreat as I stifle my growing desire.

This is indeed a first.

She really is changing me.

"Damina," my tone catches on the last vowel of her name as her fingers linger too long at my waistline. If I don't get her attention now, I know nothing will stop what happens next. Not even Jackson.

"Yes," she answers softly, moving her hands back up to my chest and my body freezes with pleasurable delight.

The phone rings again and the reminder of the loophole of her past singes my rage once more.

Repeating her name, she sits up and away from me

and I see a slight pinch of annoyance mar her perfect face. "What's wrong?" Damina asks.

Grabbing her phone from the nightstand, I offer it to her and ask, "Do you think you can answer your phone now?" She looks at the phone and her eyes grow wide as her face reddens at the sight of his name.

Damina rolls her eyes as she props herself up on the bed and exhales deeply. It's obvious she's more annoyed at his lingering presence than I thought. She also looks irritated with me as well. "Dalcour are you mad at me because he called?"

Jumping up from her bedside, I mumble, "*Please give me the strength!*" in Arabic. I need strength not to find this feign, Jackson, and end him. I also need strength to endure being in the same space with Damina without ravishing her body repeatedly.

"Of course not, Damina. But I need to know what you will do about it?" I respond, reining in my rage.

"Dalcour, with everything that has happened tonight, I haven't given him a second thought," Damina answers.

"Well, he's obviously had plenty of time to think of you."

"What do you want me to do about it? I've told you everything from the beginning I'm in a complicated place right now."

"Complicated, huh?"

"Wow! You're actually mad at me?"

"No Damina, I'm not mad," I counter. Everything in me wants to tell her I'm afraid of losing her to the shadows of her past, but I cannot. "But I need to understand where I fit in your world. I've made no mystery of my affection for you, but I need to know how long this *complication* of yours will last."

"Dalcour, I—"

"... *I want to be with you.*" Her thoughts are loud as her heart calls to me from across the room and I am instantly at her side. Knowing that she wants to be with me is all I need to know. The truth of her longing for me calls to me like tidal waves rushing an ocean floor. I just need to be patient. She deserves that and so much more.

"Damina, I don't want to rush you. I know this is all sudden. But you must know the thought of him and his lingering presence in your life is discomforting at best. What can I do to help you break from your past?" Leaning my body against her, I rest my forehead on hers and enjoy the same sweetness of our first non-kiss.

"There's nothing more you need to do, Dalcour. I think the past is breaking away all its own. And well, with the ever-changing landscape of my life as it is, I think you and I have more that connects us than anything or anyone in my past."

"That's good to hear, Damina. Like I said, I don't want to rush you. But I have no plans of sharing you either."

"Good. I'm not too keen on being shared," Damina adds while gazing up at me with her big bright eyes. Still, it's the glistening sheen of her parted lips as she stares at me that is my undoing.

This time the non-kiss doesn't suffice.

I need more.

In fact, I need all of her.

Pressing myself against her, our mouths are locked together as one and the sweetness of her nectar-like kiss entices my tongue and the aromatic scent of her vanilla and eucalyptus fragrance permeates my being. Strumming my fingers along her neckline, I test my resolve and plant sinfully satisfying kisses around her neck.

Vibrant electricity flows between us and our bodies draw together like magnets. The only thing separating us is the thin fibers of cotton our clothes are made from. Damina sighs in my ear and she inhales my scent, igniting a frenzy within her as she places a tight hold at my back, pulling me closer to her. Lifting my face slightly to meet her eyes, I detect no objection from her, and I know she is ready.

The power of my manhood concurs, and her name escapes my lips as she tugs me tighter, forcing an alliance between her preciousness and the strength of my masculinity.

Does she know what she is doing to me?

How can she even fathom what she is asking?

Once more our lips are locked as one and our tongues swirl with delight. Strangely, I don't feel the beast making his presence known and I inwardly wonder if this moment can actually happen apart from *him*.

Perhaps it is possible to know her in the most intimate way without the savagery of the beast lurking within? Maybe the love I feel for her is capable of taming the wild wickedness of my dark soul?

Passion overrides my intellect and my indecisiveness fades in the aching desire burning in my loins to be one with her. Again her thoughts invade my mind and I am confident she wants this—she wants me! Damina pushes her body up against me, tugging my back so that every part of me is touching every part of her. Her tongue lashes through my mouth, taming every inch of my being, whipping me into the willful submission of her lure.

While I can't help wondering whether I'd be her first—I almost don't care. Though I'd never consider myself prideful, I'm more than confident that what I want to do to her will make it as though she were a virgin all over again—and with that thought I take great delight!

The fervency of our passion fills the atmosphere and shimmering embers of light hover around us and I know our Altrinion nature is fully in sync and all my instincts are heightened with a needful craving like a starved man. I want to partake of everything that is Damina Nicaud and I plan to share all of me.

Yet, despite my need to give in to my desire, our moment is cut short when Braelyn barges into the room unannounced. As I shout her name over my shoulder, she gasps and exits quickly, leaving a flurry of profane curses while slamming the door shut.

Damina chuckles, nestling her head in my shoulders and it's the best feeling in the world. While my longing for her remains sure, both Braelyn and Jackson's interruptions are reminders there's still unfinished business. I've never been one to leave loose ends open, and with Damina now in my life I will ensure every loophole is closed.

Chapter 20

Jackson

Having the den council committed to strengthening our stance as Primes in the supernatural community is good, but how can I be happy with the distance between Damina and I growing with every passing moment. My patience has certainly reached the end of its rope and I no longer have a desire to tie another knot only to cling to the notion that she just needs space.

Something has changed.

She has changed.

With an unprecedented amount of supernatural activity occurring since her departure, my mind grows weary hopeful she isn't the epicenter of it all. Worry grips my being at the thought of any harm coming to her while she remains uncovered by the cloaking of her aunt and me. Now she's out in the world all alone and vulnerable.

Worst of all, our conversation didn't go as I had expected last night. I know she's still upset with me, and rightfully so—but she seemed distant. Cold. In our years together, I've experienced what it's like for her to be mad at me. Heck, I even know what her silent treatment feels like—but this is nothing like that.

What's more confusing is when I ran into her boss, Stephen, he told me he received a letter of resignation from her via email. Supposedly, her email cited she's taken a position with another company. Although I didn't go into details when I spoke with Damina, she denied quitting her job and I believe her.

Despite everything that has happened to us, Damina has never been a liar—especially to me. Besides, it isn't her style—at all. I know her well enough to know she'd never quit a job via email. Even if she didn't want to return home, she would at least call Stephen. They had a great working relationship, and she has never been one to burn bridges. Considering she also introduced Stephen to his wife, and her college roommate, Courtney, I can't imagine her treating him so coolly.

So it's no wonder everything inside me is confident that Allyson is behind this somehow.

We've had no luck finding her since that night. While I know she's had to go to her condo from time to time, she's evaded our efforts at every turn. Ever since *that day* she stood full of self-righteous indignation outside of Damina's condo, taunting me of our impending doom, I've known Allyson is also somehow involved in the demise of my relationship with Damina.

Yet, there was no evidence to Allyson's presence when I spoke with Damina last night, but I still felt as if there was someone standing between us.

My mind rages with wonder as images of Damina in the arms of another plague not only my thoughts, but my entire being.

Not that I think Damina left me for someone else, but I'd be a fool to think any man wouldn't jump at the chance to offer himself a willing vessel for her to pour her love. That man is supposed to be me!

The only glimmer of hope is her promise to call me today. Though I have no idea when she plans to call or how our conversation will go, I can be sure of one thing: I will do everything I can to win her back to me. Even if it means crawling on my knees and begging for her forgiveness.

Thankfully, I've had the power restored to her condo which has made my stay here bearable. A few of my guys have kept watch at my place just in case she pops up. Mostly, I like being at her place because it helps me feel close to her.

At least a little.

Still, despite the pain I've caused her, there's a small part of me that believes an equally small part of her was happy to talk with me—or at least hear my voice. There was a softness in her tone as our conversation ended compared to the coldness I felt from her in the beginning of our call. And I can only hope I haven't lost her completely.

As I pass the time waiting for her call, I watch one of her favorite shows, *Vampire Diaries,* and I find myself extremely annoyed she enjoyed watching this love triangle unfold. I can't help wondering whether she was merely entertained or saw something more.

Crap!

What's happening to me? I've never been jealous—ever. Quite frankly, Damina never gave me a reason to doubt the veracity of her love toward me. I'm no fool. Throughout our relationship I've witnessed the jaw-dropping and drooling manner in which she affects anyone who encounters her. It's for that reason I've always counted myself fortunate just to be in her presence, but there's now a gnawing in my gut making me wary—and watching this show isn't helping matters.

I've never seen how it all ends, but I wonder whether I'm Stefan or Damon. Hopefully, I'm the one who gets the girl.

All I want is a happily ever-after and I want it with Damina!

"Jack-O!" Gregory says now standing at my side. *Strange.* I didn't hear him come in. Although I want to answer him, my gaze is bleak. I can't shake feeling like I'm losing her and waiting for her to call is driving me insane. "Jackson!" Gregory barks once more, tugging on my shoulder.

"Yes, Gregory, what is it?" I answer, shrugging him

off me as I stand and pace around the room.

"Brandon's pulling the car around now. He's got Kyra with him."

"What for? And why are you bringing her here of all places? The last thing I need is for Damina to come home and find Kyra here!"

"Well, I doubt Damina is coming home anytime soon, Jackson." Gregory's matter-of-fact tone is annoying, but I'm more intrigued in what Kyra has to say. It must be important for him to bring her here.

At least it had better be.

"Look, Jackson, I—I um, didn't mean it like that. I'm sure she'll be back home where she belongs soon," Gregory continues mildly as he watches over me with a sincere look of concern.

"Thank you, my friend. Now tell me, what did she find out?"

"Well, it's about your *friend*, Allyson. Apparently, the guy who drove the getaway car that night is a Dunes Wolf named Perry."

"A Dunes? In this area? Does he live here?"

"I'm not sure, but Kyra's people have good reason to think he's been here for a while."

"Does anyone know where he's from?"

"Now, that's the part I know you won't like. He's from New Orleans."

"What!"

"Look, I know what you must be thinking, Jack-O and I've thought the same thing: this can't be a coincidence."

Dread and panic fill my being as my mind swarms with all manner of possibilities and none of them are good. Knowing that Damina needed to get away from me is one thing, but for her to be in New Orleans with Dunes wolves, the Marchand brothers, or otherwise stirs my soul with a vehement malice I never thought possible.

Here I am, trying to give her some space and repair what's broken among the wolves, meanwhile that wretched Allyson has done everything possible to foil my good fortune with my beloved! For all I know she's aligned herself with Keiron for no other reason than to see to my downfall!

Once again, my complacency has brought me to ruin!

"There's more Jack!" Gregory gruffly announces, rounding the corner to regain my attention.

"What more could there be?"

"Oh, there's much more, Jackson. Much more," Kyra reveals from the doorway with Brandon just behind her.

My heart falters seeing Kyra at Damina's entrance and I suddenly feel as though I'm betraying her by just Kyra's presence. Yet, despite every ounce of ambivalence I feel for Kyra, the moderate but genuine look of concern etched on her face tells me I need to hear what Kyra has to say.

Before I have a moment to answer her or Gregory in reply, my phone rings and I yank it out of my pocket. The number on the screen isn't the one Damina has been calling from, but once again the gnawing within heightens my alarm, and I answer the caller quickly, rushing to the threshold of Damina's bedroom.

My first hello goes unanswered and I pull the phone away from me with every intention of ending the call until a slight sniffling whimper in the background catches my ear and I know this is the call I've waited for.

A jolting flutter rampages my heart and I finally exhale, unaware I've been holding my breath and answer, "Baby is that you?"

Dalcour

TONIGHT IS the night I announce to the world that Damina Nicaud is mine! Joy fills the merry beating of my heart as I relish in the fact that for the first time in my life I am in love. I am totally enraptured by the presence and awe of this woman more than I ever thought possible.

If this is the love Decaux challenged me to find, I take great delight in obliging his request. Perhaps my doing so will finally end his bloodthirsty quest. Although, now that I have Damina I can only imagine how he felt the day they took his beloved Calida from him. I suppose that's why he made my ability to find such a love a challenge—and it has taken me all this time to finally find her.

It's taken a lot to get her to me too.

While it pains me to think of her broken heart at the hands of Jackson, his loss is more than my gain—it is my love. Not only that, she's had to learn in a matter of days what it means to be in my world. She's discovered the truth of her Altrinion lineage, the Order of Altrinion, some history on Dunes wolves and she's even had to fight and be fought for.

I've learned a lot too. She isn't as frail or weak as those in her family must think. Damina has fought Scourge vampires all on her own and won; demonstrating she is more than capable at defending herself. All I need to do now is show her the complete Altrinion arsenal at her disposal.

Taking her to the Civility Center last night was bold of me, but I knew after everything she could handle it. Though I'm sure knowing I was by her side gave her assurance, she stood strong in the presence of Titan in all his allure and even challenged Trieu with a diffidence that gave pause to the Great Storm Rider herself.

Over the last few days, we've learned openness, trust, and shared unrivaled heights of intimacy.

Still, the one thing I never considered when she revived my heart is how sadness affects it. As she recounted the day of her parent's death and it being the reason for her disdain of the color red, my heart collapsed to the pit of my being. With her thoughts ravaging my mind, I saw her parent's deaths as though I was there and the horror of it still clings to me.

It's for that reason I do what I do now.

Holding the red gown in my hands I can only imagine how lovely she will look when she finally wears it. But it is not this day. She's not ready.

I hear her singing in the shower and I hang the gown back in the closet and replace it with the more ethereal teal colored gown. While I hope it's not too presumptuous of me, the last thing I want to do is rush her.

Especially not tonight.

Tonight, I intend to show her to all the world and make my declarations clear. Not only for her sake, but for even the likes of Colin DeVeaux who propositioned me just moments ago, while Damina slept, to wed his daughter. Hopefully, I made it clear to him that I have no intention of aiding his dismal desires to be part of the supernatural community. He and his daughter will just have to live out their lives the old-fashioned way or find another suitor. In any case, it's not my concern.

Damina is my only concern.

"Now, isn't this an infraction of employee— employer relations?" Jerrica teases from behind me in the hall outside Damina's suite. She stares at the teal gown in my hand and strains to smile.

"Hey! When did you get here?" I answer surprised. As much as I want to hug my friend, I don't.

"A little while now, but I didn't want to interrupt anything. Is Damina okay?"

"Yes, she's fine," I answer quickly closing Damina's closet door and exiting her room. "She's just showering before the ball."

"Ah, I so I gather you two are *going together*?" Jerrica's tight smile does little to hide her clipped tone.

"That's the plan." Jerrica watches my face hard and I try not to outwardly display my glee.

"How splendid for you both!" Jerrica's forced happiness stabs my heart, but it's the sincerity of her smile, that bridles my unease. I can't imagine how she must feel. The good thing is I know she means no harm.

"Hey D!" Braelyn says from the end of the hallway. Wrapped in an oversized terrycloth robe, her wet feet slap against the hall floor and I chuckle as Jerrica's turns her attention away from me as her obvious frustration with Braelyn grows. "Titan called. He's got some news from the breakout at the CC last night. I think he wants you to come by before you head to the ball."

"Completely out of the question. No way! Tonight is about me and Damina. It's our night—my chance to introduce her to all the supernatural world."

"Oh stop being dramatic, D! It's not all the world— just all of Louisiana!" Braelyn quips.

Before I can rebuke Braelyn, Jerrica grabs my arm, redirecting my attention. "It's quite all right, Dalcour. Why don't you tend to your business? I'll ride with Damina and I'll make sure she arrives safely."

"Are you sure?" I question, searching Jerrica's face. Sensing Brian's presence nearby, he's cloaking her truth from me so I can't finger through her mind.

Jerrica offers a wide smile that meets her eyes, and sighs, somewhat disappointed in my apparent mistrust.

"Yes, I'm sure. Besides, I look forward to catching up with Damina."

"So you see, boss, no need to worry. And you can still show her off to all the world, as you say. Because of course a woman in love wants nothing more than to be paraded like a circus animal." Braelyn adds shaking her wet hair loose from its towel. As much as she'd like me to believe there's truth behind her cynicism, I know better.

"Then should I suppose that's why you're smelling like cotton candy—so you can parade yourself in front of Abraham's boy?" I tease.

"You know what? I'm not even going to dignify that with a response!"

"Braelyn, darling, I think you just did," Jerrica mutters with her hand over her mouth.

"Great! Now you both are ganging up on me. I see what this is! Anyway, I just came to check on my girl!" Braelyn says over her shoulder as she charges into Damina's suite.

Jerrica and I both laugh, and I feel myself relax, knowing that somehow, I haven't completely lost my friend.

It was all worth it for this moment.

Watching the graceful swan-like movements of Damina as she makes her way toward me on the stage seizes my heart only to remind me, she controls it all. Every jaw is dropped as her willowy motion sends the breeze of her calming and sweet fragrance throughout the hall.

While there are beautiful works of art adorned throughout this great hall, none are fit to be her rival. There has never been a work of art more lovely or as awe-inspiring as Damina Nicaud.

She is the pure personification of art in motion.

Extending my hand to hers, she looks up at me with her beautifully bright eyes, fueled by a glint of the Altrinion flame, and my heart skips a beat. Per usual for my Beautiful Queen, her luscious lips part slightly as takes her first step up toward me and takes everything within me not to delight myself in the pleasure of her kiss.

For she is indeed the sweetest thing I've ever tasted.

"I knew you'd look ravishing in that gown!" I whisper in her ear as she mounts the stage. No worries, Beautiful, I won't make you say anything. I just had to have you at my side." I add.

Damina smiles and issues a sigh of relief and looks back at the crowd and waves as if she was raised in the royal court. Once more I'm impressed by the elegance of her manner. Wrapping my hold tight at her waist, she nestles her head into me, resting there as though it were her home.

And like any couple, our would-be bliss-filled evening is marked by highs and lows. Damina wasn't pleased when I revealed Colin's plan for me to wed Claudia, but knowing I am far from interested seemed to settle her impending anger.

Dealing with the Braelyn, Mark, and Dauphine fiasco didn't help either; neither did Jerrica for that matter. Still, Damina handled her crash-course into her newfound world like a trooper. Like Melvina always says, "she ate the meat and threw away the bones."

Thankfully and despite it all, I've found a way to salvage our evening. Now that I've showcased the love of my life to the supernatural community, it's time to spend a little time away from the noise of the ball.

Taking her hand, I lead us out to the patio. Her eyes grow wide with amazement as she sees floating glass balls of light illumine the walkway with tiki torches placed at either side of the garden. Situated in the middle of the garden gazebo a small stringed quartet plays softly as two women arrayed in white with veiled faces dance ceremoniously tossing white rose petals in the air.

Holding her close to me, we dance slowly to the music and giddy feeling of Christmas warms over me again.

"Damina, I love you." After a flurry of confessions, all headlined by my endless devotion and affection for her, those precious and sacred binding words escape my lips.

I can hardly believe it myself, but my own truth rattles my brain in an endless stream of emotion and thoughts, and they all point to Damina. She rests her head deeper in my chest and I feel her cast away the remaining weightiness of her past as though she tossed it to the far-reaching corners of the ocean.

The glowing embers of the Altrinion force shine brightly through her and my body instantly mirrors hers as our streams of light glow as one. I can't help but marvel at the sight of her and smile, knowing I have found what so many have longed for. True love.

No longer does the thought of such a force as true love haunt or torment. Instead, like Damina, I've allowed it to become my guiding light. Our brilliance shines brighter and in an instant our lips are locked together as one. Rippling currents of electric energy pulsate through our bodies with each touch and kiss.

Wrapping my arms tightly around her, we drift above the ground as I relish in the sweet scent of her aroma as it bedazzles me with the wonderfulness that is Damina. A foggy, steamy cloud forms at the fusion of the night's chill and the warmth we emit and her name drips like a faucet my mouth and I realize her name is synonymous with love. Saying her name is akin to the word love itself.

This time it's Damina's lips trailing the ravine of my neck and her tongues caresses my clavicle, and she inhales my scent wholly. Her body convulses in my firm grip as she thrusts herself against me and a golden iridescent mist rises over us and I am overcome in the entirety of her.

If it weren't for the voyeurs looming about, I'd take great pleasure in sharing the highest level of intimacy with her in the shroud of passion surrounding us. Damina's head flings back and her mouth gapes open and my desire holds strong as I keep a firm grip around her waist. She cups her head at the nape of my neck, and she exhales, moaning ever so sweetly in my ear a butterfly-like sensation flutters through my entire being.

In all my years I've never felt anything quite like this—ever. If I didn't know better, I'd swear that indeed connected at the highest level of intimacy—but with our clothes on. *How is this possible?* I ask myself.

As our kiss fades, Damina slowly pulls away from me and her panic-filled expression fills my heart with dread.

"Dal! Are you doing this?" She screams, now aware of levitating motion.

"We are doing this. Don't worry beautiful, this is all us," I reply softly, cupping her chin in my hand.

"Put me down now!" She demands.

"Calm down, Damina. It's okay. I've got you," I reply, trying to ease her discomfort.

"Dal! Now!" Damina yells back.

Damina now regards me as a stranger as her flame-fueled eyes stare at me with both uncertainty and alarm. While it's evident she fears what is happening in this moment, it's not me she fears most.

Chapter 21

Jackson

"Baby, what's wrong? What happened? Whose phone is this?" A flustered series of questions rush through me all at once and I know I'm more than rattled. Something truly is wrong.

"I—I need you. I want to come home, Jackson," Damina cries.

"Yes, baby that's all I needed to hear," I answer softly, slamming her bedroom door behind me. "Please, tell me where you are, and I'll be right there. Just please promise me you're not hurt." The mere thought kindles a fire stirring deep within me.

"No, I'm not hurt—at least not how you think. I just need you, Jackson—everything is just so messed up! I need you!" Damina exclaims through her moaned cries.

Though I still know something is actually wrong, I know better than to push the issue. The important thing is that she called me. I need to find a way to help her however I can.

"You got it, baby. Okay, listen, everything is going to be okay—give me a minute, Gregory!" I shout over my shoulder as my hulking companion stands in the doorway of her bedroom, calling my name through the cracked door.

"Jackson, you're gonna wanna see this!" Gregory continues.

I put my hand up in warning and rush across her room and push the door shut.

"Okay, Damina, sorry about that. Now, tell me where you are, and I'll come and get you."

"No, Jack. I just want to come home. You don't need to come here. Can you just arrange something for me to get back home? I don't have my wallet with me. Pull some strings with TSA—anything?"

"That's fine baby. You know I'll get you back to me safely. I'll get Sophie and Gregory right on it. Where's the nearest airport or train station? I can get them to make a few calls if I—"

"Jack, dude you really need to come out here!" Gregory is back at Damina's bedroom door, with his head pushed through the opening.

"Gregory not now! What?" I yell back.

"Look, Jackson, I'm trying to be helpful here, but I can just go!" Kyra snaps, forcing the door open past Gregory before turning back to the living room.

"Kyra, you're gonna have to wait just a moment, please! Can you all give me a moment?" I shout at Gregory, Brandon and Kyra. Kyra rolls her eyes and heads toward the front door. "I'm on a call. Gregory, go see what she wants so I can finish with Damina please!" I demand.

"All right, baby, where were we?" I question. The phone is silent, and I barely hear Damina breathing in the background and fear strikes my soul once again.

"Finished. We are finished, Jackson!" Damina declares.

"What? What are you talking about, Damina? Come on baby, tell me where you are?"

"You just said it so lovely, Jackson. You need to finish with me, so you can get back to her. Well, don't let me stop you! I don't know why I thought anything had changed. But no worries, you can have all the time you need with Kyra, Mr. Nash! We are finished. More than you know!" Damina screams and the sound of the phone crashing against something rings aloud in my ear.

"DAMINA!" I yell to unyielding ears and the call ends with only Damina's screams echoed in the distance.

Crap!

I knew having Kyra here would only make matters worse.

Gregory charges back in the room only to find me in the same desolate state as that of my wedding's eve. My body grows cold and blood leaves my face as the haunting images of Damina in her anger flash through my mind. I redial the number she called from and it just rings and goes to an auto voicemail.

Once again, I have authored her pain and I fear the dreaded pages turning in my heartbreak's story.

"Jackson, man you've got to get out here now—before she leaves!" Gregory shouts at me, shaking my shoulders.

This time nothing but anger singes my rage and even my best companion looks to be my enemy.

"I only asked you to keep Kyra away for a few minutes! A few minutes, Gregory! If I have truly lost Damina this time, I will never forgive you!" I scream, pushing Gregory up against the wall, sending a picture of Damina and me on her wall crashing to the ground. We both look down at the broken glass now at our feet and the imminence of my doom is sure and Gregory gazes back at me with a grief-stricken glare.

"Jackson, please," Gregory says, gently removing my hand from his collar. "Talk with Kyra," he breathes his words as though it is his last.

Scanning his face, I still see the same sincerity and friendship I've seen a thousand times.

Back off. This is your friend, idiot!

Loosening my grip from his neck, I rush toward Kyra and she steps back behind Brandon, keeping a wary eye on me. "Jackson," she mutters over Brandon's shoulder.

"Careful Kyra! Your next breath could cost you your very life. Now tell me, what was so important?"

"Listen, I don't know how much time we have so I'll

be brief," Kyra begins.

"Be *very* brief." My seething tone is less threatening than I intend. Every ounce of me wants to end Kyra.

"You were right to be wary of Damina's friend Allyson," Kyra says walking around Brandon.

"What about Allyson? Gregory told us her boyfriend was a Dunes—we already know that, Kyra."

"There's more Jackson," Gregory adds from behind me.

"What more?"

"She's a Jadeite, Jackson!" Kyra exclaims, now standing right in front of me. Her expression is more genuine than it's ever been.

"How can you be sure?" I question, fear once again invading my presence.

"Excuse me, what is a Jadeite?" Brandon says, staring around the room confused.

"The Jadeites are extremist. A faction of humans loyal to the Vitreous Order, and the most dangerous of Altrinion and Altrinion vampires," Kyra answers in a low tone, but her gaze is set on me.

"Just how dangerous are we talking?" Brandon questions.

"If there were Nazis of the supernatural world—it would be the Vitreous; which makes their followers even worse," Gregory states in a calm yet somber tone.

"*That would explain a lot.* How can you be certain she's a Jadeite?" I ask.

"Well, Merle did as you asked and had her followed which lead straight to a secret Jadeite location."

"Was her Dunes boyfriend with her?"

"No, that was the strange part. We can't find him either. My trackers went back to his regular hang outs, and no one has seen him in a few days. Even they seemed pretty worried about him."

"Him? I couldn't care less about him!"

"But he's still a wolf, Jackson! Didn't you just say we needed to begin reengaging with the Beta Primes!"

"Are you serious, Kyra? You think I care about the Betas right now? That is not my concern tonight!"

"Then it very well should be! Because I'd hate for his fate to become Dacari's—or even Damina's!" Kyra lashes back.

My hands are gripped at her shoulders in an instant as my wolf struggles to break loose, making me work hard to subdue his will to be free.

"Tell me! What do you mean? What does this have to do with Dacari?"

"Dacari has spent a lot of time with Allyson since Damina's departure—they've become fast friends. And just as we arrived tonight, I thought I spotted Dacari going into Allyson's building."

"Why didn't you tell me that, Kyra?" Gregory barks, his concern for Dacari's well-being evident.

"It doesn't matter. Allyson's not home; she hasn't been for a while, so I'm sure Dacari will be fine," Brandon remarks with reassurance, now postured at Gregory's side. I try to shrug off my new discovery at Gregory's fondness for Dacari—but I'll come back to it when we know she's well.

"Well, maybe she is and maybe she isn't. But if the Dunes disappearance and the beating Merle and my trackers took is any indication of how dangerous it is to be associated with this Allyson character; you'd do best to scurry." Kyra's portentous posture doesn't go unnoticed by any of us, but we ignore her and race out of Damina's condo toward Allyson's building.

"Brandon! Stay with Kyra! Don't let her out of your sight!" I shout over my shoulder on my way out.

"No worries, I'm not going anywhere," Kyra answers in a low tone that still catches my ear.

Arriving in front of Allyson's building we see Dacari's Jeep parked out front and we make our way to the steps when we see Dacari racing down the hall.

She's running but thankfully we spy no one behind her. Gregory pulls me to the side of the building near a large set of bushes and we keep out of sight as she bounces down the staircase. From the looks of it, she doesn't seem hurt, so we keep a watchful eye on her.

Dacari looks up and down the street and squinches her nose up before pulling her phone out of her purse. Walking toward her Jeep, she makes a call. Gregory looks at me, hunches his shoulders, unsure if we should continue our stalking. Before I have a chance to weigh in, she starts talking.

"Damina! Where are you, chica? Look, I've called you a thousand times and you haven't answered your phone yet! I surely hope you didn't forget about your birthday promise to me. If you did, oh well! I'm sure I will have fun in New Orleans with or without you...

who am I kidding? You know I only want to spend my birthday with you. Alrighty then, tell the Big Easy to duck for cover, I am on my way!"

As Dacari jumps in her jeep and speeds off, my shooting ache burns in the center of my chest and I know exactly what I must do.

"Gregory, make the arrangements for the company jet. We're going to New Orleans."

Dalcour

"DAMINA!" CALLING her name outside of Bessie's Tavern, I knew she would be here. Following the tempest of the storm trailing her was easy. Even if it weren't, I'd surely span the entirety of the globe to find her.

The terrace doors swing open and Damina gazes down at me and I behold her in all her luminous glow. Despite the torrential pouring rain that I'm almost certain is her doing, I can see every inch of her perfected frame above me. The brilliant light shining through her is almost brighter than the sun and the warmth of her being calls to me like a siren.

Damina smiles down at me and I know the fear that once held her state is now fleeting.

"Hey beautiful! Odd weather we're having tonight, don't you think?" I tease, smiling hard against the rain. "I believe you owe me a dance! I told you I would have you dancing in the rain before long. And well, seeing as though you skipped out on me earlier, I suppose now is as good a time as any!"

Damina laughs, shaking her head. I'm glad to see she's still amused by my charms. She glances over her shoulder and I hear other voices in the background. But it's the loud and incessant noise of a phone ringing that churns a tinge of melancholy within me. It doesn't take a genius to know it's probably Jackson!

I've grown quite sick of the mongrel's constant intrusion. This morning Nara emailed me all I needed to know about this *would-be* Prime Alpha. While it closes the loophole on the kind of wolf strong enough to cloak an Altrinion as powerful as Damina, it does little to assuage my disgust. As not only a wolf, but a prime, he had one job—to protect Damina, and he failed. Miserably.

But it is his misery that gives me great company.

Although, as I watched television waiting for her to awake this morning, after our crazy night at the Civility Center, I couldn't shake the feeling I might end up like Denzel's character in *The Preacher's Wife*. Being destined to give back my heart's one true love because it's the *right thing to do*, doesn't sit well with me.

Thankfully, Damina doesn't give me long to ponder my premonitions further when I see her climb onto the railing, I know she'll be back in my arms where she belongs.

This is no mere trust fall. She knows I will always catch her. *I am not him*. It doesn't matter how many times lightning strikes the shores of our love; we will not become as tenuous as glass. I'll never let her break. Not now or ever.

As she freefalls toward me, I glide upward, and she lands gently in my embrace. Her illuminating presence is as if she is encapsulated in flames, but she is not burned. The heat emitting from her is too hot for mortals and would almost set me ablaze if our Altrinion nature wasn't synchronized.

Damina smiles at me and the flaming brightness around her subsides slightly, just enough for me to see her face without squinting. "Well hello, beautiful," I say offering a smile bright enough to match hers.

"Hello yourself," she says with a soft smile before gently thrusting her mouth onto mine.

"Are you okay? Why did you run?" I question, keeping her body close to mine. Though I have to work hard not to gawk at how her rain-drenched gown clings to her beautifully wet curves, I need to make sure we are good.

Damina's face falls and her teeth chatter in the freezing rain and my heart races, fearful of her response. "I—I was afraid. I couldn't imagine any of this—that you were actually *real*."

"And now?" I smile, hopeful her response doesn't break my newly beating heart.

"Now, I know more than ever this is where I am meant to be. Here. With you. I wasn't ready to admit it before, but I love you, Dalcour. I love you!"

Damina's confession overtakes me in a windfall of passion, joy, and a zealous love I never thought a wretched man like me capable. Gazing into the depth of her fiery eyes, I know without question that this woman is more than my love; she is my home. Cupping her chin, I pull her face to mine and once more delight in the sweetness of her lips.

"Come now, let's get you out of this rain. Let's go home," I say staring at her perfectly wet body.

"I thought you said the mansion wasn't your home?"

"No, I said home is where the heart is. Now that my heart beats for you—you are my home, Damina Nicaud."

The strength of the storm dissipates as we soar through the night sky. While it's not the first time Damina has drifted asleep in my arms, tonight there is a calming peace exuding through her that is different from before. Although it's been clear for some time that she cares deeply for me, tonight is the first time she allowed herself to admit it.

As much as I want to search her mind and uncover what changed since she left me at the Hall until the moment she confessed her love for me outside of Bessie's Tavern tonight, I dare not. Rather, I am merely thankful for whatever pivotal and transforming factor is responsible for her declaration.

Nearing the mansion, a swarm of butterflies seem to invade my being as nervousness takes over. With her body sodden with her drenched clothes hugging her and revealing all her glory, I have no desire to take her through the mansion for all eyes to see. So I'm taking her straight to my bedroom. Everything in me tells me this is a bad idea; but I can think of no better option.

"Almost there," I whisper in her ear, beckoning her to awake.

As she awakes, we land on the balcony and she stares around, her face full of curiosity.

"Where are we?"

"My room," I quietly reply as I open the doors to my suite.

It doesn't take long for Damina to get comfortable. Perhaps too comfortable.

Something has changed. She has changed.

There's a slightly new confidence to her stride as she walks around my room. She seems genuinely intrigued at everything from the sacred scrolls to the ancient mercy blades above my bed.

While I'm happy to oblige her interest, I can tell she's become interested in more than my relics and artifacts.

She wants me.

Try as I might to avoid her advances through playfulness, my impressive music collection or even revisiting her declaration of love—it's clear Damina Nicaud has one thing on her mind.

As desperate as I am to finally be one with her, I can't help fear the wicked churning from my inner beast. I almost wonder whether this was Decaux's wicked plan all along. I'm sure he knows I'm fated and as such I could only love one such as I. I can only imagine how the sinister hole of his would-be heart would delight should I kill the very one I loved with my entire being!

Anger fills my mind as I see the makings of his grand scheme at work!

Unfortunately, Damina isn't making this easy. Her overpowering effervescence permeates my entire suite, making it difficult to breathe without her invading my pores wholly. The way she looks at me, touches me—hell, even the way she says my name makes me want to both devour and ravish her!

Oh, how I wish I were pure like her! If only blood didn't call to me with such a primal force, perhaps my lustful longing toward her wouldn't be so dangerous. But here I stand, a cursed soul, unable to enrapture myself in my heart's pleasure without fear or pain.

Radiating heat seeps through my skin and a waterfall of feverish sweat covers my forehead as I work hard to resist awakening the darkness within me. Though I've asked for her to leave and give me time to compose myself, she remains defiant.

"Just—just go, Damina!" I shout at her and it's all I can think to do to get rid of her.

"Dalcour, you're scaring me. Tell me what's wrong with you!" She demands.

"You—you need to go, Damina! Now!" I yell once more, toppled over at my waist as I feel my fangs protrude as a burning red film coats my skin. Staggering to the bathroom, I temper my tone just enough and say over my shoulder, "I'll be okay in a moment. Come back after you change, okay. I promise I'll be fine."

Slamming the bathroom doors behind me, I try to catch my breath. Looking into the mirror, I see the makings of the malevolent mask crushing from beneath my face. Crimson and blood-stained eyes stare back at me in the mirror as razor sharp fangs rut through my canines and incisors. The stinging pain of blood-lust calls to me and I work hard to stifle the venomous creature within. If it weren't for the bottles of blood Braelyn stored in the bathroom for me after my last faux pa with Claudia, I'd have to make my way to the CC to get a fix.

After crushing three bottles like the ravenous animal that I am, I gaze back in the mirror and see my normal Cherrywood hue frame my face. Thankful for only the usual crimson glint in my eyes, I smile knowing once again I've deterred the dark duplicity that desires his release.

"*I won't let you hurt her*," I declare confidently to my reflection and exit the bathroom.

Yet, as I see blood dripping from Damina's palm I am certain my pronouncement is premature.

The pulsing of my heart fades and my vision is cloaked in blackness. Only a sliver of light remains, and my sight is set on the steady stream of blood pouring from Damina's hand. A shiny red tint covers my skin and thick, barreling muscles erupt all over my body.

Taking thunderous steps toward her, I can no longer resist the blood-fueled invitation that calls to me. Her trusting eyes stare back at me, but I can't withstand the lure of both her body and her blood. I want to drink her and fill her with me—all of me. The thought of her pleasurable screams as I take my refuge inside of her while partaking of her innocence sends me into a frenzy.

She sits like prey on the bed and I am on the hunt. Watching her squirm gives me merciless delight.

While I feel my better part pleading with me to turn from my savage pursuit, snarling hisses are my only recourse as my tongue lashes toward the blood seeping through her flesh. Even as she tries to hide her self-inflicted wound, I can still smell it. And despite the shrouded darkness of my vision, the glorious revelation of her nakedness shimmering through her wet gown engorges the strength between my thighs, returning my intent to relentlessly ravishing her body without release.

Though, unlike any prey before her, she somehow maintains her resolve. No longer does she seek an escape or even wriggle away from me. She is resolute. Calm. Perhaps she has accepted her fate? If that be her choice, I'll take pleasure in making her beg for me to end her suffering.

Oh, the ways I want her to suffer! I want to bring her to the highest heights of ecstasy, take her to the edge of her demise and do it all over again.

With the fitting song, *Demons* playing in the background, I hiss once more as my tongue thrusts toward her. Nonetheless she remains unphased.

What is happening?

Through the dark fog clouding my view, a bright, sun-scorching ray exudes from her being and mysteriously calms the raging force rampaging inside of me. The light is almost blinding, but she remains in center view.

With her hand outstretched toward me, she gently touches my chest and utters my name, "Dalcour," in a tone so sweet it's almost too pure for my ears. She repeats my name but this time speaking in a long-lost Altrinion dialect too harmonic for mere ears to detect.

What is she doing to me?

I try hard to withstand her loving entreat, but I cannot. The darkness that once encapsulated my sight, gives way to the brightness of her light as the red sheen along my skin recedes. Her calmingly sweet vanilla and eucalyptus scent overpowers me, and I am lost in her trance.

The beast submits to her will and I feel a soothing shower that is the dew of her presence drift upon my body. As her hand rests on my chest, the loud thumping of my heartbeat resumes and I open my eyes, returning to the man she loves.

For the first time, it feels as though a thousand weights have lifted from me. The heaviness of my carnality and the wretchedness of my past fall away as a feathery freedom flows through me like I've never felt before. *This must be love.*

Chapter 22

Jackson

The Big Easy. It's been eons since I've ventured the streets of New Orleans. Despite the glorious charm of this City, I know I will not be able to indulge in its many pleasantries.

We barely made it into Louisiana as a hurricane-like storm ripped through an unprepared New Orleans. While it was hardly reminiscent of Katrina's impact, it caught everyone unaware. Though I'll never admit it to anyone, I am certain Damina was indeed the eye of the storm. Haunting images of her blazing through the City in a furious rage because of what she perceived to be my duplicity wreaks havoc on my heart. This time, I won't let her go until I make her understand the truth. My truth.

Following Dacari around isn't easy. We kept our distance, but close enough to ensure her safety. Gregory is surprisingly inclined to keep her in his sights. I've been too worried about Damina to ask him about his affection for her; but I'm sure I'll get around to it.

Still, nothing could prepare me for this. The one thing I dreaded is now a reality. Dacari's path to Damina has taken us from a colorful tavern in the heart of the French Quarter to the one place I never wanted to find her.

The mansion of Dalcour Marchand.

What is she doing here? Why is she here? How long has she been here?

A cascade of panic, fear, anger, jealousy and rage floods my emotions and it takes all of Gregory and Shawn's brute strength to keep me from marching up the steps of the mansion with Dacari to snatch Damina from this hell hole!

I'm surprised to only see a group of women at the door. From what I can see, they don't want to let Dacari in, but I can also tell they are all human. That helps my angst a little.

"They're foolish to think they can keep her from Damina!" Gregory scoffs.

"When did you become such an admirer of Ms. Peyroux?" I ask while never taking my eyes off the front door. Gregory shrugs his shoulders and laughs, doing his best not to look at me.

"Hey look, there's Damina!" Gregory says, pointing at the front door. "She looks—um happy," he adds and my heart falls to the pit of my stomach.

After all the worry she gave me last night and the wrecking ball she took to the City, I expected to see her less jolly than she appears. While everything in me only wishes for her happiness, I'm more concerned with *why* her demeanor has shifted and *who* is responsible for this change.

As the door closes, fierce feelings rage within me and it takes everything in me not to allow my wolf his release.

"Hey, Jackson! Stay calm, dude. Now we can go ring that bell if you want, but you and I both know if you ring that bell things can go a completely different way. We still don't know what she knows or if she has even tapped into her Altrinion nature yet. This is not how you want to introduce her to your wolf."

"Look around, Gregory! Of course she has! And even if she hasn't, it doesn't mean she's not in any danger. Just being in that place alone is reason for worry!"

"I get it! Really, I do. But let's think about this for a moment. This is Damina we're talking about—and not just her, but Dacari as well."

"Dacari?"

"Yes, Dacari. Do you actually think if Damina thought there was danger here she would let her cousin in? You and I both know she loves Dacari more than anything! She would never put Dacari in danger."

"I suppose you are right," I say as I think on Gregory's words. "So what am I to do? Should I just sit out here forever? Waiting?"

"Dude, haven't you learned anything from your time with Damina? If I've learned anything about those two is that there's no way they'll be trapped in that mansion for long. Dacari will have Damina out shopping in no time!"

We both laugh, shaking our heads in agreement. "So tell me, Gregory, when did you become an expert on all things Dacari?"

"I'm no expert, but I do pay attention."

"Obviously," I tease.

"Yep—hey—wait! Who is that guy?" Gregory barks as we watch a large, muscular man pick up Dacari's luggage from the porch.

"Whoever he is—he is—"

"He's a dead man!" Gregory shouts back, pulling the door handle.

Tugging his hand from the door, I squeeze his shoulder and laugh. "I was going to say that he must be a Dunes wolf—at least according to that tattoo on his arm. Now, what did you just tell me? Stay calm?"

"Whatever!" Gregory snaps back and keeps gazing out the window.

As we wait for them to come out of the mansion, Shawn catches a hitch ride with Tye in tow and looks for a place for us to rest. I haven't slept in a full twenty-four hours and I will stay awake another twenty-four if it meant just one chance to make Damina mine again.

Thankfully, Gregory's inclination was right and within the longest ninety minutes of my life, the door of the mansion opens. A small group of young people resembling the cast of an after school special are the first to exit. Most seem bubbly and upbeat, save the two girls who prevented Dacari's entry. Two young men are among them and a part of me hopes Damina hasn't indulged in their likeness. They are far too young—but they are wolves—Dunes wolves.

Dacari and Damina are the last to emerge from the mansion. Dacari makes it down the staircase of the porch first and Damina remains at the top. She smiles broad and waves sweetly, making me wonder who is on the other end of the door. Kneeling down in the limo, I get a better view of inside the dark mansion. Luckily, my enhanced vision grants me laser focus, but joy does not fill my heart at the sight.

My heart falters once more as I see Dalcour Marchand standing at the top of the stairs. His smile is broad as he stands next to a vampiric-goth girl, waving farewell to Damina. But it's the freely given smile she gives in return that brings me to near death.

I thought that smile was mine. Heck, I even thought her air-blown kisses were only meant for me.

Less than seven days ago we were to marry. Now, someone has stolen my bride.

But I have every intent on reclaiming my bride for my own.

Crap!

"Not yet, Jack-O. Not yet," Gregory says holding me back from my exit. "Let's just see where they're going. It's better if we do this away from this mansion and it's prying eyes," he recommends.

Gregory was right again. Following them through the City as they shop, gives me time to quiet the erratic energy building inside me. My emotions pivot from an irrational ire to grief, making it hard to make sense of the point of it all.

Just when I thought I was only endangering my alpha status; I now see that perhaps my focus was misplaced. What good is it to strengthen my pack to aid me in protecting my beloved, if my beloved is no longer mine?

When they finally stop for lunch at a local bakery, I dash out of the limo. I can't wait any longer. As I walk down the sidewalk, the loud sound of *Missing You* by Case taunts me from a passing car as I near the front patio of the restaurant.

How à propos?

Damina and her cousin saunter outside and look for seating as I round the gated entrance. Her name escapes my mouth before I can formulate my next thought. Halting her motion, she slowly turns about.

"Damina," I say once more, and we are now face to face. Her lovely face is full of surprise and marred by disgust. Who can blame her? As far as she's concerned, I cheated on her. But it's time for the truth.

While I'm not sure how it's possible, she looks more radiant before me now than ever. There's a confidence in her posture that is unfamiliar to me. Damina's hair is thicker and longer than when last I saw her. Even her curves are more pronounced. And with the way her clothes hug her body, unlike her normal, oversized garb I can't help the spring of jealousy welling within me.

But more than anything, my heart longs to be near her and it's taking everything in me to resist carrying her away.

"It's good to see you, baby. You look beautiful." I know what I have to tell her won't be easy to hear. If my suspicions are correct, I am sure what I will tell her will turn her world completely upside down.

One thing is sure, I'll gladly spin the Earth on its axis a thousand times if only it returns her heart to me.

Dalcour

I NEVER knew love could be like this!

Had I known true love would feel this good, I would have spent the last five hundred years searching for her. Waking up with Damina next to me brings a joy to my once darkened soul I thought impossible. Now, however, I know nothing is impossible.

With Damina by my side there is nothing we can't overcome!

I know this because I did what a monster like me never dreamed of doing. Restraining myself from making love to her because it was the right thing to do, was the hardest thing I've ever done in my five hundred years! It wasn't because I didn't want her. Nor was it because I feared taking her virginity for the whole mansion to hear. No. It was simply because there's a part of her that still clings to Jackson.

Sure, I have no doubt that our moment of passion would erase any inkling of Jackson from her mind forever, but that's not how her first time—our first time should be. She needs to be free. I don't want her to feel as though she's settling in the least bit when we come together.

Yes, it pains me to admit I know the truth of her continual love for Jackson, but I respect her too much to act as though he doesn't exist. Besides, since we are Fated, it's best for everyone if we don't take that step unless we are absolutely certain. If not, the consequences could be dire.

Instead, I held her in my arms, delighting in just the beautifulness that is her until the sun arose.

That's when I knew that I truly knew love!

For the first time in over four centuries, I felt the sun arise on my face and I did not burn. No smoldering lava-like rash erupted on my flesh, nor did smoke rise from my body as the brightness of the sun's light covered both Damina and me.

Jumping from my bed, I dashed to the window, fully prepared to pull the drapes down on both the terrace doors and windows. As I stood there, I realized for the first time—I could stand in the sun.

While I never thought anything could rival the thump of my newly beating heart, being able to rest in the sunlight once more, swells me with both delight and the purest joy!

All of this is because for the first time, I know love

and her name is Damina.

I'd like nothing more than to drown myself in the sweetness of her love, but with her cousin Dacari's arrival this morning and my brother's growing threats I'll have to press pause. Just as Dacari was getting settled I received word of another breach at the Civility Center. That makes two this week! Thankfully, Damina has agreed to take her cousin shopping long enough for Titan and the others to visit and discuss the incident.

I've also asked Lux to come by and check our security here at the mansion. Jerrica's used some outside contractor to install cameras, but I hardly think it's sufficient. As much as I hate asking Damina to leave my side, it's all I can do to keep her away from this mess! Luckily, our resident and upcoming young alpha, Mark agreed to tag along and keep her safety. Between him and Damina's personal praesidium, Vonnie, at her side, I'm sure she'll be fine. Not to mention her cousin, Dacari, is quite a spitfire. I doubt she'll let anyone get close enough to hurt her big cousin.

Dacari is an interesting conundrum all her own. While I didn't have the heart to confirm whether I believe Dacari is an Altrinion-wolf hybrid, there was something very different about her. Like both Bessie and Alana it's clear she has a hybrid lineage, but I still detected something more. *Something strangely familiar*. Unfortunately, It's likely she's just as unaware of her supernatural state as Damina. With my brother stirring trouble and the unfinished business of the mansion looming about, I don't have time to dig deeper into understanding Little Miss Peyroux, but I vow to soon help her and Damina discover her truth.

"We've got to get the Dunes in position now!" Titan barks, breaking my musing of all things Damina Nicaud.

Titan and Mikkel have been arguing since they've arrived. Fortunately, my blissfully good mood has muted much of their ruckus.

"The Dunes? Seriously! We don't need those primitive mutts for anything!" Mikkel hisses back.

"Lord Marchand has a plan and we need to stick to it!" Titan growls.

"Yes, and where has that plan gotten you? Dranoel is locked up now because you trusted him!" Mikkel lashes once more.

"Both of you stop it! Look, Mikkel, we don't know that Dranoel is responsible for the breaches at the CC or that he was ever involved at all!" I shout, coming between both men. These two have never gotten along. I've worked hard through the years at keeping them apart but leave it to my brother's machinations to bring them together.

"All we know is Dranoel was the last one there. Now, Dalcour, I admit he does look guilty. But that could be a distraction."

"Then why did you lock him up if you didn't think he was indeed to blame?" Mikkel questions in his normal slithering tone.

"I locked him up to prove otherwise! If he's in a cell,

the next move Decaux or anyone makes will be their own," Titan counters.

"Agreed, Titan. But it also leaves Trieu vulnerable."

"She's a tough old broad, my lord," Lux says from behind us, leaning against the parlor doors. "If anyone can protect themselves, it's the Great Lady Trieu. But, if you're worried, I can take some of my company with me to watch over her."

"That's a great idea, Lux. Thank you. How about you send a delegation instead? I need you close. The mansion open house is tomorrow, and I can't risk a scene. Titan, can you get word to Trieu that we're sending aid her way? Mikkel, we can shut down the Hall for now. I'm sure we still need to recover from the Ball last night. Once we've secured everything with the mansion, we can finally get the Dunes in position. And with it, bring a finality to this battle for balance once and for all." Despite a few groans and gripes shared between Titan and Mikkel, everyone nods as I give my orders and they take their leave.

As they leave, I send a quick text to Mark and Damina, letting them know it's safe for them to return to the mansion. *I can't get Damina back here fast enough!*

"Well, you're certainly chipper today!" Jerrica says at the doorway of the parlor. Her smile is bright, but I can tell she's still working hard to be happy for me. Seeing her in such disarray pains my heart. She's still my friend and I want to see her just as happy as me.

"I suppose I have a lot to be chipper about," I

respond, snatching the final proposal documents Braelyn gave me from the desk, waving them in the air. "It looks like we're headed for the big show!" I say cheerfully. I'd rather keep her attention on the mansion than my love life.

Her expression softens, and she smiles wide, "Well yes, I think everything will pull together just lovely!"

"Yes, and it's all thanks to you, my friend."

"Oh no, I can't take all the credit," Jerrica answers shaking her head in protest.

"Yes, you most certainly should! I know I haven't had a chance to thank you for everything you've done. You almost singlehandedly put the Dunes in position to prosper while driving a continuous stream of income to their cause. And that, Ms. Jeffers, is no small feat!"

"Don't you dare make a fuss! Please, I only did what anyone with an innovative spirit would do! We're business owners, after all!"

"Yes, we are but you are more than that, Jerrica Jeffers," I say taking a firm hold of her hand in mine. "You are not only a wonderful woman, but an amazing friend! Even when I thought I was unlovable and undeserving of love; you saw fit to bring the one person into my life proving just how wrong I was. Because of you, Jerrica, I am happy. I just want you to know that! It takes an amazing woman to want to see her best friend truly in love. I'm just glad to be your friend," I say softly as I squeeze her palm in mine.

Jerrica smiles and stares up at the ceiling, hopeful to push back the tears from their release. Just as she parts her lips to respond, Braelyn and Mark rush into the parlor.

"Big D! We've got trouble!" Mark exclaims, as he rounds the chair trying to catch his breath. Braelyn is at his side in an instant and I see the remaining of the team coming into the foyer, but I don't see Damina or Dacari.

"What happened?" Brian barks, pushing his way through the team, looking for Dacari.

Darkness creeps over me and a feverish dread pulsates through me, gripping my heart so tight it's hard to breathe. Dilano races behind Brian with Alana at his side.

"Vonnie stayed behind, she's trailing them now," Dilano says, looking up at me with fear in his eyes.

"Trailing who?" Jerrica questions. "Will someone tell us what is going on?"

In a millisecond, my hands are clutched at Dilano's throat and everyone cries for his release. My ears are unyielding to their screams. I have no quarrel with him, but I do believe in killing the messenger should their message bring me grief.

"Where is she?" It's the only question requiring an answer and the only answer capable of breaking my heart.

Chapter 23

Jackson

This should be the best feeling in the world! It's the first time I've been alone with Damina in almost a week. I've waited so long to finally have my beloved back with me, *but she's not with me just yet.*

I've probably spit out more than she could handle in the few moments we've been alone. There's not much left hidden. She now knows that I'm a wolf, that I know she is an Altrinion, and that my wretched brother, Keiron, is the root and cause of all our pain.

As much as it pains me to know she's likely given her heart to another, I will take ownership in my part. Had I been truthful, perhaps we would never be in such disarray. Because of my duplicity, I now must work hard to douse my irritation with her newfound demeanor.

It's clear she is not quite the same woman I once knew.

She has changed.

And so have I.

Still, with the nightmarish images of Kyra in my arms and over the phone last night, it's still the biggest elephant in the room.

"Damina! What are you talking about? I don't want to be with Kyra! You misunderstand me—I have only ever wanted to be with you! There's no me without you!"

"But—I—I—thought—"

"You thought wrong! I don't care if you're Altrinion or anything. Baby, from the first day I lifted that paddle in the auction hall, I knew then what I know as I stand here before you now—I love you! I always have, and I always will," I declare taking her face in my hands gazing deep into her beautifully flame-filled eyes. My eyes water knowing I've caused her so much pain. It hurts me that she could even fathom my heart belonging to another.

All that I am is hers!

Clutching her face in my hands sends tremors through my soul. *I've waited so long just to touch her!*

The heat from her skin is warm and inviting and her enchanting scent makes me weak in my knees. As she looks back at me, her trusting eyes return to their normal hazel view and she watches me and smiles, melting my heart. I want to surrender everything that I am to her and bow in her presence. I want to beg for her forgiveness and her mercy.

I want to do everything I can to make her mine again.

Slowly, she pulls away, likely hopeful I don't see her tears. But I do. If only she would allow me to comfort her, I'd ease her suffering.

"So you're telling me that you don't love Kyra?" Damina answers with a confused glare.

"Precisely, baby. I never have. We were only together for a short time and I never shared with her what I have with you!" I respond. I need her to know I've never loved anyone the way I love her.

"I don't understand. Then why did she come to our luncheon? She's obviously carrying a torch for you!"

"No. Kyra is only carrying a torch for Kyra. She is a Dunes alpha and her pack is in trouble. The lavish living she and her mother have lived has finally caught up with her. Now, she's looking to align herself with anyone who she thinks can save them from ruin. That's where my brother comes in. He promised her if I got cursed, he would take her as his bride and protect her pack," I explain.

"So you don't love her?" Damina repeats. She grabs her chest, staring around the room as though she needed to catch her breath.

"Love Kyra? Of course not! I've never even uttered those words to her. That's why she used a changeling to transform into you. But Keiron didn't count on Kyra texting my phone. You came over as a result of her text. And your arrival is what broke the enchantment."

"How is that possible?"

"Because a changeling cannot occupy the same space with the source from which they imprinted on. The minute you came into the room, I could see things for what they were. That's when I knew what had happened," I reveal. Reliving that fateful night is not on the top of my list, but I'll answer any question, if only to regain her trust.

"That's why when the hourglass broke you looked genuinely surprised to see me—" Damina mutters, her voice barely above a whisper.

I smile, nodding in agreement, hopeful I am getting through to her. But it is clear that she is not ready to give in so quickly.

"And now you want me to believe you? After all these lies? You want me to believe some enigmatic creature poofed into your house, tricked you into thinking it was me and that's why you made out with Kyra? Why should I believe you? How do I know you're not lying as we speak?"

"Oh, but you can believe that wolves and vampires exist? Makes sense!" Gregory mocks from across the room. A low snarl rumbles through me and I shake my head in disapproval.

Smiling once more, I take a few steps closer and block her view of Gregory. "Do you remember the honey-do list you gave me? The list of all the things you wanted me to do before you moved in after our wedding—"

"I do, but I don't understand what that has to do with anything, Jackson!"

"What was the number one thing on your list?" I ask, with my hands resting on her shoulders.

She shakes from me, ambling across the floor. "Huh? What? I—I don't remember. I can't think of that right now!"

"Well, I can remember. As a matter of fact, I remember you wanted to get a new doorbell. That was scheduled to be fixed while we were away. You wanted all hardwood flooring for your allergies and in case we had to babysit Doodle. But the number one thing on your list was a security system. You were worried about some reported burglaries, so you asked me to get one of those video camera systems," I recount with a broad smile.

"I don't understand. Jackson, what does that have to do with anything?" Damina questions, trying to comprehend what is going on.

"I had the system installed weeks ago. And as a result, everything from that night was recorded. Here's a card with our login information. You can see what's happening at the house now and you can check all the saved recordings. You can see that night. There's even audio with it. And if you watch closely, you'll hear me say one thing repeatedly—*Damina, I love you*. I thought it was you, baby! I swear I would never, ever cheat on you!" Pleading with Damina, I try to give her the small card with the login information, but she turns away, refusing to take it, but Dacari snatches both Damina's card and the one meant for me, stuffing it into her zipper pocket as the other falls to the ground.

I want to pick it up, but I keep my sights on Damina.

Damina stands frozen and I know her newly strengthened Altrinion mind can recall all the hidden things her mortal mind was too weak to comprehend. She gazes up at me, her face full of both awe and regret. Her breathing quickens and her eyes water.

She now knows the haunting truth of that night.

I want to reach out to her and shake her from the torment of the frightening flashbacks of the pain from that night, but my wolf's senses kick in like a spider and I know a dark danger is near.

In that moment, the sun drifts behind the cover of the clouds as darkness fills the afternoon sky. Gazing at her, I wonder if it's Damina's pulse on nature's new course, but I know it's not her. Damina's eyes grow wide and I know she too feels the impending peril looming in the distance.

A wild flowery aroma that's almost repugnant to me wafts pass my nose and my body instantly stiffens in alarm. Both Shawn and Gregory tighten their posture and even Tye wriggles to push his back against the wall.

I feel the threat growing closer and I rush across the room, hopeful to keep Damina from whatever harm seeks entry to the hostel, but I am too late.

He is here.

Dalcour

Summoning every ounce of the Altrinion force within me, I soar through a newly darkened sky as nature concedes to my will. Though I can surely stand in the sun, the last thing I need to do is tempt fate. With Braelyn on my six, I can't risk her safety either. While I'm happy to see the sun and sky obeying my command, I can hardly take pleasure in it.

My only thoughts are of Damina.

I have no idea what the wretched mongrel has to say to her, but his words may be his last.

Breaking through the long glass window of the hostel, I crash into the unit using nothing but my speed and strength to aid my flight. Braelyn yanks on the dusty gray curtain as she rounds into the room behind me as both Brian and Mark speed up the stairs and bust through the front door.

"Are you okay, Beautiful?" I ask, resting a soft kiss on her forehead. Damina shyly nods in reply, but her eyes remain on Jackson. Jackson keeps his sights set on me as deep growls rumble through him as he watches her curled in my embrace.

"Take your hands off her, Marchand!" Jackson demands through a roaring growl. His chest swells and his eyes flash in a greenish-golden hue, letting out another deep grizzly sound and both his minions echo in kind. Both Brian and Mark try to maintain their posture, but I'm slightly annoyed how they almost shrink in Jackson's presence.

SON

But it's clear that he is the Prime Alpha and they are caught in the middle.

"You know him, Jackson?" Dacari asks from across the room still shielded by his largest comrade. Brian is noticeably bothered by the wolf's clutch on Dacari, but he only casts a wary glance in her direction but retains his stance at my side.

"No, but I *know of him.* I know all about Dalcour Marchand, his treacherous brother and their evil deeds. Wasn't it you and your brother who hunted families of the Prime Pack into near extinction?" Jackson shouts with a daring wicked glare. "But now, look at you, with Dunes puppies at your side. Now let my wife go!" Jackson demands.

"You're wife? Huh? That's funny because if I recall, wasn't it you who cheated on this beautiful woman the day before your wedding? So I don't think that makes her your wife. Besides, how could *my lady* be *your wife*?" I retort with an unwavering smirk. "However, if I recall my histories, you are from the Nashoba pack of primes. Am I correct? The same pack that was too chicken to stand unified with the other packs and fight. Who, instead, hid among the villages of men? That's right, your ancestors fled from my brother and me on all fours. But you should know, he never bought your disappearing act—he only ended his raid at my request—so I guess you owe me!"

"I owe you nothing! Now let Damina go!" Jackson's eyes narrow as he shouts once more. His eyes are locked on me and Damina and I know he wants to snatch her from my grasp, but he's hesitant and rightfully so.

"How do you know who Dal is, Jackson?" Damina questions.

"*Dal*?" Jackson says through gritted teeth. Good. He didn't like that. I can't help how happy his discomfort makes me. His eyes flash brightly once more at Damina's admission, but he closes them quickly and swallows the thick air in his throat. "Once I found out where you were and who you had been with it was easy to figure out the rest. But, Damina, these people aren't who you think they are. They aren't what you think they are."

"And you are? Jackson just ten minutes ago, I thought you were just my cheating ex—and now I've learned you are a wolf? I mean that's not something you just omit when you're planning to marry someone. So, what? When was I going to find out? When I had your first litter? At the next full moon? When Jackson?" Damina shouts back.

"No, Damina, it's not like that. I was going to tell you—" Jackson pleads.

He's pathetic, and she's certainly better off.

"More lies, Beautiful. All he has is more lies. Let's see he's had, what, almost five years to tell you the truth, but he doesn't until now. Because he's a liar, Damina! And just like a Nashoba—big and bad in name only but when it gets tough all they do is hide," I scoff. He's almost making this too easy.

"I don't know about my ancestors, but I can tell you

that I'm not hiding anything right now! Listen Damina, he's not what he seems. He's not just an Altr—"

I know he wants to tell her of our Fated lineage. I haven't been able to share that with her yet, but I won't let him get ahead of me. I must stop him in his tracks. Now.

"No worries, *Nashoba*! Unlike you, I didn't cut my name in half to hide my identity. She knows exactly who and what I am. *She has already seen my face!*" I say as I step out of the shadows in the direct sunlight as the passing clouds now reveal the sun. Jackson's mouth gapes open at my confession and he ambles backward as a look of horror frowns upon his face.

The room erupts in a series of gasps at my admission. Even Braelyn, Mark and Brian look at one another shocked by my revelation as I maintain my stance in the sun.

Damina, however, isn't impressed. I know she's not happy with my reveal, especially after I asked her to keep my newfound state between us two. She knows exactly my aim, and she's not happy. Thankfully, Jackson still seems to be the focus of her rage.

Jackson clears his throat and saunters around the room with his hands in his pockets before turning to face us once more. This time, he wears his assurance in full stride. He's not going to go down easy.

Well, I guess the mutt has got a brazen brass pair after all.

"Well, you see that's funny, Marchand. You say *she's seen your face*, but maybe that's because she doesn't know everything. I mean, you certainly play the part well, with your entourage of vampires and baby wolves—"

"Puppies!" The large one scoffs gruffly, moving closer to Jackson's side. Mark and Brian both stare at them but keep their cool as Jackson glares at them sharply.

"Exactly! However, Gregory we must remember they are still our kin—so I'm more than willing to exercise some degree of control. But, as for you, Marchand—does Damina really know who you are? Did you compel these gentlemen to be at your side or do they willingly submit to you?" Jackson haughtily questions.

"No one makes us do anything!" Brian barks back at Jackson. His nostrils flare and his eyes grow wide with rage, but he holds his place at my side.

"Now, see, that's good to know. I'm glad it was your choice to make," Jackson says in a demeaning tone, patting Brian's shoulder. "Although I do have to wonder if Damina was afforded such a choice. Then again, Marchand, you can read my mind—what am I about to say? Well, for the benefit of all of us non-mind readers in the room, please tell us, have you been reading her mind the entire time, or did you just compel her and make her fall for you?" Jackson contends with a grimaced sneer.

I lunge at Jackson, but Mark jumps in front of me, holding me back. I almost have to wonder whether Mark is protecting me or Jackson.

"What? Dalcour, what is Jack talking about? You can read my mind?" Damina asks, curiosity filling her face.

"It's not how he's trying to make it seem, Beautiful, I assure you," I reply refuting Jackson's claim.

"Really Marchand? Because the stories I've been told all speak of the seducing Marchand brothers. Roaming from town to town luring women from their families, compelling kings out of their treasuries, and willing governments into their submission. How is this any different?" Jackson retorts in a daring stance, goading me to react.

"Dalcour, is this true? Have you been reading my mind this entire time?"

"It's not what you think, Damina."

"Then what is it, exactly? Because now that I think of it, I've been blurting things out that I wouldn't normally say and confessing things way more than I'm comfortable. You always seem to anticipate what I need even before I ask. I thought we were just in sync, but all this time you've been—"

"No, Beautiful! Don't let him twist this around! Can't you see what he's doing? He's trying to keep you from the truth. He's *been* keeping you from the truth— and for years! Now, in an act of desperation he throws accusations around so that you won't confront the one fact he refuses to admit; why he never told you the truth!"

"But you've been reading my mind? Compelling me to do what you want? I thought what we had was real! And Jackson, I thought we were ready to unite as husband and wife. I was wrong. I was wrong about both of you. Neither of you deserves me," Damina lashes out, glaring at us both in disgust.

Jackson continues to beg and plead his case, but his unrelenting plea goes unforgiven and I almost feel sorry for him. Almost. *But I must admit, I slightly admire his relentless tenacity.*

In his final act of desperation, he races across the room and holds Damina's face firm and everything in me bucks. Time sits in slow motion as he releases the Altrinion orb of her father to her and reveals her hidden truth.

My heart sinks to the pit of my being as Jackson exposes her father's wishes for him to be not only her protector, but her covering—her husband. Her everything. Not only that, but she is a Duacin—of an equally high Altrinion branch like me. Unlike me, her father wanted better for her—someone better than a wretched Altrinion-vampire like me. And he commissioned Jackson to be the one to care for her in such a way.

A chain of mixed emotions flood Damina's entire being and she looks at me and we both know—everything has changed. All I know is this: my love for her remains. I just hope she feels the same.

Chapter 24

Jackson

Seeing Damina free-fall from the eighth floor of the hostel wreaked havoc in my heart with a relentless pain. Weak to almost near death, it took everything in me to show her the Altrinion orb from her father. As excruciating as it was to endure, I would go to death's door as many times as needed to prove my endearing love for her.

Dalcour's screams as she glided through the air were almost as agonizing to watch. If he is indeed Fated as she I know her departure was tormenting to watch. Why I feel any sympathy for the one who seeks to take from me the only love I've ever known is beyond me. I suppose the truth is simply that I understand.

Neither Dalcour nor have any words left to say.

There are no words capable of describing our pain.

"Jackson," Gregory says tapping me on the shoulder, trying to break the forming face-off between me and Dalcour. "We should get out of here. I just got a notification from the hotel. They're ready for us."

"Good job, Gregory," I reply over my shoulder as I keep my sights on Dalcour. No matter how I may empathize with his pain; I still don't trust him. "Shawn, get Tye and let's head out."

"Got it!" Shawn answers.

"Dacari, let's get your things," Gregory says turning to Dacari. Her face is still frozen from watching her cousin fly out of the window. She's obviously in shock. I can only imagine how she must feel.

"Get your hands off me, jerk!" Dacari yells, pushing Gregory away.

"It's okay, Dacari. Let us get you back to Delia," I softly reply.

"I am not my cousin; Jack and I don't need your help!" She snaps back.

Gregory pulls her hand, and she shoves his shoulder. Brian jumps in between them and growls at Gregory. Both men's fangs hang from their mouth as their chests swell and their stance stiffens. I suppose Gregory had a right to be worried about this guy when he first saw him outside of the mansion.

"Dudes!" The vamp girl screams with bubbly sarcasm. "She's a lady, not some shiny little toy for you to claim as your own. Maybe that's something all of you should think about—perhaps neither of these gals want you brawling on their behalf. How about just ask them what it is they want? Ha! What a novel idea! Dacari, dear, would you like to go with me? Vonnie is waiting for us downstairs with a car."

Dacari shakes her head in agreement and heads off with the goth-vamp girl. Even though I should keep a watchful eye on Dacari for Damina's sake, I think it's best to let her go on her own accord.

As they exit, the goth-vamp turns around and smiles, "See how that's done boys?"

Gregory, Shawn, and I leave shortly afterward with Tye and head to the hotel.

"Hey Jack-O, Dacari mentioned Damina has a big show at the mansion tomorrow," Gregory says.

"Good to know. I guess I better go get a new suit. Gotta look the part when I get my girl back."

Dalcour

"ARE YOU okay, Big D?" Mark turns and asks.

As much as I want to reply, I cannot. I have nothing to say. With Damina gone, the pulsating of my heart subsides, and I feel numb all over. I can only hope she will return to me, but after what Jackson showed her, I am no longer convinced.

"She will return, my lord," Brian quietly says, placing a firm hold at my shoulder. His reaction to everything surprises me. Just the other day he fought me as a foe, and now he regards me his ally. I'm not sure what changed between us, but I am thankful for his sentiment.

A smile is all I have to offer in return and both he and Mark return the gesture.

Still, I refuse any more sympathetic overtures. And while the beast within no longer holds sway over me, I am still a force and I still take pleasure in reminding anyone just who I am.

But this time I am the one who needs the refresher.

"Mark, contact Cedric and have him and Lux come by and square this place up. Can't have my city torn apart by savages," I laugh, knowing I'm referring to myself. Mostly.

Climbing to the window's ledge, I take in a deep breath and enjoy the lingering presence of Damina's sweet scent. As I do, a newfound hope wells within me and a small surge in my heart strengthens.

"My lord, what are you doing?" Brian calls to me with a worried glare.

"No worries, B," Mark begins, "I think the big guy just needs to let off a little steam." Mark bright smile is reassuring as he pats Brian's back.

"I'll meet you all at the mansion. I just need a little drift."

"And what of Damina?" Brian asks.

"As long as her cousin is with us, I know she'll return."

"How can you be so certain?"

"Because I can feel it in my heart," I reply, and take my dive in the cloudy afternoon sky.

Chapter 25

Jackson

All my life I've always played it safe. I've never been one to color outside the lines. In my upbringing, protecting the ones you love meant staying on the straight and narrow and avoiding confrontation wherever possible.

My father always said, "A good man starts few fights, but wins them all." That is exactly what I plan to do tonight. I plan to win it all. First, however, I need to pick a fight.

It's not my proudest moment, but I know it is near suicide to go headfirst into the lion's den when the lion is on the prowl. So the first thing I need to do is throw him off my scent.

Our contacts in Louisiana informed us there have

been several hotspots popping up. While I know it's likely due to Damina's presence, tonight I'll use the illusion of these occurrences as a diversion. I need to get Marchand out of the mansion long enough for me to talk with Damina. Although I had every intent to barge straight through the front door, Gregory talked me off the fence.

"How do I look?" I ask Gregory and Shawn.

Both men smile admiringly. I think they're genuinely happy to see my spirit lifted. After arriving at the hotel, we paid a serviceman handsomely for me to use the basement laundry room for a quick and proper phasing. I was still wearing my last fight with Tye and the crew on my face and my unsightliness didn't go unnoticed by her.

"You clean up rather good," Shawn says warmly.

"Thank you," I reply.

"Well, you had better woo your lady love— especially since you're sending me out as bait!" Shawn states.

"Aww, don't be such a wuss, Shawn," Gregory teases. "You only need to make it look like a break in—just long enough to draw Marchand and his gang out."

"I know—I know," Shawn snips.

"I do appreciate it, Shawn. Gregory, you gotta keep watch too. Even though Marchand might vacate the property, I doubt he'll leave Damina for long. If nothing else, I'm confident he'll leave his wolves behind to keep her and Dacari safe," I add.

"His wolves—too easy!" Gregory laughs.

"Do not underestimate them, Gregory!" I shout back. "They may be young Dunes, but that alpha has prime blood in him. He's a Beta. He's stronger than the rest. Though I doubt he knows just how strong he is, we shouldn't take him for granted."

Gregory nods in agreement and we leave for the mansion and Shawn sets toward the Civility Center.

We arrive at the mansion at the same time a few small wolf packs as the humans depart. Shawn calls and informs us that Marchand fell for the bait and he and his team conduct their search. I ask him to stay until he confirms their departure, if possible.

Meanwhile, I make my way through the mansion, working hard not to be too obvious to the young wolves partying with their alpha. Gregory finds Mark near the DJ table and nudges him for a favor.

Then I see her.

She's adorned in a lovely red gown; a color I've always known would suit her. Just staring at her from behind soothes the trepidation of my heart and I once again, I'm falling in love.

I'm happy to see her alone. I'm also proud of her.

Earlier today, I spent time researching this revitalization project and proposals provided. I even saw a digital composite she designed for not only this home, but several others in the Garden District. I've always known she was talented, but her skill is unrivaled. Though I'm happy she got to do something she's always wanted to do, it just pains me that she must do so under such circumstances.

The wind carries Damina's inviting fragrance to me and it is heaven. As Mark cues, *"Everything,"* by Lifehouse at my request, I know it's now or never.

"Hey babe," I say softly, taking pleasure in watching her posture twitch at my call. "You look beautiful. I always knew red was your color," I add with a broad smile to match as she turns to face me.

"What—what are you doing here? I thought you left." Damina whispers over her shoulder, as she digs her heels into the ground, attempting to dampen my pull.

"No. Gregory found us something a tad better than the hostel. Baby, I would never leave like that. We have a lot to discuss."

"Jack, you shouldn't be here."

"This is exactly where I belong. With you. I should've never let you leave that night. I should have told you the truth a long time ago. I've made a lot of mistakes. You aren't one of them. You are the best thing that has ever happened to me and I'm not gonna let what we have slip away."

"Jack, you're right we need to talk—like how did you show my father to me? Why were you so drained afterwards?"

"Damina, baby we can talk about that later," I respond. I don't know how much time we have.

"No, Jackson. I need to know. You owe me that much." Damina is right, she deserves to hear the truth from me.

"You're right. I do owe you. Do you remember how

odd I acted on our drive home from our wedding shower?"

"Yeah, but what does that have to do with anything."

"I called your aunt while you were at the spa and told her I was going to tell you the truth. I didn't like the idea of marrying you without you knowing everything. But she begged me to wait. She said the transference would take better after we consummated our union. I told her I didn't care if I had the orb—I wanted to just tell you everything. It was eating me up inside keeping it from you."

"That's why you were so handsy with me."

"I thought I could—but I couldn't."

"Why? What changed?"

"Everything changed, baby. Seeing you in Marchand's arms. The way he looked at you and the way you looked back—I knew I had one last chance to prove to you that I would never hurt you. One last chance to make you mine—again. It was supposed to be my gift to you on our wedding night—at least that's what your father requested. But I couldn't wait until then because I was afraid that if I waited there would be no wedding. So I dug deep. Every ounce of love I have for you and all my fear of losing you was enough to channel the orb."

"It looked like it almost killed you."

"I suppose it could have, if I held on any longer. Especially since we weren't in harmony at the time. But I'd do it all over again if I needed. I just needed you to see—"

"Jackson, I'm so sorry. If I had only stayed in D.C."

"Baby no tears," Jackson says cupping my chin in his hand. "Not tonight. Tonight, I want to dance with my lady, my love. They're playing our song! Do you remember it?"

"I remember. We danced to it at the Crab Claw. It's one of the few times you were okay with public displays of affection. Wait, a minute—you did this?"

"I had a little help." I bow my head over my shoulder where Gregory stands next to Mark in the window.

"Please, Damina, take my hand." Pulling her hand in mine, vibrant streams of golden electricity rivet through our bodies.

We dance as the song plays and I squeeze her tight in my arms. Everything about this moment feels right. Damina nestles her head into my shoulder and I realize just how much I've missed this.

Tears rush from behind Damina's eyes as she ponders our conundrum. Though it's painful to admit, I know she loves both me and Dalcour. Somehow in their short time together, he's captured her heart. Now it's my time to reclaim it.

Precious tears fall from Damina's eyes again and I wipe her face. Tracing the outline of her luscious lips with her tears, my eyes grow wide with desire and I plunge my mouth onto her.

Kissing her is like heaven and everything in me wants to claim my bride.

"I love you," I whisper in her ear. The pace of my heartbeat quickens as we press our bodies together tight.

A crowd of onlookers' gawks at us through but they are the least of my concern. All I know in this moment is that Damina is mine. All mine and I have no plans of sharing.

"Nothing matters more to me than you, Damina. Nothing. Do you understand?" I utter, holding her face in my hands, forcing eye contact.

Keeping a firm hold of my beloved, I lean into her ear and say, "Listen, baby, it doesn't matter what happened with you and him this week—"

"Jackson, no, let me explain. It's not what you—"

"No, it's all my fault," I protest. "I can lay everything that happened at my feet. If only I had been honest from the beginning. My actions drove you away—to this." I reply, looking around the mansion with disgust.

"Look, Jack, I need to explain what really happened."

"No. You don't owe him an explanation, Beautiful," Dalcour says in a strong and sturdy tone. He gazes at me with a such an ominous glare a weaker man would both fear and faint.

Luckily for me, I am not that man.

Well, perhaps I did pick this fight, but I also have every intent to win.

Dalcour

SOMETHING ABOUT tonight's breach felt different. Wrong. There wasn't a trace of my brother's handiwork, which made me suspicious the moment we left the mansion. And it is without question that Nashoba and his crew are at the epicenter of tonight's alleged misfortune.

Now, facing Jackson with his arms wrapped around Damina, I know without question, he is to blame. But it's seeing how Damina stands torn between me and Jackson that tears my heart in two.

"Look, Marchand. I don't want to make a scene. This is between Damina and me. I only came to get my fiancé." The arrogance in which he speaks offends me more than anything.

"That's just it, Nashoba. She isn't your fiancé. At least not anymore. So why don't you and your *puppies* leave!" I shout back. I've grown quite tired of his pompousness.

"Both of you stop it! And stop talking as if I weren't standing right here. I, and I alone decide where I'm going and where I belong. But this isn't happening— not this time." Damina shakes her head at both me and Jackson and Braelyn's words from yesterday plague my mind. "Now, both of you, listen. Dal, I'm sorry I've brought my troubles to your door, but this conversation is between Jackson and me."

"Beautiful, I won't let him hurt you more than he already has. Besides, I know you aren't really considering going back to him. At least not now. Not after all we've shared. *What about us?*"

She's breaking me.

Does she know how much power she has over me?

"I need time. If nothing more, I need to stop running

and face the issues. I owe it to myself and Jackson."

"Thank you, baby," Jackson says kissing her cheek. She frowns and I know she is uncomfortable between the two of us. I want to run and pound my fists into his perfect jawline, but Lux grabs my arms keeping me away from Jackson.

"Don't thank me too soon. Jackson, you know I love you and I always will. But a lot has transpired since we've been apart. I need time to sort through it all. Even more, I made a promise to my friends and they are counting on me. I will not leave them now."

"Bravo! Bravo! Well said, my lady!" A thunderous clap turns our attention to the edge of the garden maze. A man, who I detect is a wolf, with a resemblance to Jackson appears out of the darkness ambling through the vaulted columned lights near the fire pit. He bellows a wicked laugh and continues clapping as he walks up the steps.

Jackson jumps in front of Damina, shielding her at his back. "What are you doing here, Keiron?"

Quickly, I am at Damina's side but my lips curl at the sight of Jackson's grip around Damina's wrist, but I stifle my fury and keep my sights on this new intruder.

"You mongrels sure do travel in packs!" I sneer.

"Answer the question, Keiron! Why are you here?" Damina says, pushing herself between me and Jackson. Her skin glows brightly, and I instantly know this intruder has something to do with her heartbreak.

"Oh, my lady. Don't lose your venom on me! Like I

told you before, I gain nothing at the cause of your displeasure. For it was not I who deceived you all these years. That would be my brother's doing!" Jackson snarls at Keiron's claim.

"At least the mutt speaks the truth!" Crossing my arms at my waist, I can't help laughing at the sibling quarrel.

"Well, I wouldn't laugh too quick if I were you, Lord Marchand. I mean, it is you that has the lovely Ms. Nicaud glowing so brightly, is it not? It's that very light that has attracted every Scourge and Skull for miles. All of which are dying to sample her tasty flesh!"

Pure rage fuels me and I leap toward him, "They'll never get in an inch of her!" A shimmering red current shines through me as my fists lock at my sides. Titan and Lux maintain their position and their growls echo my fury.

Keiron laughs once more, rubbing his hands together, unmoved. "To the contrary, my lord, they already have! At least two times if I'm correct. Let's see, there was the time at the Civility Center and the night at the cemetery."

"Three times if you count the alley." Mikkel's snake-like voice speaks beyond the darkness of the courtyard and his pale, luminous frame appears at Keiron's side. Mikkel's wide, devious grin ignites an inferno-like eruption within me.

Traitor!

"It was you!" Damina shouts as images her running from him in the alley adjacent to the Tavern invade my mind. A burning fire sizzles inside me at the thought of Mikkel's treachery.

"Why yes? Our encounter at the Hall of Isis was only our second. The oracles had long foretold of your coming. You caused quite a torrent when you arrived. Once I discovered its origin at Bessie's Tavern, I knew I had to find you. I underestimated you to my own demise. But my hand will heal—in time!"

Lifting his injured hand, it's translucence reveals his duplicity. *He's a Vitreous-Altrinion traitor!*

Damina charges Mikkel head on, full of rage but me and Jackson hold her arms, preventing her attack.

"Well someone's become a spunky little sprite, haven't you?" Keiron chuckles and claps his hands once more.

"Wait a minute—what oracles? Why were you even after Damina in the first place?" Brae says from behind.

"Oracles have foretold of Damina's arrival long before your scourged soul came into this world!" Mikkel's motions are quick like a phantom as he saunters up the steps in a flash. He sneers in Brae's direction, unleashing his long, reptilian-like tongue, showing his fangs. Brae grimaces but maintains behind Mark. "The ever-beautiful Ms. Nicaud is nothing more than an obstacle that must be extinguished!"

Gasps echo as Mikkel implies Damina's demise and I feel the beast rising within me and my crimson eyes burn like fire. "So it was you all this time, Mikkel? You compromised the CC and the Hall, making it look like Dranoel's doing. For what? Were you afraid I'd find true love? Working with my brother—against me!"

"I care not for who you love or your worthless grandstanding competition with Decaux! But as the last of the pure Altrinion line, her very existence threatens our way of life." Mikkel lashes back.

As he speaks, all else becomes silent to me. Only the memory of Trieu's warning haunts my mind. She forewarned there were others who would only want Damina's demise. She told me threats would come.

Why did I think just finding love would make everything okay?

To be Fated is to live with a constant target on not just your back, but your entire being. What pleasure can come from a love without peace?

Perhaps Damina is better off with Jackson?

If only he could have protected her as he should have—no one would know of her lineage!

I'd gladly give my life for hers!

As much as it pains me, I would rather see her with Jackson if it meant preserving her life.

I'll choose her life before another—including my own. And I'd do so every time!

Chapter 26

Jackson

This is not how I expected to spend this evening.

Watching Keiron take the life of a young human girl only confirmed he is no longer my brother. He is an enemy to me. However, fighting alongside my wolfen-kin reminded me I have a brotherhood that far extends my birth order.

Holding one Skull by the throat, I rip out his jugular and fling him across the parlor. Blood splatters across the glass pane of the parlor doors and I laugh as another Skull falls in the pile of carcasses I've amassed.

"Are you soulless beasts good for anything!" Keiron sneers to the remaining wolves around him.

"That's what you get little brother, when you send Goliath for David." I say with bated breath.

"The hubris that emits from you, brother, is reprehensible! Being our father's favorite has gone to your head. You are no more deserving to be Alpha Lord than any of these incapable canines at your feet. Yet, somehow, you've convinced yourself you can have it all! The title. The pack. And the love. But you can't! And why should you? You don't even want it!"

"And you want it too much, Keiron!"

"So what? Would you rather live as father and those before him did—hiding instead of being a true leader!"

"A true leader knows how to lead by keeping his people safe!"

"Oh, like you kept Damina safe?"

"Mention her name one more time—"

"And what? What will you do? Nothing. You'll do nothing. The power of Alpha Lord lives in you and you refuse to be what you really are!"

"What do you know of it, Keiron?"

"We should live as gods among men. As Alpha Lord, every creeping thing would be subject to your command."

"Is that all you want, Keiron? To have control. That's not power, little brother. We are not gods—just another created thing!"

"Then accept my challenge and fight! I'll show you what a god looks like!"

"No brother, I will not fight you. We both know there's only two ways for you to assume the role as alpha. You'd have to kill me through challenged combat and or succeed me in death. And the battalion you've sent so far has been no match for me—"

"Well, we shall end this archaic tradition tonight! Now, this, Keiron is how we put an end to such trivial pursuits!" Mikkel's shadowy form emerges from the dark corners of the parlor as he slices through my abdomen from behind. Four Scourges pounce on me. Two Scourge lick the forward side of the knife as blood pours from my body while two other clamps onto my arms with their teeth.

I look up and see Damina standing at the doorway and I know for the first time she has forgiven me as burgeoning grief fills her lovely face. Smiling at her weakly, blood seeps from my mouth as Mikkel rips the blade from my body.

Two more Scourge jump on me, but I kick free of them with my remaining strength, keeping my eyes on Damina. I want to tell her to run, but I don't have the voice.

While I'd hate for her to see me leave her like this, I want her to know I'll happily fight for her to my very end.

"End him!" Mikkel's shrieking command echoes through the parlor and a pack of Skull appear from the corner of the parlor hall.

Coldness sweeps over me and the pulsing of my heart declines. The gnawing of the wolf within me lessens, but he pounds like a caged lion in my chest, begging for his release. Just as my eyes close, a bright warm light fills the room. A hurling hurricane force of wind rattles the sediment, shaking the foundation of the mansion with the force of an earthquake.

The luminous light shines like the sun, but my eyes are too weak to see it in full. Peering through the cracks of my eyes, I see a sliver of a face smiling down on me. A small burst of a calmingly sweet aroma wafts past me and I know with all certainty it is Damina. I feel her hands on my chest and a warm heat like the kindling of fire crackles through me and the life that once sought its retreat, slowly returns to me.

I awake to find Damina, glowing brightly but eerily still in my arms.

Dalcour

WHAT WE didn't chase off the property we killed. Nothing was left alive with any mal intent.

Rushing back into the mansion, I search for everyone—and for Damina. The mansion is quiet, but the stench of spilled blood fills the atmosphere. Mark and Gregory are at my side as we search around the mansion looking for everyone. Titan remained outside with Lux, Dilano and Shawn to ensure the perimeter is safe.

As we near the foyer, a bright golden light shines under the parlor doors. Mark slides the doors open and a blinding glow reminiscent of the sun's light blazes through the mansion with an intense heat. Mark crosses the threshold with Gregory, but I cannot. The radiating light emitting from the front of the parlor, scorches my skin. Smoke rises from me, burning my arms and feet.

"Ow!" Braelyn screams from the foyer.

"Get away from here now!" Mark shouts over his shoulder at Braelyn. I turn and look at her and see red blisters layer her face and hands.

"Braelyn do what he says! Go, now!" I yell.

Although it hurts, I can withstand some of the light, but it's obvious it would be too dangerous for Braelyn.

"What is it?" Gregory says.

"It's her. Damina," a faint voice calls from the front.

"Jack-O? Is that you?" Gregory questions, stepping further into the light.

"Yes, it's me," Jackson answers.

My heart sinks to the bottom of my gut as I now see Jackson holding Damina's limp body in the background. Gazing around the room I see nothing but the remains of dead Skull and ash husks of the Scourge. Peering through the light I even spot Mikkel's sword on the floor next to Keiron and I am sure Mikkel's treachery has met its end.

Trying once more to cross the threshold, Gregory raises his hand to my chest as he sees smoke singe my forearms. He shakes his head in caution.

"We'll go get her, Lord Marchand," Gregory states and I'm surprised by his sudden kindness.

"We got her, Big D!" Mark echoes. "Get back toward the terrace and keep Brae with you until we get her settled," Mark orders.

"I'll make certain they call you to her once this

subsides," Jackson says from the distance. Despite every ounce of animosity I feel for him, I know his sentiment is true.

I race to the back terrace, taking Braelyn with me. Braelyn looks up at me with tears pouring down her face and slams into my chest and cries.

Chapter 27

Nothing has been the same since that night. The woman who should have torn their worlds apart has now merged them into one. New alliances are forged while old enemies remain. A truce born from tragedy has turned their worlds upside down.

All that matters is their love for her.

At least for now.

"How did your time go in the Taming Wells? Do you think Kate will make it?" Jackson questions Dalcour as he saunters slowly down the hall.

"She's coming along," Dalcour begins. "Titan's made good progress with her so far—so has Braelyn."

"That's good. Well, Keiron still isn't talking—at least nothing more than his usual request." Jackson replies as he responds to texts on his phone.

"It's been over a month and he still asking for her?" Dalcour shakes his head and chuckles at the irritable scowl now etched across Jackson's face. Jackson nods his head affirming Dalcour's question, but never looks up. Quietness brews between them and Dalcour paces the floor, staring back and forth at Damina's suite. "What do we do when she wakes?" Dalcour asks staring at Jackson while leaning on the doorframe of the room across the hall.

"We help her find her cousin. That's what she would want," Jackson answers with his arms folded at his lap.

"And, what do we do about us? When she chooses one or the other?" Dalcour replies, now sipping from the new smoothie bottle Braelyn gave him after the brawl.

Pushing away from his chair, Jackson stands and smiles at Dalcour and says, "When that time comes, Lord Marchand, whoever is not chosen will bow out gracefully and clean up the mess our brothers have made. While the other keeps her safe until that mess is no more."

"I see," Dalcour responds with a deep sigh. "One thing is sure, Lord Nashoba, when she does awake, for one man she will be his redemption and the other his reckoning. I just hope we are strong enough to endure our fate—whatever that end shall be."

Both men stare at one another, take a deep breath and smile before laughing quietly.

As they laugh, the door to Damina's room opens and Delia rounds the corner and smiles. Jackson and Dalcour stand, gazing at Delia with frozen expressions.

"What is it, Delia?" Dalcour questions, his heart thumping loudly in his chest.

"Is she..." Jackson begins, his voice trembling.

"Yes, gentlemen, Damina is awake."

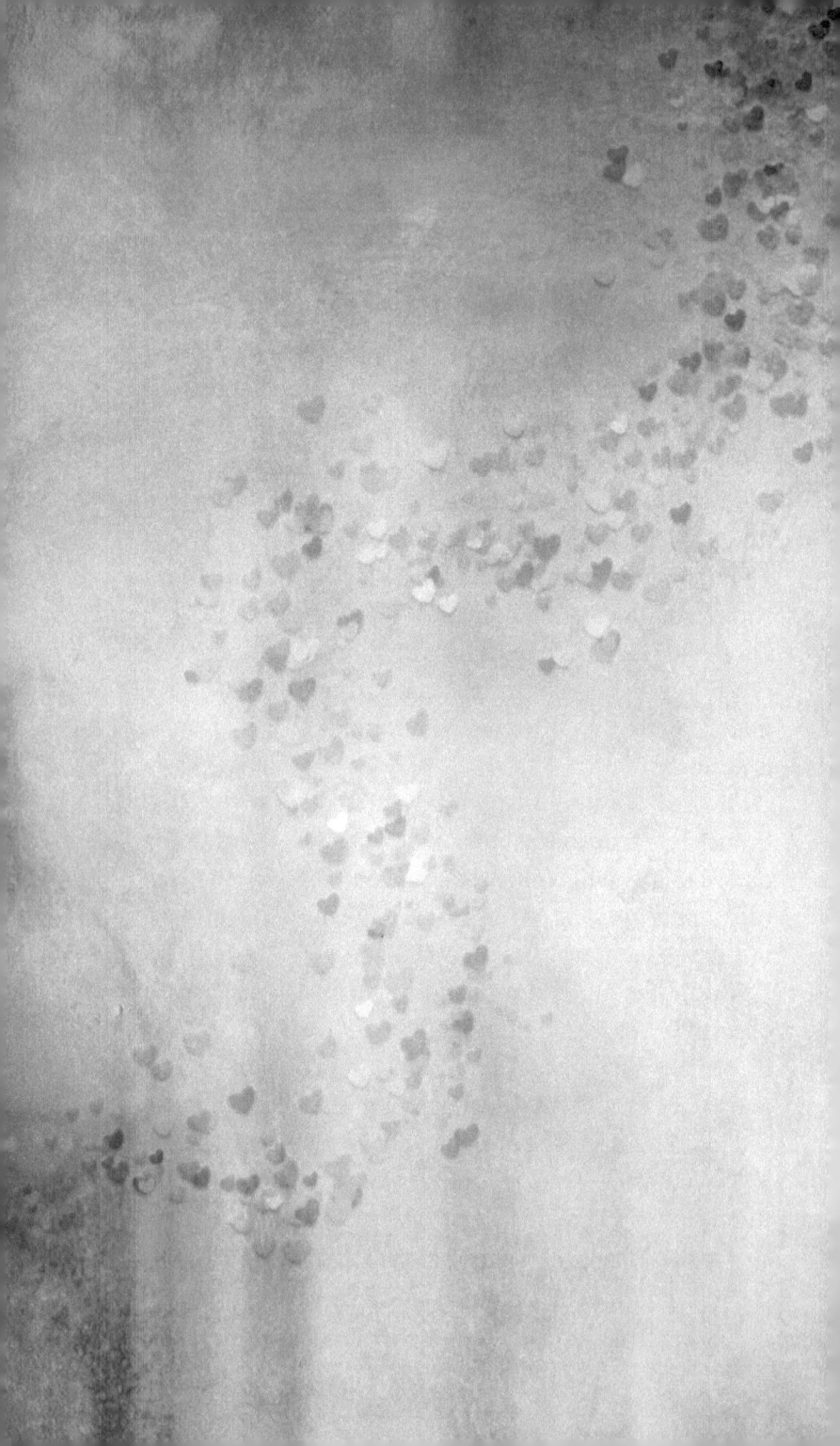

About the Author

L. C. Son has the life she's always imagined and more. A wife to one and mom to three kids and a very regal Beagle, she would say she is living a life full of awesomeness!

Growing up, she spent hours reading comic books she "borrowed" from her older brother which inspired her love for heroes and all things fantasy and paranormal. Much like the characters she adored, she lives a duplicitous life. By day she works tirelessly to champion the employment of persons with severe disabilities. By night she puts on her wife-mom cape, sharing with her husband at their church and juggling their kid's very active schedules.

Writing has always come second nature to her and a skill she uses in her professional career. *Beautiful Nightmare* is her first published work and she's thrilled to finally bring to life the characters that have lived in the creative corners of her mind. Presently, she's working on the next installment in the Beautiful Nightmare series and an anthology in the Beautiful Nightmare world named Origins.

Before You Go!

Thanks for your readership and support. There's more on the horizon for the world of Beautiful Nightmare and I'm excited to share with you what's planned next in the series:

BEAUTIFUL NIGHTMARE (BOOK ONE)-
- RELEASED FEBRUARY 2019
HEARTS ECLIPSED, A BEAUTIFUL NIGHTMARE NOVELLA
- NOVEMBER 2019
AWAKEN: BEAUTIFUL NIGHTMARE (BOOK TWO)
BREAKING CURSES: A BEAUTIFUL NIGHTMARE NOVELLA
-PLANNED
ORIGINS: A BEAUTIFUL NIGHTMARE ANTHOLOGY
...MORE TO COME!

As always, stay connected with me online at www.LCSonBooks.com and be sure to sign up for member only exclusives and information!

Join the Beautiful Nightmare Book Group.
WWW.FACEBOOK.COM/LCSONBOOKS

www.ingramcontent.com/pod-product-compliance
Lightning Source LLC
Chambersburg PA
CBHW020920110726
47900CB00001B/225